Aunt Bessie Believes

An Isle of Man Cozy Mystery

Diana Xarissa

Text Copyright © 2014 Diana Xarissa

Cover Photo Copyright © 2014 Kevin Moughtin

All rights reserved.

ISBN: 1500229350
ISBN-13: 978-1500229351

Author's Note

Welcome to book two in the Aunt Bessie – Isle of Man Cozy Mystery series. While I recommend reading the books in order, each book will stand alone if you prefer not to do so. I have just a few notes, mainly for those of you who have started with this book instead of the first.

Aunt Bessie's life story was originally told in my Isle of Man Romance, *Island Inheritance*. Bessie was the source of the inheritance that prompted the heroine to visit the Isle of Man. That meant, of course, that in that book she had recently passed away. Readers get to learn her life story thanks to letters, diary excerpts and through stories told by other characters in the book.

When I started thinking about writing a cozy mystery, I knew I needed to create the perfect protagonist. And then I decided that I already had one. Aunt Bessie was the perfect cozy heroine, I just had to bring her back to life.

I've chosen, therefore, to start this cozy mystery series about fifteen years before the romance, circa 1998. In that way, Bessie is still happily alive to get unhappily mixed up with murder. I've worked hard to try to make sure I haven't accidently given anyone technology that didn't exist in the late 1990s, but I can't promise I haven't made any mistakes.

As with the first book in the series (*Aunt Bessie Assumes*), readers might spot a character or two who have wandered in from my romance series. Obviously, they are younger versions of themselves here, and they are blissfully unaware of the future that you may have already read about.

I've used British spellings and British and/or Manx words and terminology throughout the book. A couple of pages of translations and explanations for many of them, especially for readers outside of the United Kingdom, appear at the end of the book. It is entirely possible that the odd American spelling or primarily American word usage has snuck into the text. If that is the case, I am sorry and if you let me know about it, I will correct it.

A note on the setting; this story takes place on the uniquely beautiful Isle of Man. The island is located between England and Ireland in the Irish Sea. While it is a Crown Dependency, it is a country in its own right, with its own currency, stamps, language and government.

This is a work of fiction. All of the characters are a product of the author's imagination. Any resemblance to actual persons, living or dead, is entirely coincidental. Similarly, the names of the restaurants and shops and other businesses on the island are fictional. I have taken considerable liberties with my locations, adding various shops and other businesses that simply don't exist on the island, or at least not where I've put them.

The historical sites and other landmarks on the island are all real; however, all of the events that take place within them in this story are fictional. Manx National Heritage does exist and their efforts to preserve and promote the historical sites and the history of the island are extraordinary. All of the Manx National Heritage staff in this story, however, are fictional depictions.

I never get tired of writing or talking about the Isle of Man. It was my home for over ten years and I write about in order to have an opportunity to, at least mentally, revisit a place I loved. It is a truly unique and fascinating location, steeped in history and endowed with its own distinct culture and traditions. I look forward to one day having an opportunity to spend much more time there.

CHAPTER ONE

"Why do these things always have to be on the first floor?" Doona grumbled as she slowly climbed the stairs, holding tight to her friend's arm.

"Marjorie said they were having trouble finding space to hold the class this time. We're lucky they found a room for us, even if it is up a few steps," Elizabeth Cubbon, "Bessie" to nearly everyone, answered. She was unbothered by the climb.

"If it was only a few steps, I wouldn't complain."

Bessie laughed. "Why don't you let go of my arm? Then we don't both have to try to squeeze together on the same step at the same time, and the trip will be easier for both of us."

Doona shook her head. "It's fine," she replied, not meeting Bessie's eyes.

"For goodness sake," Bessie said crossly. "I'm perfectly capable of climbing up any number of stairs all by myself. I do it at home at least a dozen times a day, you know. All this mollycoddling is starting to get on my nerves."

Doona flushed and didn't reply. The pair reached the top of the stairs and headed down the short hallway towards the only open door. Bessie could almost feel the dust in the air. The hall smelled musty and disused, which wasn't surprising since the club that owned the building didn't use the first floor very often.

A few steps away from the door, Doona paused and gave

Bessie a tentative smile.

"I'm sorry, I don't mean to mollycoddle you," she said softly. "I still feel so badly about what happened last month, you getting nearly killed and everything, that I feel like I need to watch over you constantly. Besides, whatever you say, I know that nasty fall you took left you battered and bruised."

"I suppose I should appreciate the fact that you didn't say anything about me being so old that I will take longer to recover," Bessie replied, smiling to take any sting out of the words. "I know that my fall and subsequent events were very stressful for all of us, but I just saw my doctor this morning and he says I'm 'fit as a fiddle.' You need to stop worrying about me so much."

"I'll try, but it won't be easy," Doona said.

Bessie thought of a dozen replies, but she didn't get a chance to say any of them as they were interrupted by loud voices floating up the stairway behind them.

"I can't believe that I had to pay for this course and now I'm expected to climb up all these stairs as well," a loud and churlish voice said.

Bessie struggled to hear the reply, but could only just make out a quiet murmur.

"I don't care how much trouble you had finding a space," the angry voice came again. "I'm not supposed to climb too many stairs, not with my bad heart. Maybe I should just get my money back and not take the course."

The voices were getting closer and now Bessie recognised their owners.

Marjorie Stevens worked as a librarian at the Manx Museum and was in charge of organising and teaching the class that Bessie and Doona were there to take. Somewhere in her thirties, she was a natural blonde with light blue eyes that were always hidden behind fashionable glasses.

Many years ago, when Marjorie first arrived on the island, Bessie had heard rumours about a love affair that had gone disastrously wrong. Bessie had hopes that Marjorie might meet someone special at some point in the future, but by all indications, the woman was determined to remain single. That was a position that Bessie could well understand. It would have been Marjorie's voice speaking quietly and calmly in between the heated outbursts from the other woman who now appeared at the top of the stairs.

"Oh, goody," Doona whispered softly to Bessie as Moirrey Teare's miserable countenance came into view.

Moirrey was a thirty-something hypochondriac who made sure that she was well known throughout the town of Laxey. Although she was not unattractive, Bessie wasn't sure she had ever seen the woman smile. In all the years she'd known her, Bessie had never seen her wear any makeup or seem to put any effort into her appearance.

Today, Moirrey's dark brown hair hung limply over her shoulders, looking as if it hadn't seen a brush in at least a week. Her matching brown eyes were flashing angrily and her face was flushed from the effort of climbing the short staircase. She was rail-thin and wearing what Bessie knew had to be very expensive clothing, although the style didn't suit her. She was carrying a fancy handbag that undoubtedly had a designer label inside.

Bessie forced herself to smile as she greeted the new arrivals. "Marjorie, I'm so excited to be taking your class again," she told the woman who was carrying a large box full of books and papers in her arms. "I just hope I do better this time than I did the last two times I tried."

Marjorie smiled. "I'm sure you'll do well," she said politely. "Pardon me." Marjorie disappeared through the open door, no doubt eager to put down the heavy box.

Bessie turned to greet the other woman. "Moirrey, how lovely to see you again," she fibbed graciously. "I didn't realise you were taking this class."

The other woman looked at her for a long moment before speaking, seemingly reluctantly. "I hadn't planned on it," she told Bessie. "But I thought I ought to get out more."

Doona turned a laugh into a cough at the unexpected comment. Moirrey turned and gave her a cold glare before she turned back to Bessie.

"I must say I'm surprised to see you here," she said coolly. "At your age I would have thought you were ready for a little flat in

Douglas with doctors on call."

Bessie bristled and counted slowly to ten before she trusted herself to reply. "I'm doing just fine, thanks. I love learning and I think that the class will help with my research."

Moirrey shrugged. "Are you still playing at being a historian, then? My family history is so intimately tied up with the island's own history that I can't quite imagine trying to study one and not the other. My health being what it is, however, quite precludes me from doing any serious research, of course."

Bessie breathed deeply. "Have you met my friend, Doona Moore?" she asked, changing the subject.

"I don't believe I have." Moirrey extended her hand limply, allowing Doona to squeeze a few fingers.

"Actually," Doona told her, "we have met. I work at the Laxey Constabulary at the front desk. You were just in last week to file a complaint about your neighbours."

Moirrey frowned deeply. "You can't expect me to remember you from that?" she demanded. "I meet so many people and I can only remember a handful of them."

Doona drew a deep breath. Bessie jumped in before her friend could speak.

"I'm sure it will be a fun class," she said. "I've already taken it twice and couldn't wait to take it again."

"It doesn't say much about the skill of the teacher if you've had to take the same class multiple times, does it?" Moirrey answered. She wrinkled her nose. "Maybe this is a sign. Maybe I should just quit now and get my money back."

"It surely isn't Marjorie's fault that I'm just not that quick at languages," Bessie said, torn between defending her friend and hoping that the unpleasant Moirrey would drop out of the class.

"That's easy for you to say," Moirrey snorted. "You got the senior discount for the class. My full-price tuition is supplementing your place here."

Bessie flushed and bit her tongue before she could say what she felt.

"I paid full price," Doona interjected. "And I think it will be worth every penny."

Moirrey looked Doona up and down slowly. "Are you sure you don't qualify for the discount?" she asked in an incredulous tone. "Well, anyway," she sniffed, "I suppose the stairs will be good for you."

With that she swept her way through the open door, leaving both Doona and Bessie in shock.

"What did she just say?" Doona choked out.

"I'm sure I'm not repeating it," Bessie tried to joke. "And you shouldn't pay her a bit of attention."

Doona smoothed her slightly wrinkled top over her generous hips. "I know I could stand to lose a few pounds," she admitted, "but I didn't think I looked that bad."

Bessie gave her friend a critical once-over. Doona was somewhere in her mid-forties, with liberally highlighted brown hair and gorgeous, if artificially enhanced, green eyes. Bessie had always kept herself slender. Doona was a few inches taller and maybe forty pounds heavier than her friend.

"You look wonderful," Bessie said. "Don't pay any attention to that horrible woman."

"She implied that I wasn't important enough to remember," Doona complained. "And that I looked old and fat."

"Aye, she did at that," Bessie laughed. "In between telling me I'm too old to be taking classes and criticising my research efforts."

The remark, accompanied by the face that Bessie made, had Doona laughing. With their equilibrium restored, they now made their way through the door into the classroom. Marjorie smiled at them as they carefully selected seats as far away from Moirrey Teare as they could get in the small space.

Eight plain wooden tables, each with a pair of plastic stacking-type chairs, were arranged facing towards the front of the small and neatly rectangular room. Two windows were spaced uniformly in the wall at the front, but it didn't look as though they had been washed in a great many years. A glimmer of sunlight from the setting sun struggled to work its way through the years of accumulated grime.

Between the windows stood a large desk with a comfortable

looking chair behind it. Marjorie had placed her box on the desk and was busily unpacking it.

"I think everyone will agree that I should have that chair," Moirrey said, rising to her feet from behind the front table on the left side. "I do have a heart condition, after all."

No one spoke as she pushed the hard plastic seat she had been using to one side and then carefully rolled the cushioned chair into its place. Bessie exchanged looks with Doona as they settled into their own seats at the very back of the classroom on the right side. The silence in the room was just becoming unpleasant when another face that was familiar to Bessie appeared in the doorway.

"Oh goodness, I'm not late, am I?" the newcomer demanded. "Only traffic was all in a tangle around the school and then I lost track of where I was going and missed a turning and had to go back around again." She laughed. "Oh well, I'm here safe and sound anyway."

Bessie smiled at her. Joney Quirk was almost always slightly flustered; it was a part of her personality that sixty-plus years of life hadn't managed to change. She'd been a teacher for many of those years, teaching reception classes full of four- and five-year-olds who probably didn't notice that their teacher was always mildly atwitter. She was pleasantly plump and casually dressed. Her grey hair was tucked, as always, into a neat bun and her brown eyes sparkled with both intelligence and fun behind lined bifocals.

Moirrey sighed loudly. "I wondered what we were waiting for," she said grumpily. "According to my watch we should have started three minutes ago."

Marjorie looked at her own watch and shook her head. "According to mine, it's still a few minutes to seven. Hopefully, our other two class members will get here in that time."

Moirrey sighed loudly again. "Perhaps I should have my driver stop at everyone's house and collect them all next week?" she said sarcastically. "Since getting here on time seems to be such an issue."

"You're rather preaching to the choir," Doona pointed out.

"We're all here on time."

Moirrey opened her mouth to reply but was interrupted by a man rushing through the door.

Henry Costain was red-faced and apologetic. "We had a late tour bus," he explained. "Pensioners over from Morecambe who were so excited to see the castle that I just didn't have the heart to rush them."

"And inconveniencing all of us was, presumably, perfectly acceptable?" Moirrey demanded petulantly.

"Oh no, of course not," Henry stammered out. "If traffic had been a bit better I would have been here on time anyway, but getting around Douglas was a nightmare."

Bessie smiled sympathetically at the man, determined to soothe his ruffled feathers. Henry was a sweet bachelor in his mid-fifties. He had thinning grey hair, muddy brown eyes and a physique that tended to run towards chubby.

Not often the smartest man in the room, he was kind-hearted and a very hard worker. He had started working for Manx National Heritage as soon as he had left school and he was very popular with locals and tourists alike, always cheerful and happy to show people around at whichever site he was working. Additionally, he was always full of lots of specialist knowledge that he had accumulated over the years.

"Are you working at Castle Rushen at the moment, then?" she asked him.

"Oh, aye," Henry flushed even more. "After all the trouble at the Laxey Wheel last month the boss thought I could do with a change. Not that anyone blamed me for anything...." he trailed off.

"I should think not," Bessie said stoutly. "Anyway, Castle Rushen is so beautiful in the spring, it must be wonderful to be there."

"It is, aye," the man beamed. "It's just the commute that's a bother, although I know most people across have it much worse."

"We do get rather spoiled here, don't we?" Doona chimed in.

"I hate to interrupt this lovely bit of catching up," Moirrey said in a poisonous voice, "but I came here to learn beginning Manx, not find out what the little man who picks up rubbish at the heritage sites has been doing with his time."

Henry flushed again and looked agitated. "I don't pick up rubbish," he muttered under his breath.

"Okay, then," Marjorie spoke loudly to forestall any further conversation. "Let's get started on learning Manx, shall we?"

"I thought we were waiting for one more," Bessie said, happy to be annoying Moirrey.

"I think we'll get started," Marjorie answered her. "We don't want to waste valuable class time."

Marjorie passed out a small pamphlet with basic Manx words and their English translations, as well as several photocopied sheets with more vocabulary on them.

"Manx Gaelic is a Goidelic language, that is, it comes from Primitive Irish. Modern Irish and Scottish Gaelic share the same roots. I'm sure you're all aware that the Manx language suffered a decline in...."

"Pardon me," Moirrey interrupted. "I thought this was a language class, not a history class."

Marjorie flushed. "I thought it would good to start with some basic background into how the language developed," she said, a bit defensively. "If you're not interested, we can just dive right into the language however."

Everyone exchanged glances, but no one was willing to challenge Moirrey. Bessie, of course, knew the history of the language well enough to teach a course on it herself so she didn't argue, even though she was annoyed that Moirrey was upsetting Marjorie.

"Okay then, we're going to start with the basics," Marjorie began again. "The focus of the class is on 'Conversational Manx' rather than on reading or writing in the language. I encourage you to take notes of how the words are pronounced rather than worrying over exact spellings, at least at this point."

Bessie pulled a pencil from her handbag and set it on the table in front of her. She smiled to herself as she recalled doing the same at every class she had taken in the difficult Gaelic language. Maybe this third attempt would be enough to get her competent enough to move up to the "Intermediate Manx" class that Marjorie was teaching next.

"Fastyr mie," Marjorie said to the class.

"Fastyr mie," the class chanted back to her.

"Very good," Marjorie smiled. "That's 'good afternoon' or 'good evening.'"

For the next fifteen minutes or so Marjorie took them slowly through a range of greetings. Then the class was instructed to walk around and exchange polite conversation in Manx with one another for a few minutes. Bessie laughed as she said "good afternoon" and "how are you" politely to the other members of the class, who, for the most part, supplied the appropriate responses.

"Honestly, Henry," Moirrey exploded as the session continued. "I said 'kys t'ou,' you're supposed to reply 'ta mee braew,' not 'quoi uss.'" She sighed dramatically.

"I'm sorry, Ms. Teare, really I am. I just got confused, like, and mixed up my sentences."

Moirrey rolled her eyes and flounced away from him, heading straight for Doona, who was sitting on her own, having just finished her chat with Joney. Doona turned her head and silently mouthed "help" towards Bessie, who was busily stumbling over her words with Marjorie. Doona was saved when the classroom door suddenly burst open.

"Oh my goodness, I'm so very late, I'm so very, very sorry."

Bessie looked at the stranger curiously. She had never seen her before. The woman was very young, maybe in her mid-twenties, with long, blonde, windblown hair and pretty blue eyes. She was slim and well dressed, but she looked frazzled.

Doona was closest to the door and she leapt up to greet the new arrival. "No worries," she told the woman. "I'm sure Marjorie understands, don't you, Marjorie?"

Marjorie laughed and walked over to the pair. "Of course I understand. Kys t'ou?"

"Oh, um, ta mee braew, I think."

Marjorie laughed. "Very good, I don't think you've missed anything." She turned to the rest of the class to perform the necessary introductions.

"This is Liz Martin. She's my next-door neighbour, and I've

been teaching her Manx over the garden fence for the last few months." Marjorie introduced each of the others in turn, getting to Moirrey last.

"So nice to meet you," Liz said politely.

"Where are you from, dear?" Moirrey asked.

"I grew up in Bolsover," Liz told her. "But I met my husband at uni in Liverpool. He works in banking and got transferred here in January."

"So many banks suddenly seem to have forgotten that we have many talented men and women living here who need jobs," Moirrey sniffed. "If I was in charge of the work permit committee there would be a lot fewer people like you coming over here and taking jobs away from the native Manx people."

Liz looked at Marjorie uncertainly. "I don't work, actually," she said in an apologetic tone. "I'm at home with the kids."

"How many children do you have?" Bessie asked, smiling kindly at Liz.

"Two," Liz beamed. "Jackson is two and a half and Kylie is sixteen months."

"I'll bet they're a handful as well," Bessie said. "You must have pictures?"

Moirrey sighed deeply. "If this is what every class is going to be like, I can't see much point in my being here," she grumbled loudly.

Marjorie flushed and swallowed visibly before she spoke. "Let's get back to our conversations, then," she suggested. "Has everyone had a chance to talk with everyone else? We'll leave Liz out of this round."

A few minutes later everyone had had enough of trying out their very basic greetings and Marjorie called them back together. "Let's work through talking about drinks and drinking and then we can take a tea break and discuss what we're having in Manx."

Bessie took careful notes, writing her own unique phonetic pronunciation guide to each word or phrase as Marjorie took them slowly through them.

At one point Doona leaned across to glance at Bessie's neatly written notes. "What on earth does that say?" she hissed at

Bessie.

"By vie lhiam ushtey," Bessie whispered back.

"Really?" Doona peered more closely at the paper and then shook her head.

She began to speak again, but was interrupted by a loud "shhhhhhh" from Moirrey. Silenced, Doona rolled her eyes at her friend instead and the pair struggled to choke back giggles as Moirrey glared at them.

Another fifteen minutes ticked past before Marjorie announced that it was time for a tea break.

"Oh, thank heavens," Bessie exclaimed.

"I hope there are some chocolate biscuits to go with that tea," Doona said as everyone rose from their seats to gather around the tea table in the left front corner of the room.

"I hardly think you need biscuits," Moirrey said to Doona in a disapproving tone.

"Oh, I definitely do," Doona answered, sharing a wry smile with Bessie.

"So do I," Joney said, smiling at Doona. "Chocolate makes life so much better."

While everyone waited for the kettle to boil, Liz, at Bessie's insistence, pulled a few snapshots of her children from her handbag and Bessie, Doona and Marjorie cooed over them. None of the three had any children of their own; indeed, Doona was the only one of the three who had ever been married. Even though Doona had tried matrimony twice, she was currently single and remained childless.

Joney pulled out a few snapshots of her newly arrived granddaughter, her first grandchild, and everyone fussed over those as well.

"I just wish Peter were here to share the joy with me," Joney said, sniffling slightly. Peter, her husband of many happy years, had passed away a year earlier.

Bessie patted Joney's hand. "He'd be ever so proud of that little one," she told Joney. "Every time I saw him anywhere he always bragged about his children. I'm sure he'd be even worse with the grandbaby."

Bessie never minded not having children of her own. Instead, she had happily taken on the role of honourary maiden aunt to just about every child in Laxey. Once those children reached school age, parents could count on every one of them running away to "Aunt Bessie's" at least once in a while. Bessie usually had biscuits, frequently had cake and always had a sympathetic ear for children who felt misunderstood or under-appreciated at home.

In all of her years of opening her doors to the neighbourhood children, there had only ever been one child that she'd ever asked to leave. Disagreeable and difficult even as a teen, Moirrey Teare had never forgiven Bessie for the slight, a fact that bothered Bessie not even the tiniest bit.

As everyone fixed themselves cups of tea and selected a few biscuits to pile on their plates, Moirrey set her handbag on the table and began fishing bottles of tablets from deep within it. Doona's jaw dropped and Bessie counted nine different bottles, each with its own neatly typed label from the local chemist.

Moirrey looked up from her collection, appearing surprised to find herself the centre of attention. "I did mention that I have heart trouble," she reminded the others. "I'm kept alive thanks to modern medicine and this collection of tablets. They have to be taken in the right order and at exactly the right times or I could die."

Bessie and Doona exchanged looks, but both kept quiet.

"But why do you carry them all around with you all the time?" Liz asked. "I mean, why not just put the ones you need into one of those little carrying cases and leave the big bottles at home?"

Moirrey shook her head. "I like to keep track of my tablets myself," she replied. "And the best way to do that is to keep them all with me."

Liz looked like she wanted to argue, but she took a sip of tea instead. Everyone watched with bizarre fascination as Moirrey lined up the bottles in some order that, presumably, had significance for her. After they were all perfectly aligned, Moirrey counted them a couple of times. Finally, she opened the first bottle, removed a tablet and washed it down with a sip of tea. She skipped over the second bottle, retrieving a tablet from the third.

This one too she swallowed with her tea. Then she skipped all the way to the very last bottle, removing two tiny tablets from it. These were quickly dispatched with the last of Moirrey's tea. She frowned as she held up the empty cup.

"I need a refill," she said crossly.

Marjorie was quick to pour more tea into the proffered cup. Bessie finished her own drink and smiled at Marjorie.

"Please, may I have some more tea?" she asked politely.

Moirrey's frown deepened as she added sugar to her cup.

Bessie said a loud "thank you" as Marjorie passed the now full cup back to her. Moirrey nibbled a biscuit and ignored the interchange.

After Moirrey finished her second cup of tea, she opened her handbag fully and, with a sweep of her arm, brushed all of the bottles of tablets into it. One managed to escape, bouncing off the table and rolling across the floor. Doona quickly picked it up and returned it to its owner.

Moirrey took it with a suspicious look on her face. She opened the bottle, checking its contents, before closing it tightly again.

"You're welcome, I'm sure," Doona said tightly.

After an uncomfortable silence that lasted several minutes, Marjorie cleared her throat. "Okay, let's try practicing our conversation about drinking," she suggested. "Everyone take a turn to talk to everyone else and try out at least three or four of our new phrases."

As Bessie stood up to grab her notes, Marjorie gave her a wicked grin. "Don't use your notes," she told the class. "Let's see how much you can remember from earlier."

Bessie frowned ruefully. She didn't remember much. The next twenty minutes were a blur for Bessie as she struggled through a conversation with each of her classmates that only seemed to reinforce how little she could recall. One thing became almost immediately apparent to her. Young Liz was going to be the class star. Her Manx sounded fluid and effortless, especially compared to Bessie's hesitant and garbled struggles.

She was just about finished talking to everyone, heading

towards Marjorie for her last chat when Moirrey started shouting.

"We haven't learned that yet," Moirrey yelled at Liz.

"I'm sorry," Liz said, her tone desperately apologetic.

"We don't all have the benefit of free lessons from our neighbours," Moirrey told her sharply. "Some of us have to pay full price to get access to a few minutes of instruction interspersed with endless chitchat and unnecessary tea breaks."

Marjorie called the class back to order after the outburst and spent the last hour lecturing. Bessie's hand began to cramp as she tried to keep up with the angry pace that Marjorie kept. When nine o'clock finally rolled around, Bessie put her pen down with a sigh of relief. She was going to have to dig out her notes from previous classes and bring them next time. They could help supplement what she could manage to scribble down as Marjorie raced through vocabulary and pronunciation.

Bessie had little doubt that Marjorie would feel forced to keep up the uncomfortable speed in order to keep Moirrey happy. Not that anything ever made Moirrey happy, but if she crammed as much as possible into each lesson, Marjorie might at least keep Moirrey from complaining to the continuing education department about the class.

"Everyone is more than welcome to stay and chat in Manx with me after class," Marjorie told them. "And if you can ask in Manx, you can have another biscuit before you go as well."

Doona laughed. "Even though I really want another biscuit, my brain gave up about half an hour ago," she told everyone. "I guess I'd better just go home."

Everyone gathered up their things and began to head towards the door. Liz stopped to talk with Marjorie, but the others simply waved or said a quick "goodbye" before leaving.

Henry was in the lead as they left, but he stopped at the top of the stairs. "Ladies first," he said, with a small bow.

Bessie smiled approvingly and started towards the first step. She nearly fell when Moirrey shoved her to one side and started down the stairs.

Doona opened her mouth to shout after Moirrey, but Bessie held up a hand. "Please don't bother on my account," she told

Doona. "You'll only cause an ugly scene and make yourself feel bad. Moirrey is incapable of feeling like she did anything wrong."

"Was she badly brought up or is this something she's grown into?" Doona asked as she and Bessie began their slow descent.

"Oh, she was badly brought up," Bessie told her. "She was hugely overindulged by parents who worried excessively about her 'weak heart.' I'm sure they thought they were doing the right thing, but they spoiled her rotten and never taught her manners or basic decent behaviour."

Doona sighed. "I suppose it's too late for her to learn any of that now."

The group reached the bottom of the stairs and crossed towards the front door of the building. Doona pulled the door open and held it for Bessie. From outside they could just make out angry voices.

"What on earth is going on out there?" Bessie wondered.

She and Doona paused, waiting while Joney and Henry came up behind them. All four were listening carefully when someone shouted loudly from the car park.

"I wish you would just drop dead!"

CHAPTER TWO

"I'd better go see what's going on," Henry said in a tentative voice.

"I think we should all go," Bessie said. "There's safety in numbers."

Henry hesitated a moment longer before nodding. The four cautiously made their way through the door and into the car park. It was dark and overcast outside and the wind was cold and strong enough to feel uncomfortable. A single light stood in the centre of the car park, providing a small amount of illumination and casting eerie shadows in all directions.

Moirrey was standing in front of her late model luxury car, glaring at someone. Her driver stood beside the vehicle looking anxiously from Moirrey to the person standing near her. The other person had his or her back to the building, so Bessie and the others couldn't see to whom Moirrey was speaking. Bessie and the others stopped just outside of the doorway, unsure of what to do next.

"You can wish whatever you like," Moirrey was telling the other person. "But wishing me dead won't change anything. We have a signed legal agreement, after all."

"I'm just asking you for one more week," the other person pleaded. "I'm working two jobs and Jack is across working sixty hours a week. We just need one more week to come up with what we owe you."

Moirrey smiled nastily. "Our agreement is clear," she said. "You are over two months late with your payments and that means the property reverts to me. My advocate will be making arrangements tomorrow to take possession. It would have happened today if it hadn't been Easter bank holiday."

"Please, Ms. Teare, I'm begging you now, please don't throw us out of our home.

"I think you'll find that it's my home. You were meant to be purchasing it from me, but you haven't held up your end of the bargain."

"Your father must be spinning in his grave, watching you," the other person said bitterly. "You know he wanted my father to have that house after all of his years of service."

Moirrey shrugged. "If he wanted him to have it, he would have given it to him. He didn't though; he sold it to him. Admittedly at a ridiculously low price, but still."

"And that's what this is all about, isn't it? Money. You'll get a bunch of lovely money if you steal the house out from under us and then sell it to someone else, won't you?" the stranger demanded.

"Of course," Moirrey answered. "I'm not denying that. You owe me, what, a thousand pounds for two month of late payments. After that, you keep paying me another five hundred pounds a month for five more years and then the property is yours under the old agreement. When I take the house back from you, however, I can sell it for considerably more."

"How much more?"

"Would you believe a developer just offered me a quarter of a million pounds for the property?" Moirrey asked, smiling nastily.

Bessie and the others gasped along with the still unidentified person.

"That's a lot more than the thousand you owe me, isn't it? Of course the developer isn't interested in the house. No, he'll tear that down and build a new housing estate instead."

Bessie could hear sobs coming from Moirrey's adversary.

"Tear it down? That cottage has been my home since I was

born in its back bedroom. I can't believe you'd let them tear it down."

"You'd better believe it," Moirrey said. She paused and then spoke again. "Look," she said in a saccharine-sweet voice, "if I were you, instead of standing around arguing, I'd be at home enjoying my little cottage as much as I possibly could."

With that, Moirrey nodded to her driver, who jumped to open the car door for her.

"Of course," she added as she slid into the plush leather interior, "you really should start packing as well."

Moirrey's driver shut the door behind her before the other person had an opportunity to reply. Bessie and the others watched silently as the expensive car drove from the car park, purring quietly.

As soon as the car was out of sight, the stranger began to sob loudly. Bessie could see his or her shoulders shaking in the dim light. She walked quickly towards the dark figure, ignoring Henry's awkward attempts to stop her.

"Anne Caine, what are you doing here?" Bessie asked, as the crying woman turned when Bessie touched her arm.

"Bessie?" Anne said in confusion. "I didn't expect, that is, ohhhhh."

She burst into a fresh set of tears. Bessie felt around in her handbag, trying to find a packet of tissues. Doona beat her to it, though.

"Here we are," Doona said, handing Anne a tissue and patting her arm gently. "It's going to be okay," she said soothingly, passing out yet another tissue and rubbing the woman's back.

Doona worked at the Isle of Man Constabulary's Laxey station, manning the front desk. She got plenty of practice consoling everyone from parents of temporarily missing children to fighting spouses to confused seniors who had been found wandering lost. She was ideally suited for dealing with a sobbing Anne Caine.

No introductions were necessary. Everyone in Laxey knew the crying woman, even Doona, who'd only lived in the town for a few years. Anne had always been a fixture at the local shop at the top of the hill above the beach where Bessie's cabin stood. There were few residents in Laxey who didn't stop and visit the shop at least once or twice a week. For Bessie it was a somewhat steep climb up, but a pleasant stroll back down. She had been in the habit of shopping there at least three times a week, grabbing lottery tickets, fresh bread and other odds and ends to keep her going between trips to the much larger grocery store in Ramsey.

About six months earlier, however, Anne had been let go. The owner of the shop had decided to replace her with his own daughter, a stroppy, ill-mannered girl of around seventeen. She was sullen and sallow-skinned and she always seemed to be on the phone, complaining to her boyfriend about the customers.

"Oh, I've got to ring up some bread and lottery tickets for some old cow," Bessie heard her say the last time she was in the store. "Not sure why she wants to win the lottery, wouldn't do her any good, all that money, would it? She's got to be nearly a hundred."

Bessie had bristled but remained silent. She wasn't anywhere near a hundred yet, preferring to think of herself as late middle-aged. In truth, once she passed her sixtieth birthday she had stopped counting, but she was aware that she had reached that specific milestone before the girl in the shop had even been born.

That particular encounter had taken place several months earlier and Bessie had since found alternative sources for whatever she needed between proper grocery store trips. She'd only been in the shop once or twice lately. From what she heard, she wasn't the only one who had been put off shopping at the local store and Bessie wouldn't be surprised if the shop found itself out of business before the owner's daughter had worked there a full year.

Now, as Anne sopped up tears with Doona's tissues, Bessie stepped to one side and waited for the other woman to reign in her overwhelming emotions. Once the sobbing had stopped and Anne had more or less composed herself, Bessie couldn't help but ask a few questions.

"What on earth was that all about?" she asked. "What were

you and Moirrey arguing about?"

For a moment, Bessie thought that Anne might tell her that the fight wasn't any of her business, but the woman didn't have enough energy left to argue.

"I suppose I might as well tell you," Anne shrugged. "It'll be all over the island tomorrow anyway."

They were interrupted when Liz and Marjorie walked out of the building. The pair took one look at the scene and rushed over.

"What's going on?" Marjorie demanded.

"It's a little bit complicated," Bessie told her.

Liz frowned. "I promised Bill that I would be home by now," she said apologetically. "He isn't great at putting the kids to bed. He ends up playing with them until they're overtired and then they just cry until I get home."

Marjorie gave her neighbour a quick hug. "Off you go," she insisted. "We'll get everything worked out here."

As Liz hopped into her family-sized saloon car and drove away, Henry gave the others a nervous look.

"I'm not sure I'll be much help," he said hesitantly.

Bessie took pity on the man, who looked desperately uncomfortable at witnessing Anne's tears.

"You head home as well," she urged the man. "I'm sure you have to work early in the morning. You need your rest. It's just the start of the tourist season. If you fall behind on your sleep now, you won't catch up until November when the sites close."

"Aye, you're right about that," Henry smiled at Bessie and then quickly nodded at the others and scurried away. He drove a battered hatchback that didn't seem to want to start. By the time he'd managed to get the car going and exited the car park, Anne appeared much calmer.

"I'm sorry," she told Bessie, Doona, Joney and Marjorie. "I wasn't expecting to bump into that bi..., er, witch here tonight and when I saw her I'm afraid I just lost control."

A loudly ringing mobile phone started them all. Joney quickly dug into her handbag. "Hello?"

The others stood patiently as bits of conversation drifted their way.

"Are you sure it's a fever?"
"Did you try...?"
"What about...?"

Joney clicked the phone off and turned to the others. "I'm really sorry, but I have to go. That was my daughter. The baby had her first jabs today and she's not feeling very well tonight. I think my daughter is more upset than the baby, but I need to go and offer some grandmotherly advice."

She was gone before the others could speak, leaving Bessie to turn to Anne with her questions.

"What brought you here at this hour anyway?" Bessie began.

"I'm working," Anne replied with a sad smile. "Not that it matters, but I'm being paid a bit to clean up after your class tonight."

"In that case," Bessie smiled, "why don't we all go in and have a cuppa? Once we've all had a drink we can give you a quick hand with the tidying."

"Oh no, I'm being paid for the job. I'll do it," Anne insisted.

"Nonsense," Bessie gently overruled her. "We're going to take up your valuable time getting all the skeet on Moirrey. Helping you clean is the least we can do."

Doona laughed at Bessie's honesty as the foursome made their way back into the building. Doona hovered right behind Bessie as they climbed the stairs for the second time that night, but Bessie was grateful that she didn't fuss further. Back in their classroom, Marjorie quickly boiled another kettle of water and made the tea. Doona arranged four chairs in a circle around the table and opened another box of biscuits. Then the foursome settled in for a chat.

Bessie sat back and took a good look at Anne. She was shocked by what she saw. Anne had always been slender, but now she was almost emaciated. She had been a plain child, who had grown into a plain woman. Her dark brown hair was littered with far more grey than Bessie would have expected for a woman of forty. The grey stopped abruptly about two inches from Anne's unflattering centre part. Clearly she had been accustomed to colouring her hair in the past. Anne's eyes were red and swollen from all the crying. Bessie knew that normally Anne's eyes were a dark brown that had matched her hair, before the grey had moved in.

Anne sighed as she quickly finished her tea and poured another cup. "I suppose I should just tell you everything," she sighed.

Bessie patted her hand. "We may be able to help," she told her in a gentle voice.

"No one can help," Anne countered. "But there's no point trying to keep secrets on this island, anyway." She sighed again. "I know my life story isn't exactly a secret but I don't know how much people know about the arrangements that were made for my cottage."

Bessie shrugged. "From what I heard, your father bought it from Ewan Teare, Moirrey's father, at a bargain price after many years of service as his estate manager."

"That's about right," Anne replied. "Except I'm not sure the price was such a bargain. Dad signed a thirty-year loan note with Mr. Teare. The cottage would have been paid off this year, when dad would have turned sixty-five. Unfortunately, dad and Mr. Teare had a bit of a falling out towards the end of 1973 and dad went a little bit off the rails for a while. Once they made up, dad was something like six months behind in his payments. Mr. Teare renegotiated the terms through his new advocate, Matthew Barnes, and part of the deal extended the term of loan for an additional five years."

Bessie drew a sharp breath. "I'm sure your father didn't get a fair deal with that conniving, sniveling, back-stabbing cretin drawing up the agreement."

Anne shrugged. "I guess you've heard of him, then."

Bessie intercepted Doona's questioning look and shook her head gently. She could fill Doona in later.

"Bessie, I don't like the man any better than you do," Marjorie interrupted. "He certainly has never done the museum any favours. But I don't know that he's all that bad."

Bessie shook her head. "You won't change my mind about him," she told Marjorie. "There's no point in discussing it."

Anne shrugged. "Whatever your opinion of the man, he drew up a new agreement and my father signed it. It was designed, I was told later, to help keep my father sober. Dad loved his drink a bit too much; that was one of the causes of the fight he had with Mr. Teare. The new agreement had strict penalties for late payments. Mr. Teare wasn't having dad get six months in arrears again."

"Did your father have his own advocate check over the agreement?" Bessie asked.

"Dad didn't think he needed to do any such thing. Mr. Teare would have been insulted and dad trusted him completely." Anne shrugged. "When dad signed it, I was fifteen and planning for a brilliant future as a schoolteacher," Anne sighed. "Everyone knows how I fu..., er, um, messed that up."

Bessie grinned at the aborted curse. Anne had been brought up properly. It was unfortunate she had made one small mistake that had had such long-term and devastating consequences.

"Anyway," Anne continued, "I never thought the agreement was a bad deal until recently."

"What happened recently?" Doona asked.

Anne flushed. "You all know I lost my job," she said quietly. "That was the first bit of bad luck. Jack's always struggled to hold down steady employment." Anne turned an even brighter red and took a long drink.

Bessie and Doona exchanged looks. Everyone did know that Anne's husband, Jack, had trouble holding a job. The only thing that Jack held down successfully was the third bar stool from the left in *The Cat and Longtail* pub in downtown Laxey. He'd been a fixture there since the place opened in the nineteen-eighties. He'd get odd jobs here and there, whenever Anne put her foot down, but it was never long before he was turning up to work drunk if he bothered to turn up at all.

"Anyway," Anne continued, "for the first few months we assumed I'd find something else fairly quickly, but it turns out no one is looking for a middle-aged woman without even a single O-level to her name. After a while, we started to try to cut back on our expenses, and we started selling whatever we could, but we'd always pretty much lived from month to month. We didn't have any savings and not much of value to sell. By February we'd run out of money and couldn't pay Moirrey."

Bessie shook her head. "You should have come and talked to me," she told the woman. "I would have helped you somehow."

Anne shrugged. "I don't know what you could have done," she said sadly. "But I appreciate the offer."

Bessie kept silent. She had been fortunate to receive an inheritance in her youth that had allowed her to buy her small cottage and make a few cautious investments. Her advocate, Doncan Quayle, had acted as her financial advisor, something at which, it turned out, he was quite proficient. Bessie had never had to find paid employment; instead she had been able to live relatively comfortably within her small income in her tiny cottage, which she was able to extend twice, thanks to her advocate's moneymaking talents.

Her only real extravagance, aside from her home, had always been books. After years of watching every penny and rationing her purchases, she had found herself a relatively wealthy woman in recent years. For her, the very definition of wealth was being able to go to the local bookstore and buy whatever she fancied without worrying about the prices.

She definitely could have helped Anne Caine with her financial difficulties, as she occasionally helped others in the small and close-knit community. Her only stipulation, when she did help, was that the recipients of her kindness not tell anyone from where their assistance had come. The last thing Bessie wanted was everyone on the island talking about her generosity.

"So what happens now?" Doona asked.

"I guess I need to move," Anne said sadly. "I've no idea where I'll go, or how I'll afford anything else, though."

"Didn't you say something to Moirrey about only needing another week to get the money together?" Marjorie asked.

"I did," Anne agreed, "but I was lying. I was just hoping that that woman might give me just a little bit more time. I am working two jobs, but neither one pays much of anything. There's no way I can find a thousand pounds in a week. My only hope was Jack.

He's across trying to find Andy to see if he can help us out. Andy's been living across for five years and we're hoping he's doing well enough to loan us some money."

"So Jack didn't go over to find work?" Bessie asked.

Anne laughed hollowly. "Jack? Work? After all these years of sponging off of me, why on earth would he start working now?"

"So that he doesn't lose his home?" Doona suggested.

"He'll tell you that the cottage has never really been 'his' home," she sighed. "I've lived there my entire life, but he claims he's always felt like an intruder there. I don't know, maybe he shouldn't even bother coming back to the island now."

"I suppose Moirrey is still using Mr. Barnes for her legal affairs?" Bessie checked.

"Yes, at least that's who keeps sending the threatening letters."

"I shall have young Doncan get in touch with him first thing in the morning, then. If the agreement between your father and Moirrey's isn't fair then it shouldn't be legally binding. Moirrey is about to find that she has a fight on her hands."

Anne shook her head. "I appreciate the idea," she said, "but young Doncan Quayle's father is the man who drew up the original agreement between my father and Moirrey's. I don't know what was in the original, but it might not have been any fairer than the second one. I can't see young Doncan battling against something his own father set into place."

"You might be surprised," Bessie answered. "Young Doncan didn't always see eye to eye with his father when it came to the ethical side of the law. He might well relish a chance to right old wrongs committed by his father."

"Sorry," Doona interrupted, "but how many Doncan Quayles are there?"

Bessie laughed. "Three. Doncan James Quayle was the first Doncan. His father, William, was actually my first advocate on the island, but he died young, not long after his son was called to the bar. Doncan James had one son, whom he also named Doncan, but he called him Doncan William, so he wasn't, strictly speaking, a junior. Doncan William is now known as Doncan Quayle, Sr., but I still tend to think of him as 'young Doncan.' Young Doncan also has a son, whom he called Doncan William, Junior. Junior is in his mid-twenties and working towards his law degree. Young Doncan, who is at least fifty, is my advocate now, and he's a lovely man."

Donna nodded. "I think I get it," she said uncertainly.

"I think young Doncan can really help," Bessie told Anne again.

Anne shrugged. "If you think he can help," she said with a sigh, "I guess we can try. I can't afford to pay him for his time, though."

Bessie waved that away. "I'm sure Doncan will defer his fee until everything is straightened up and you're back on your feet again," she said. And if he won't, I'll pay the fee myself, she added silently.

After that the foursome got busy. Bessie washed and dried cups and plates and Marjorie carefully put them away while Doona walked through the room with a duster and Anne ran the vacuum through the space.

"I don't have to do the rest of the building," Anne told them when they'd finished. "Really, Kate just gave me this job because she feels sorry for me."

Kate Christian ran the organisation that owned the small building.

"One more thing, and then we can go," Bessie said, sitting down at one of the desks. "Do you pay Moirrey the loan money directly or do you pay it through someone else?"

"I pay Moirrey directly, why?" Anne asked.

Bessie reached into her bag and pulled out her chequebook. She wrote carefully for a moment and then tore out and handed a cheque to Anne. "There's a cheque for Moirrey for fifteen hundred pounds. That covers February, March and April, so you have a little extra time to get caught up before your next payment is due at the end of May," she explained to a bewildered-looking Anne.

"But I can't take this," Anne stammered.

"Of course you can," Bessie told her. "Take it to Moirrey first thing tomorrow and tell her to stop making threats."

"But according to the agreement, she doesn't have to take the cheque," Anne argued. "I've already failed to keep my side of the agreement."

"She'll take it," Bessie told her. "Or she'll have to answer to me and my advocate. You'd better believe she isn't going to want to do that."

Anne looked uncertain, but she didn't argue any further. Instead, they all made their way out of the building. Anne locked the door behind them and walked to her old compact car. Marjorie climbed into her own estate car that was always filled with boxes full of paper, and the two were already pulling away by the time Bessie and Doona were safely buckled up into Doona's two-year-old mid-sized auto.

"That was awfully nice of you," Doona said to Bessie as they made their way out of the car park.

"I wasn't about to let Anne lose her house," Bessie answered. "That child has had a hard enough life."

"Go on then, tell me everything," Doona demanded.

Bessie nodded. "You know I don't usually gossip," she told Doona. "But, as Anne said, there aren't any secrets on this island. You would know the story if you had been smart enough to live in Laxey your whole life."

Doona laughed. "I suppose I should apologise for my parents' bad judgment," she said.

"Indeed," Bessie shot back. "Although I'm not sure Laxey has been so good for Anne Caine."

"Go on then, tell me the whole story. Start with how Anne messed up her own future."

"She did that in the most common way," Bessie replied. "She got pregnant at sixteen. Her own mother had died in childbirth and, while her father, Robert, did his best to bring her up well, she really needed her mother. Mrs. Teare was the closest thing she had to a mother figure and she was, well, not especially maternal, at least not until Moirrey came along. And after that, Moirrey absorbed pretty much one hundred percent of Mrs. Teare's time and attention."

"I didn't realise Anne even had children," Doona said.

"Just the one," Bessie replied. "And Andy couldn't wait to turn eighteen and get off the island. He quit school as soon as he could and then worked every odd job he could find and saved every penny until he had enough saved to fund a move to London. That must have been five years ago, and as far as I know he's never been back, not even to visit."

"It sounds like he's not afraid of a little hard work, at least. Not like his father."

"Yes and no," Bessie sighed. "From what I've heard, he didn't make a lot of effort at school or help out at home. He was only motivated when he decided he was leaving."

"With that father of his, it's hardly surprising he wanted to get away," Doona said. "Do you know every time I went in *The Cat and Longtail* Jack Caine tried to chat me up? From what I've heard, he tried to sleep with every woman who walked in the place and a few who were just strolling past. I don't reckon he had much luck, though. He isn't exactly an attractive man, is he?"

"You should have seen him in his younger days," Bessie told her. "When he was eighteen he had all the girls running after him."

"And he chose Anne?" Doona asked incredulously. "I mean, she's a really nice woman, but even in the first flush of youth she couldn't have been all that beautiful."

Bessie laughed. "No, she was never beautiful. I don't think Jack chose her as much as tried to get together with every single girl he met. He was just unfortunate that Anne was the one who ended up pregnant. There weren't as many options in those days for unexpected pregnancies, of course. The story goes that Anne's father and Ewan Teare got together and went to see Jack. Apparently he wasn't given a whole lot of choice in the matter, but then again, neither was Anne."

"So they've been unhappily married ever since?" Doona asked.

"Indeed," Bessie replied. "Although I don't know that they were all that unhappy, at least in the beginning. When Andy was small and Ewan Teare and Robert Hall were both still alive, Anne and her little family seemed to be doing okay. It was only after

Ewan passed away that money seemed to start to be an issue. I'm not sure what exactly was going on over there, though. The Teares have always fiercely guarded their privacy."

"That can't have been popular on an island that thrives on skeet," Doona laughed.

"Everyone had their own opinions about the family, and I doubt they've stopped talking about them even now, when Moirrey is the only one left."

Doona nodded. "Someone rang in a couple of weeks ago to report seeing lights on in the old Teare house. We sent a patrol over but they didn't find anything suspicious. But why doesn't Moirrey live there anymore?"

"That's one of the big questions that everyone would love an answer to," Bessie told her. "All she's ever said is that the house is too large for her, especially with her heart condition. She claims she can't be going up and down all those stairs all day."

"And what do you think is the real reason?" Doona asked.

"Money, or lack of it," Bessie answered. "I don't think dear old Ewan left his only daughter as well off as everyone seems to think. I can't imagine she's happy living in one of the former servants' cottages while her grand mansion sits empty, I just don't think she can afford to run the big house. I think that's part of why she's pushing Anne so hard. She needs the quarter of a million pounds."

"I would rather think she just a nasty person," Doona laughed.

"Oh, don't get me wrong," Bessie assured her. "She is a very nasty person, too, but in this case I think there's more going on than just nastiness. And I'm sure Mr. Barnes has a hand in the trouble between Anne and Moirrey as well; he simply must."

"Oh yes, what's the story with him?" Doona asked. "I've never heard you mention him and I certainly didn't know how badly you dislike him."

Bessie sighed. By now they had pulled up in front of her small cottage and were sitting with the engine running. "If we're going to talk about him, you'd better come in for bit," she told Doona. "It's a long story."

Doona shook her head. "It's half ten already," she said. "As much as I hate to say it, I need to get home and get my beauty sleep. I've got to be to work at seven tomorrow."

"Oh dear," Bessie answered. "I didn't realise that. Off you go."

Doona insisted on seeing Bessie safely inside her small cottage. Bessie stood patiently in her small kitchen as Doona rushed through the cottage, checking for hidden intruders.

"Okay, you're good," Doona said as she came back down the stairs and through the kitchen.

"There was never any doubt in my mind about that," Bessie told her.

Doona opened her mouth to reply, but then snapped it shut.

Bessie thanked her profusely for the ride back and forth to class before Doona headed home.

In her little cottage, Bessie carefully locked her doors, a precaution she was far more careful about in the last month or so. She grabbed her latest mystery novel from the small side table in the sitting room where she had been reading it before Doona arrived to take her to class.

Upstairs, she changed into her nightgown and brushed her teeth and hair. She studied her face in the mirror after she washed it. She had been told more than once that she had been beautiful in her youth and she figured she wasn't holding up too badly.

She kept her grey hair cut short, and the style suited her face. Her eyes had always been grey and while they had often seemed to fade into the background when her hair had been darker, they seemed to have become the focal point of her face now that they matched her hair. She had always had perfect vision and now only needed reading glasses, although she could usually get by without them if she absolutely needed to.

She smiled at herself in the mirror and took herself off to bed. She read just one more chapter in the her book and then, with more self-discipline than she usually had when it came to reading, she forced herself to turn off the light and get some sleep.

Tuesday morning saw her up at six as normal, in spite of her late night. She showered and then patted herself all over with her favourite rose-scented dusting powder. It was an old-fashioned habit, in today's world teeming with designer perfumes, but she had never found any perfume that could match the scent of the powder she loved so much. Matthew, the man she had loved and lost before her eighteenth birthday, had always given her roses, usually stolen from his mother's garden, but once or twice he'd actually found the money to buy her a small bouquet. Every morning, as Bessie patted powder on her arms and legs, she closed her eyes and thought, just for a moment, about Matthew.

Dressed, she ate a quick breakfast and then took her customary morning walk along the beach just outside the back door of her cottage. She walked as far as the "new" cottages, smiling and nodding at a young family that was just emerging from one of the cottages as she walked past. Now that Easter was past, the cottages would just get busier and busier throughout the spring and summer season.

On her return trip, the oldest child of the family had begun a wobbly sandcastle and his little sister was sobbing as her mother tried to brush sand out of her mouth.

"She grabbed a handful before I could stop her," the father was saying helplessly to his obviously angry wife.

"And you wonder why I don't leave you in charge of them for any length of time," the wife shouted back. "I was gone for two minutes, two bloody minutes."

The toddler looked up from his castle building and met Bessie's eyes. He almost seemed to shrug at Bessie as if to say his parents' behaviour was nothing new. Bessie sighed to herself and headed home.

The sign next to her door read "Treoghe Bwaaue," which was Manx for "Widow's Cottage." Some days Bessie wondered if she and Matthew would have done a better job of marriage and parenting than the examples she sometimes saw around her.

When she got inside, she took off her sandy trainers and then switched the ringer on her phone back on. She turned it off at night so that wrong numbers or salesmen didn't disturb her. As she reached for the play button on her answering machine, the phone rang. Startled, she picked up the receiver without waiting to hear who it was.

"Hello?"

"Bessie? It's Doona. Sit down. Are you sitting down? Moirrey's dead."

CHAPTER THREE

Bessie gasped and then sank into the nearest chair. "Pardon?" she muttered.

"I said, Moirrey's dead," Doona repeated. "We just got the call here and Hugh and Inspector Rockwell headed out to her cottage to see what happened."

"You don't think she was murdered?" Bessie asked.

"Bessie, we've had two murders in Laxey since I've lived here, both last month and both of which you know more about than most people. I can't imagine that this will turn out to be another one. Laxey is one the safest places in the world to live."

Bessie nodded and then realised that Doona couldn't see her. "Oh, er, sorry, of course. I guess, after last month, I've just got murder on my mind," she said apologetically.

"She kept telling us all that she had heart trouble," Doona said. "Maybe all that arguing with Anne was too much for her."

"Oh goodness, I hope not," Bessie exclaimed. "Anne will never forgive herself."

"She shouldn't feel like she's to blame, even if that is what killed her," Doona said stoutly. "Moirrey brought it on herself, being nasty and horrible to everyone."

Bessie chuckled. "She was rather nasty to you last night, wasn't she?"

"And to you and to everyone else," Doona reminded her

friend. "I know we aren't meant to speak ill of the dead, but I think the vicar is going to have a hard time finding anything nice to say at Moirrey's funeral."

"I hadn't thought of that," Bessie sighed. She wouldn't be surprised if the vicar rang her later to see if she could help with the eulogy. He would be out of luck this time.

"Oh, I have to go," Doona said. "Inspector Kelly just drove past into the car park and I'm sure he'll have a ton of work for me once he gets inside. How about if I come over tonight with dinner? I'll fill you in then."

"That would be great," Bessie agreed. "Maybe bring Hugh with you?" she suggested.

"I'll try," Doona promised as the call ended.

Bessie sat back and tried to figure out exactly what emotion it was that she was feeling. She wasn't mourning for Moirrey, the woman had been too unpleasant for her to feel that, but she did feel sad. Perhaps she was sorry for a life that could have been lived joyously, but was instead suffered miserably.

Bessie shrugged. Moirrey's parents had spoiled their sickly child and Moirrey had been happy to exploit her illness at every possible opportunity. Bessie had often suspected that Moirrey wasn't anywhere near as unwell as she wanted everyone to think, but in light of her untimely death, it appeared that Bessie had been unfair in that regard.

For the next hour, Bessie's phone rang every time she hung it up. Everyone she knew wanted to get the latest skeet on Moirrey, even though Bessie knew nothing more than what was already common knowledge. In between answering calls, she managed to make one.

"Doncan?" she said after his secretary put her through. "I think I might need some help for a friend."

"Please don't tell me that this has anything to do with Moirrey Teare," Doncan said with a sigh.

Bessie laughed. "How did you know?"

"I've had three phone calls already this morning from people who had some sort of legal dealings with Moirrey and are now in a state of panic as to what might happen next," Doncan told her.

"But I wasn't aware that you had any business with the woman."

"I don't," Bessie told him. "But I'm trying to help out a friend."

Doncan laughed. "I should have guessed. You're always helping out a friend. I hope you haven't offered them too much of your money this time?"

"It is my money," Bessie answered.

"I understand that," Doncan backpedalled slightly. "But my job, as your advocate, is to protect you from unscrupulous folks who might take advantage of you."

"And you do your job very well," Bessie told him. "But Anne Caine isn't unscrupulous; she's just had a run of bad luck."

"Oh, it's her you're helping?" Doncan asked. "I can't argue with that, then. She needs all the help she can get."

"Exactly," Bessie said. "She's two months behind in her payments to Moirrey. I think the agreement that her father signed might be unfair, but for now I've written a cheque to Moirrey for the arrears. The question is, with Moirrey dead, what happens now?"

"That's a great question," Doncan told her. "I wish I had an answer. Matthew Barnes is Moirrey's advocate. I'm assuming he has a will for her, although considering her young age, she might not have made one yet. Whatever the case there, however, her father's will only gave her life interest in his estate. As I understand it, on her death, the entire estate goes to her brother."

Bessie gasped. "Her brother? My goodness, I'd plumb forgotten that she had a brother."

"I suspect she might have forgotten as well," Doncan commented dryly. "He was sent to boarding school before she was two, wasn't he? She can't have had many memories of him."

"He did go to boarding school very young." Bessie tried to recall the details. "I know he came home for occasional summers and Christmases, but I also know that Ewan and Jane Teare tended to keep him busy and well away from Moirrey. They were always worried that he would be too rough with his fragile little sister."

"I remember him coming back for a few months before his gap year," Doncan told Bessie. "Junior was tiny and my wife and I were always out and about walking him around to try to get him to sleep. I remember bumping into Ewan and Andrew one afternoon in the middle of nowhere."

"Andrew, that was his name," Bessie laughed. "I'm glad you said it, because I couldn't for the life of me remember it."

"Well, you haven't had much cause to remember it lately, have you? That must have been twenty-five years ago, more or less."

"I wish I could remember more about him," Bessie said with a sigh. "The Teare family kept pretty much to themselves. They had their mansion and you only ever got inside by invitation. They weren't much interested in inviting an old spinster with no social connections to visit."

Doncan laughed. "I wouldn't describe you that way at all," he told Bessie. "But you're right about the Teares. I think I've only been in the mansion a handful of times, mostly from when I was Ewan's advocate. Of course, once he moved his business elsewhere I didn't have any reason to be there."

"I've heard it was beautiful inside," Bessie sighed. "Now it's just sitting there empty and I've heard it is very run-down."

"You know, this could be good news for Junior," Doncan told her. "He went with me on a visit there many years ago. He couldn't have been more that five or six at the time. We never got past the huge foyer, but he fell in love with the place. He's been wanting to buy it ever since."

"It must be worth a fortune," Bessie suggested.

"I'm sure it won't go cheap," Doncan agreed. "But it does need an awful lot of work, from what I'm told. Junior has a fairly substantial inheritance from my father that he's been saving for many years. I know he's made a few tentative offers to Moirrey in the past, but she always refused to even consider selling the estate. Her brother, assuming he can be tracked down, might be more amenable."

"I suppose tracking down Andrew Teare has to be Mr. Barnes first priority, then?"

"Indeed. I would suggest that Anne and her cottage are in limbo until he can manage that. Have her ring me if Mr. Barnes contacts her in any way, please."

"I will definitely do that," Bessie agreed. She hung up feeling slightly better about Anne's future. Whatever happened, Doncan was on the case and he'd never let Bessie down yet.

Bessie was due to give a research paper at a conference at the Manx Museum in Douglas in about a month's time. She wasn't in the mood to work on her research, but with time slipping away, she forced herself. By lunchtime she felt she'd worked hard enough, though, and she allowed herself an indulgent afternoon, curled up with a new book. She grinned as the murderer was revealed. The guilty party was exactly whom she suspected throughout the story.

Doona was due to arrive in less than an hour. Since Doona had promised to bring dinner with her, Bessie decided to mix up some shortbread. She'd had a handful of children visit over the Easter weekend and she'd almost run out of homemade treats. She was always careful to stock a range of store-bought goodies for just such an emergency, but she preferred to offer her guests something she'd made herself whenever possible.

Bessie's whole house was filled with the fabulous aroma of freshly baked buttery shortbread when, an hour later, the doorbell rang. As Bessie opened the door for Doona and Hugh, Hugh was already excited about pudding.

"Do I smell shortbread?" he asked, his eyes shining exactly like they had when he had visited Bessie when he was eight.

"Yes," Bessie laughed. "You can have a piece if you eat all your veggies."

Hugh was in his mid-twenties with brown hair and matching eyes. He still looked not much more than fifteen. Bessie grinned at the odd wisps of hair that poked out at strange angles from Hugh's upper lip. Perhaps he would manage to grow a mustache once he hit thirty. Bessie had learned recently that he was smarter than he often appeared and that he had high hopes of advancing in his chosen field of police work.

"I'll eat all my veggies," he now promised Bessie. She didn't doubt it; he still had the overgrown appetite of a teenaged boy to go with his appearance. That might catch up with him in later years as well.

Doona had brought several containers of Chinese food and Bessie quickly passed out plates and everyone loaded them up with generous helpings. Doona had also brought a bottle of wine and, as they all took seats at Bessie's kitchen table, Doona opened it and poured it into three glasses.

"I really shouldn't," Hugh said. "I'm driving."

"So am I," Doona replied. "But I think we need to drink a toast to Moirrey Teare."

Hugh didn't argue further. They each took a glass and clinked them together gently.

"To Moirrey," Bessie said solemnly.

"To Moirrey," the others echoed.

For a few minutes everyone ate silently, until curiosity got the better of Bessie.

"So what exactly happened to Moirrey?" she demanded.

Hugh shrugged and swallowed. "Dr. Quayle reckons her heart just gave out," he told Bessie and Doona. "She was born with some sort of heart condition, apparently. He was happy to sign the death certificate as natural causes."

Bessie opened her mouth to protest and then shook her head. She had been reading too many murder mysteries lately. Murder in real life, though, was rare. It was far more likely that Dr. Quayle was correct. Even if no one on the island was really going to miss Moirrey, no one would have murdered her.

"So that's it, then?" Doona asked. "No police investigation?"

Hugh smiled at them. "Officially, there won't be any police investigation," he told them. "But you know how Inspector Rockwell is working with some of us on investigative techniques?" he asked the others.

When they nodded, he continued. "Well, since this case has some interesting elements, the inspector is using it like a training exercise."

Bessie smiled. She'd met Inspector Rockwell only a month earlier, but so far she had found much she liked about the man. He had worked in CID in Manchester before he and his family relocated to the island. Now living in Ramsey, he had been given temporary command of the Laxey station during a recent reshuffle. When he'd been given the assignment, he'd offered to start doing some CID training with some of the young constables. Bessie was delighted that he seemed to be following up on his plan.

"So what does that mean?" Doona asked.

"Basically, after the doctor left, we processed the scene as if it were a crime scene. We carefully gathered evidence and filled out request forms for laboratory processing, things like that. Inspector Rockwell even had us collect fingerprints from all of the prescription bottles on Moirrey's dresser."

Bessie's eyes shone with excitement. "That sounds like such, well, fun isn't the right word. It sounds so interesting. I don't suppose the Isle of Man Constabulary has any interest in hiring an older woman?"

Hugh laughed. "Sorry, Aunt Bessie, but I don't think you can join the force after the age of fifty or so."

Bessie frowned. "I didn't think so," she sighed. "I should have given it a go when I was younger. I suppose I would have had to learn to drive if I joined as well, wouldn't I?"

"I would think so," Hugh answered. "At least all the constables I know have driving licenses."

"I've been thinking about getting one, anyway," Bessie told him. "Not driving is getting to be inconvenient."

"Oh, ah," Hugh took a drink of his wine and then focussed on his food.

Bessie looked over at Doona. "Do you think I should try driving?" she asked her friend.

Doona shook her head. "If you start driving, I won't get to see as much of you. I enjoy running errands with you and picking you up for our class and that sort of thing."

Bessie nodded slowly. "I hadn't thought of that," she said eventually.

"You were going to tell me about Matthew Barnes," Doona changed the subject.

Bessie sighed. "In that case, let's get our dinner dishes out of the way and grab some shortbread. I need the sugar if I'm going to be telling this story."

Bessie cut generous triangles of the still warm shortbread and piled it onto plates while Hugh and Doona cleared up the dinner dishes. When the kettle boiled, Doona made tea for everyone and they all settled back down to enjoy the crumbly shortbread with their tea.

"Matthew Barnes," Bessie sighed. "I try to avoid even thinking about that man."

"I've been told he's a good advocate," Hugh offered.

"I'm sure he is," Bessie answered. "As long as you don't mind being represented by someone lacking in ethics."

Hugh frowned. "Are you suggesting he's doing something criminal?"

"Of course not, he's an advocate," Bessie shook her head. "I'm sure he's always just barely on the right side of the law, but I think he tiptoes quite close to the edge sometimes."

"So what exactly did he do to upset you?" Doona asked.

"I've always used the Quayle Firm for my legal affairs," she told the others. "William Quayle was already established in Laxey when I moved back here with my parents all those years ago. After his death, I started working with his son Doncan, and when he passed away I was happy to stay with young Doncan. Of course young Doncan is now somewhere around fifty and I expect I'll end up using Doncan, Junior, in the future."

Doona shook her head. "Too many Doncans," she complained.

Bessie laughed. "Sorry about that. I don't know why men feel the need to name their sons after themselves, but so many of them do it and it just confuses things."

"So where does Matthew Barnes come in?" Hugh asked around a mouthful of shortbread.

"In the early seventies, he moved from London to the island and set up shop in Douglas. There's always plenty of work for advocates in Douglas, I suppose, but after a while Mr. Barnes started to look around the rest of the island. Right around then, the first Doncan Quayle died. His son, young Doncan, had only been qualified for a year or two and he was suddenly in charge of the family law firm. That was when Mr. Barnes decided to open a branch office in Laxey."

Doona shook her head. "That wasn't very nice of him," she commented. "Poor Doncan was just getting started and Mr. Barnes was there to try to get all the new business."

"If he'd kept himself to trying to get the new business, I'm sure I wouldn't dislike him so much," Bessie said. "Instead, he actively began chasing after Doncan's clients. Why, he even had the nerve to come here and sit right at this table and try to persuade me to move my legal affairs to his control."

"I'd have loved to be a fly on the wall for that visit," Doona laughed.

Bessie grinned. "I was not best pleased," she admitted. "I'm not usually rude to guests in my own home, but I didn't waste any time being pleasant to him once I realised what he was after, that's for sure."

"I suppose other clients were less loyal to Doncan Quayle?" Hugh asked.

"Indeed," Bessie sighed. "Mr. Barnes offered various incentives, including lower fees, to people who moved their business to his newly established firm. I was also told that he hinted very strongly that young Doncan wasn't really up to the task yet, that he was too young and inexperienced to handle anything more complex than basic legal practice. Doncan was struggling to keep his head above water as it was. He didn't have time to chase around the countryside trying to persuade people that he was capable."

Bessie sighed. "It's been twenty-five odd years and I still get angry when I think about it," she told the others. "Mr. Barnes came very dangerously close to driving Doncan right out of business."

"It got that bad?" Doona said in surprise.

"There were other factors at work as well," Bessie told her. "The first Doncan was fairly unscrupulous and pretty ruthless, which worked well for a lot of people. He and his son didn't always agree on matters of ethics. Young Doncan made some changes when he took over. He's less ruthless and more interested in finding fair and workable solutions that everyone can live with. Some of his clients weren't happy about that and they found a lot to like in Matthew Barnes."

"So what happened? I mean, I know Doncan Quayle is very successful today," Doona said.

"He managed to ride out the storm," Bessie replied. "A few of his oldest customers stuck by him and, slowly, over time, many of his former clients came back as well, the ones who preferred ethical behaviour in their legal dealings, anyway. I don't think Doncan regrets losing the others, quite frankly."

"And Ewan Teare went with Mr. Barnes?" Hugh asked.

"Indeed. He was one of the first to move and when he passed away Moirrey stayed with Mr. Barnes. I think she was even more devious than he is, although I mustn't speak ill of the dead."

Doona laughed. "Is there any other way to speak of Moirrey?"

Bessie sighed. "I wish I could have liked her more," she told the others. "I feel badly that I'm not more saddened by her passing."

"We can't like everyone who comes into our lives," Doona replied. "I have two ex-husbands, remember? I know all about not liking people."

Bessie and Hugh both laughed and then Bessie started talking about a new book she had just finished. Half an hour later the little party broke up with everyone in good spirits. Bessie watched Hugh waddle out to his car, full to bursting with Chinese food and shortbread.

"We need to find him a nice girl," Doona remarked as he drove away.

"After all your talk about ex-husbands, I'm sure you've put him off the idea of ever getting married." Bessie teased.

"I didn't say anything about him getting married," Doona countered. "I just want him to find a nice girl. There are a few around, but none of them seem interested in the neighbourhood constable."

"Matchmaking has never been my strong suit," Bessie told her truthfully. Actually, she'd never really tried it, preferring to let people make their own choices and their own mistakes when it came to love. Her own love affairs had been complicated and both had ended badly. She didn't want to be responsible for any such thing in anyone else's life.

"It's never been mine, either," Doona admitted. "But maybe this time I'll get lucky, or rather Hugh will."

With that, Doona had gone as well and Bessie locked up the cottage door. Tomorrow she needed to finish her research so that she could actually start writing the paper she was going to present. She needed to do some grocery shopping as well and, there was no getting around it, at some point she needed to practice her Manx.

She really should have practised with Doona over dinner, but she told herself that she didn't want Hugh to feel left out. It was as good an excuse as she could come up with to cover up for the fact that she simply didn't want to practice. Manx was difficult and she was acting like a stroppy schoolgirl, refusing to do her homework because it was too hard. She'd give herself a stern talking-to the next day, she decided. And she would practice her Manx.

CHAPTER FOUR

Bessie spent most of Wednesday working on her paper, her resolve from the previous day all but forgotten. On Thursday afternoon, she was delighted when Doona rang.

"I was thinking that we should have dinner tonight and practice our Manx," Doona told her.

"I was thinking that very thing," Bessie said untruthfully. She hadn't really been thinking about her language class at all, and now she felt guilty about it.

"I've ever so much to catch you up on," Doona said.

"Like what?" Bessie demanded.

"We can talk tonight," Doona laughed. "I'll bring pizza and chocolate fairy cakes from the new bakery in town."

Bessie smiled at the phone. "Something exciting must have happened if you're bringing chocolate." Doona just laughed.

Bessie hadn't done much housework over the last few days, devoting herself to her research instead. Now she worked her way around her cottage with a duster and the vacuum cleaner. Her least favourite job was cleaning bathrooms, but she couldn't entertain a guest if they weren't hygienic, so she took the time to clean them as well.

By the time Doona arrived, the cottage was spotless and Bessie felt like she'd earned pizza and, more importantly, chocolate. It was raining lightly by that time, so Bessie was watching for her friend. She had the door to the cottage open before Doona was out of her car. Doona rushed into the house, accompanied by the smells of spicy pizza sauce and gooey melted cheese.

"Oh, yum," Bessie said as she took the hot box from Doona and set it on the counter.

She had already pulled out plates, so the pair quickly piled slices of pizza onto them and sat down. Doona grabbed them each a can of fizzy drink from the fridge. Aside from an occasional murmur of enjoyment, they ate silently for several minutes.

After her fourth slice, Doona sat back and patted her tummy. "That was delicious."

"And we still have pudding," Bessie smiled.

She cleared away the pizza plates, discarding the now empty box.

Doona opened the bakery box of fairy cakes and placed one in the centre of a clean plate for Bessie. Then she took one for herself, carefully putting it on a plate of its own. Bessie had rules for how food should be served in her home and anyone who was hoping to be invited back made sure to follow them, regardless of what they did in their own homes.

"I'm sure chocolate has some sort of magical properties," Bessie told Doona after her first bite of cake. "Eating it makes me feel better about life."

Doona laughed. "I know exactly what you mean."

"But you had things you wanted to talk about," Bessie reminded her friend. "What's up?"

"Fastyr mie," Doona answered.

"Oh, yes, er, fastyr mie," Besse replied.

"Kys t'ou?"

"Ta mee braew, kys t'ou?"

"Oh, I'm ta mee braew as well," Doona laughed. "And now we can cross practising our Manx off the list of things to do tonight."

Bessie grinned. "I wish I could get more excited about practising," she said. "I enjoy the class and I love learning, but somehow practising seems like hard work."

"Well, anyway, we've done it now," Doona said. "Let's talk about more interesting things. You'll never guess who I met yesterday."

Bessie laughed and then looked thoughtful. "So I must guess someone highly unlikely," she said. "But it must be someone that I know or at least know of, or else you couldn't expect me to guess."

Doona shook her head. "I should know better than to tease you," she sighed.

Bessie laughed. "I guess that means I'm on the right track," she mused. "Considering recent events and your job at the police station, I'm going to guess that it was someone with a connection to Moirrey."

Doona sighed deeply. "You read too many mysteries; you're half detective yourself."

Bessie laughed. "I haven't guessed yet," she said, "but I will. I'm going to guess that you met Andrew Teare yesterday."

Doona's jaw dropped. "How, but, how could you possibly have guessed that?"

Bessie laughed again. "I wish I could say that I worked it out, but his return after twenty-five years less than twenty-four hours after his sister died is the most exciting skeet anyone's heard in weeks. I must have had ten phone calls about him today."

Now Doona laughed. "And here I was, all impressed with your powers of deduction."

"The way I heard it, he just walked into the Laxey station and introduced himself," Bessie told Doona. "Is that really what happened?"

Doona shrugged. "Pretty much. Did your sources tell you anything else?"

"Not really," Bessie said. "I think everyone was just surprised at the timing. Maggie Clague said he didn't look at all like she remembered, but she was two when he left for his gap year, so how she's supposed to remember him, I don't know. Anyway, I'm sure you can tell me more than anyone else. What did he have to say?"

"Well," Doona said with a smile, "he walked in and came up to me and said 'hello gorgeous.'"

"That sounds like a good start," Bessie grinned at the obvious pleasure on Doona's face. Clearly she had relished the compliment.

"Oh Bessie," Doona exclaimed. "He certainly doesn't look anything like his sister. He's tall, like around six foot or so, with dreamy dark hair and these soft brown eyes that look like pools of melted chocolate. He has this really sexy accent, sort of half American, half Australian and half British."

"That's too many halves," Bessie pointed out.

"Oh, you know what I mean," Doona laughed. "Anyway, he's really gorgeous and good-natured, and he was very patient with Inspector Rockwell when the inspector demanded all sorts of identification and what have you. He even said: 'you can never be too careful, especially where there's money involved.'"

"I reckon he's right about that," Bessie said. "The Teare estate must be worth a fortune, and with the number of years he's been away, I doubt anyone on the island could be sure to recognise him."

"Not even you?" Doona asked. "Surely you'll recognise him; you know everyone who has ever lived in Laxey."

Bessie shook her head. "I doubt I could identify him," she replied. "The family kept to themselves for the most part. Andrew had private tutors; he didn't go to the local school, and when he wasn't studying he used to spend a lot of time with Robert Hall. Ewan was very keen that his son learn about farming and estate management. In those days they owned a lot of farmland. Of course that's all been sold off now."

"He mentioned that," Doona told her. "He said he was shocked to discover how much of the family's land had been sold over the years. He didn't keep in touch after he left, really. He didn't even know for sure that his father had died."

"Surely he was mentioned in his father's will?" Bessie asked. "Matthew Barnes should have looked for him after his father's death."

"I don't know," Doona shrugged. "Andrew's been travelling all these years. He never did come back and take up a university place. He's lived in America, Canada, Australia, and New Zealand."

"So why come back now?" Bessie asked.

"He said that once he hit forty, a few years ago, he started really thinking about his past. He started to wonder what ever happened to his family and to his little sister."

"What's he done for money all these years?" Bessie asked, suspicious of the man's motives.

Doona shrugged. "He said his father gave him a generous amount to spend during his gap year and he was careful with it. It ran out after a few years in Australia and he started finding odd jobs from then on to pay his way. He said he did a lot of bartending, including a few years on a cruise ship. Really, he's just travelled around and enjoyed himself and not given home a lot of thought."

"Or that's how he tells it," Bessie said sharply.

Doona frowned. "You don't believe him?"

"I don't know," Bessie admitted. "I'd have to talk to him myself, rather than get it all through hearsay. I just think the timing is awfully strange. I suppose these sorts of coincidences do happen in real life sometimes, but it just seems odd to me that he would show up right after his sister died."

"I suppose it's a good thing she wasn't murdered," Doona said. "I guess he would be the chief suspect. That is, assuming he's her heir. I guess he doesn't have to be."

"Whether he is or not, he's in line for a goodly fortune, I would think," Bessie told her. "Moirrey didn't inherit anything outright. She just got a life interest in the estate; at least that's what Doncan told me. The entire estate now passes to Andrew."

"Wow," Doona said. "He's going to be a very rich man."

"Indeed," Bessie agreed. "The next question we must ask, though, is what happens to Anne Caine and her cottage?"

"I actually mentioned her to Andrew," Doona told Bessie.

"How long was he at the station?" Bessie asked. "It seems like you two talked an awful lot."

Doona blushed. "He wasn't at the station long," she muttered.

"So what aren't you telling me?" Bessie demanded.

"We had dinner together last night," Doona confessed. "After he talked to Inspector Rockwell for a bit, he stopped back at the information desk and asked me to have dinner with him. I couldn't see any reason to refuse."

Bessie smiled at her. "I thought you were done with men after your last divorce," she reminded her.

Doona blushed again. "Yeah, well, the thing is, I just felt bad for Andrew. In spite of being born and raised here, he's really a stranger. I figured having dinner with him would be the nice thing to do."

"And the gorgeous looks and sexy accent had nothing to do with it," Bessie teased.

Doona laughed as she blushed even more brightly. "Yeah, oaky, he is gorgeous and his accent makes me giddy, but still, he's a nice guy as well."

"I'm sure he is," Bessie answered. "And if he was able to satisfy Inspector Rockwell as to his identity, he may well be a very rich man as well."

"I'm not sure about the identity issue," Doona told Bessie. "I guess it's more complicated than showing your passport and collecting your fortune."

"And so it should be," Bessie answered.

Doona shrugged. "We didn't really talk about that, but I did overhear Hugh and the inspector talking about DNA testing. Andrew wasn't really pleased when I told him that, but he understood. The police have to be sure that he really is who he claims to be."

"Especially since there probably isn't anyone on the island who can definitely identify him," Bessie suggested.

"I was hoping that he was one of your guests over the years and that you'd be able to vouch for him," Doona told her.

"Sorry, he never stayed in my spare room. I don't think his parents would have let him 'run away' and besides, he was at boarding school from the age of ten or eleven. Most of my 'runaways' are older than that. Moirrey was in her teens when she turned up here."

"Moirrey was one of your young guests?" Doona said in a surprised voice.

"Just the once," Bessie answered darkly. "She was demanding and difficult and rude and obnoxious and I told her the next morning that she was no longer welcome at my home."

"I'll bet that went over well," Doona grinned.

Bessie shrugged. "I suppose Moirrey wasn't pleased, but I guess she knew better than to try anything stupid. She just stayed out of my way after that, which wasn't difficult. Her parents always wanted to keep her at home anyway. She didn't go to the local school either. She was deemed too delicate to attend regular classes."

"Andrew said that, in a way, he wasn't surprised to hear that she had died," Doona said. "He remembered constantly being told to be careful of her every time he was home. I suppose it isn't surprising that he didn't want to come back in a hurry."

"You said you mentioned Anne and her problems to Andrew," Bessie recalled. "What did he have to say about that?"

"He said he couldn't imagine throwing Anne out of her cottage for any reason," Doona replied. "He could barely remember her. She's a few years younger of course, but he had very fond memories of her father. He said he was going to have a long chat with Matthew Barnes about the matter as soon as he could."

"Well, that's a relief," Bessie sighed. "I'm sure Anne will be thrilled to have everything worked out."

"Anyway, even if you can't help identify him, I want you to meet him," Doona told Bessie. "I was hoping you could have dinner with us tomorrow night."

Bessie laughed. "You have a date with the man and you want to bring me along?" she asked.

"It isn't really a date," Doona protested. "The poor man doesn't really know anyone on the island yet, so I said I'd have dinner with him. I suggested that I could bring you along, because you knew his parents and his sister. He's eager to talk to people who might remember the family."

"As I said, I don't really remember him. I have a vague recollection of a small boy with brown hair accompanying his parents at some church service or something, but beyond that, I doubt I ever spoke to him."

"Still, come and have dinner with us, won't you?"

"If you're absolutely certain that you really want me along."

"I'm certain," Doona told her. "I think it will be good for Andrew to talk about his family with someone who knew them. He's dealing with a lot of issues being back here after all these years."

"I'm sure he is," Bessie said thoughtfully.

CHAPTER FIVE

Friday was usually Bessie's grocery shopping day, and this week was no different. She had a standing appointment with her favourite taxi service, and her preferred driver was nearly always the one who collected her after her morning walk. Dave was a safe and steady driver who always treated Bessie with respect. He took her into Ramsey and dropped her off at the large bookstore.

"Now don't be staying in there too long," he told her with a grin. "You have to get some groceries as well."

Bessie laughed. "I'll try to be good," she promised as she headed towards the store. "I'll see you outside ShopFast in three hours."

Dave didn't pull away until she was safely inside the bookstore. Bessie waved to him and then took a deep breath. There was something about the smell of thousands of books all crammed together in one space that just made her feel good.

She browsed through the shelves, not really looking for anything special, but hoping to stumble across something wonderful.

"Oh, Bessie, we've just had a new 'cat' book come in," one of the sales assistants told her as she made her way around the shop. "I haven't even had time to put it out yet."

Bessie smiled. She knew exactly which mystery series the

girl was talking about and it was just the sort of book she was in the mood for today. "I'll take it," she told the girl.

After the bookstore, she wandered through a few charity shops on her way to the grocery store. She managed to add a few second-hand paperbacks to her book collection before she arrived at ShopFast.

The twenty-minute shopping trip took about an hour, as everyone she encountered wanted to hear all of the latest news. They were all talking about Andrew Teare, although no one appeared to have actually seen the man in question as yet.

"I hear he's really fit and tan, like he's been living somewhere sunny," one woman told Bessie.

"I hear he's quite pale and not looking very well," another said. "I reckon he's as sickly as his sister was."

By the time Bessie left the store, she was tired of talking about Andrew Teare. She wasn't about to share any of the information that Doona had given her the previous evening, which meant she had nothing to add to the speculation and rumours.

Dave was waiting for her as arranged and Bessie was happy to get home with her shopping. Once the shopping was put away, she played through her answering machine messages, deleting the ones from people she had just seen in Ramsey. That left only a few calls to return and she did that quickly before making herself a light lunch. Doona had suggested her favourite restaurant for dinner that evening, and she didn't want to spoil her appetite.

Ignoring both her research and the language she was meant to be studying, Bessie spent the afternoon curled up with her new book. Aside from a short tea break, she allowed herself to fall into its pages and lose herself for the rest of the day. When the murderer was caught and everything had returned to normal in that fictional world, Bessie sighed and shut the book. She blinked a few times, slowly letting herself return to reality. There really was nothing like a good book. She supposed that was why she didn't bother to have a television.

With less than an hour to go before Doona was due to collect her, Bessie headed up to her bedroom to get ready. She took a quick shower and then combed out her short hair. She put on a pretty print dress and added a cardigan since the weather wasn't yet as summery as she might have liked. A bit of lipstick and a touch of powder on her nose completed her efforts. She had never been one for wearing much makeup; she wasn't about to start caking it on now.

Doona was right on time and Bessie was both amused and slightly worried at how nervous her friend seemed. They drove the short distance to the restaurant and Doona parked in the small car park.

"I got the last space," Doona complained. "Where will Andrew park?"

"There's plenty of parking on the roads around here," Bessie pointed out. "I'm sure he'll find something."

"He's driving a hire car," Doona fretted. "He won't want to leave that on the road."

"Why on earth not?" Bessie replied. "It isn't like it's his to worry about."

Doona shook her head. "You wouldn't believe how complicated things get if you prang a hire car," she told Bessie.

Doona had booked a table in the back room at *La Terrazza*, which would give them a great deal of privacy. There were only three tables in the back and, while the one they were given had just enough room for four people, the other two tables were only suitable for two each.

"Would you ladies like a drink while you wait for your friend?" the waiter asked.

Bessie ordered a glass of wine and, after a moment's hesitation, Doona joined her.

"I know I'm driving, but not for a while," she told Bessie once the waiter had departed. "And I think the wine might just calm my nerves a bit."

"And why are you so nervous?" Bessie teased.

"I really shouldn't be," Doona answered. "It isn't like this is a date. I just really hope you like Andrew. He seems like such a great guy."

Bessie laughed. "I'm sure he's wonderful," she told Doona. "Relax."

The waiter arrived with the wine at that moment and Doona took a huge drink of hers.

"That's better," she sighed as she sat back in her seat.

"Ah, there you are," a voice from the doorway said.

Bessie looked up and studied the man who was entering the room. He was tall, with dark brown hair that almost seemed too dark for his lighter brown eyes. He was wearing an expensively tailored suit, but he must have lost a few pounds since he'd had it made, as it hung loosely across his shoulders. She supposed that most women would consider him attractive, but he was a bit too polished to appeal to her.

He crossed the small room in two steps and smiled at Bessie and Doona. With a bow, he offered Bessie a bouquet of different coloured roses.

"I hope I have it right," he said with a huge smile. "I'm sure Doona said roses are your favourite."

Bessie smiled and thanked him as she took the flowers. He winked at her.

"If I may?" he asked. He carefully pulled a single red rose from the arrangement and held it out to Doona with a grin.

Bessie looked at him sharply, alarm bells ringing in her head. The man was entirely too smooth and superficially charming for her tastes.

Doona giggled as she took the proffered flower. Bessie frowned, but Doona was too busy gushing her thanks to pay any attention to her friend.

Andrew slipped into his chair and beamed a hearty smile at each woman in turn. "Thank you for agreeing to meet me," he told Bessie. "I'm so eager to hear about everything that happened to my family after I left the island."

"I'm surprised you didn't stay in touch," Bessie replied.

Andrew flushed. "I was such a stupid child," he told Bessie. "I really resented being sent to boarding school, and in my ten- or eleven-year-old mind, I guess I sort of blamed my baby sister for my being sent away."

"Surely she was part of the reason behind the decision?" Doona questioned.

"I don't know," Andrew shrugged. "I think my parents were considering boarding school for me long before she came along. Of course, once she arrived, she was so fragile. My parents didn't think she'd live into adulthood, you know. I suppose I can't blame them for sending away a rambunctious young boy under those circumstances."

"You were simply a perfectly normal young boy," Doona argued.

"Perhaps." Andrew squeezed Doona's hand and then left his covering hers. "But mother and father feared that even that was too much for a medically challenged child like my sister. I never really came home much after I started at school. I spent a lot of school holidays with friends' families and that just seemed to trigger even more resentment in me. By the time I finished school and was ready for my gap year, I wanted nothing further to do with my family. I took the money my father gave me and just disappeared."

"So why come back now?" Bessie challenged. She ignored the angry look that Doona sent her, focussing on Andrew.

"That's a fair question," he told her. "Really, it was only in the last few years that I started thinking about everything that happened. I realised that, in many ways, I was blaming Moirrey for things that took place when she was only a tiny baby. Even if her illness was one of the factors in the decision to send me to school, it was hardly her fault. After I turned forty I suddenly started thinking a lot more about the past. I started thinking about the things I left behind in my anger and my desire to get away from my father. And I started to regret my behaviour."

Doona sighed. "And you got here too late."

Andrew ran a hand across his eyes. "I'm sure I'm going to regret that for the rest of my life," he told them both. "I had imagined any number of different scenarios for my return, from everyone being delighted to see me to my being thrown out of the house, but I never imagined that both father and Moirrey would be gone. And I can't help feeling like Moirrey's death might be partly my fault."

"Your fault, why?" Bessie asked.

"I rang her a few days ago," Andrew answered. "She got quite upset with me on the phone. She made all sort of accusations, saying that I wasn't really Andrew Teare and that I was only after her money, things like that."

He stopped and looked down, swallowing hard. Doona pulled her hand out from under his and began to rub his back gently. After a moment he seemed to compose himself. He gave Doona a small smile and then continued.

"It was heartbreaking for me, of course, but I assumed that she'd come around once I got here. I told her that I would be arriving on the fifteenth and that my first stop on the island would be our home. I didn't realise then that she didn't live in the family home anymore. She still had the old phone number." He shook his head. "I should have come home so many years ago," he said softly. "I was worried about just turning up on Moirrey's doorstep after all these years, but now I'm afraid that the phone call upset her so much that it brought on her collapse."

Andrew's head sank into his hands and his shoulders shook. Bessie looked away, wanting to give him time to compose himself. Doona rubbed his back and murmured meaninglessly at him. After a few minutes he raised his head and sighed.

"I'm sorry," he told both women. "I promised myself I wasn't going to get upset tonight. I just can't believe that my baby sister is dead. After all these years, to finally feel ready to see her again and then to lose her just hours before I got that chance…. please, excuse me."

Andrew walked away from the table, leaving Bessie and Doona to stare after him.

"He's so broken up about losing Moirrey," Doona said softly.

"And yet he didn't feel the need to speak to her for nearly twenty-five years," Bessie replied coolly.

"You don't like him," Doona suggested.

"I don't know him well enough to have an opinion yet," Bessie said. Actually, she didn't like him, but she knew that Doona did, so she was treading carefully. "I still find the timing odd somehow."

"Maybe Andrew's right, maybe Moirrey was upset about his

returning and that caused her heart to fail," Doona said.

"Maybe," Bessie answered.

A seemingly more composed Andrew returned a moment later and Doona carefully turned the conversation to other things. They ate well, delicious Italian food that kept the conversation flowing. Bessie regaled the pair with stories of island life from the years that Andrew had been absent. She told him everything that she could remember about his father and his sister, which turned out to be not very much.

"Your parents were very private people," she told him. "And they kept you very close to home as well. Of course, they did the same with Moirrey, but her health was the issue there."

"I never could understand why my parents didn't let me go to the local school," Andrew replied. "I can't believe that I wouldn't have received just as good an education there as I did from my tutors, some of whom were really dreadful."

"I'm afraid I never got to know your parents well enough to suggest an answer to that," Bessie told him. "They were always perfectly polite, but they were, well, distant."

Andrew nodded. "That's exactly how I remember them," he said. "Except when it came to Moirrey. I think she was something of a surprise baby, but whatever the circumstances, they both seemed to dote on her."

Bessie nodded. "I remember hearing that," she agreed. "There was something about your mother being told she couldn't have any more children so Moirrey was a huge surprise, and then, with her being so ill, they did rather spoil her."

"I gather she wasn't the easiest person to get along with as an adult," Andrew remarked. "Doona was telling me that she was trying to throw Anne Hall out of her home."

"She's Anne Caine now," Bessie told him. "But yes, your sister was trying to throw her out of her cottage. Moirrey wanted to sell the land to a developer."

Andrew shook his head. "I can't believe that she would even consider selling to a developer," he said. "My father must be rolling in his grave. He wanted Robert and his family to have that house forever. Robert did so much for my father, really for the whole family. I was so sad to hear that he'd passed away as well."

"That must have been five years ago," Bessie thought back. "Does that mean that you're not going to move forward with taking possession of the cottage?"

"Of course not," Andrew exclaimed. "I don't know what my sister was thinking, but I don't have any intention of turning that poor woman out into the streets. I wasn't allowed to play with her, of course, but I spent a lot of time with her father, learning about farming and how to run the estate. I was looking forward to using those skills when I came back here. I was shocked that Moirrey had been selling off the land. I was surprised that she could do that without anyone asking me about it."

Bessie frowned. "I'm not sure that she could," she told him. "But Matthew Barnes is the one to talk to about that."

Andrew nodded. "I've already had several long talks with Mr. Barnes. I'm not very happy with the way things were done in my absence, although in many ways I suppose it is my own fault. He even told me that Moirrey was trying to have me declared dead, and I suppose I shouldn't blame her. Anyway, now that I'm back I've asked for a full accounting of the entire estate. It should make for interesting reading."

"Indeed," Bessie said. She'd love to see a copy herself.

Doona scraped up the last smidgen of her chocolate mousse, ate it and then sat back with a sigh. "That was delicious," she said.

"Everything always is here," Bessie remarked.

"I think I have a new favourite restaurant," Andrew said with a smile. "I've eaten in restaurants all over the world, and this was truly exceptional."

"What was your...?" Doona's question was interrupted by a new arrival.

"Can I clear your plates for you?"

"Anne?" Bessie said in surprise. "What are you doing here?"

Anne Caine blushed. "Oh Bessie, Doona, I didn't recognize you. I told you the other night that I was working two jobs to try to make ends meet. This is the other one."

"And we were just talking about you," Bessie told her. "You must remember Andrew Teare."

Andrew rose to his feet and offered his hand. "Anne, it's been so many years, I do apologise for not recognising you."

Anne looked at him with a confused look on her face. "Oh, but,...."

Andrew took her hand, interrupting her. "Please, may I start by saying how sorry I am for everything that my sister put you through? I understand that she was trying to get you removed from your cottage. Let me make it clear that I have no intention of following through on her threats. As far as I'm concerned, that cottage is yours and as soon as all of the legal hurdles are surmounted, I intend to make sure that the property is legally deeded to you and your heirs. Please stop worrying about the overdue payments, or indeed, any additional payments. Your father was friend, confidant and valued assistant to my father for many, many years. That property should have been given to you when my father died. Obviously, I can't turn back time, but I can fix things as soon as I am able."

Anne stood at the table, holding Andrew's hand, with a stunned look on her face. Bessie finally broke the silence.

"Anne, are you okay?" she asked.

Anne shook her head and then pulled her hand away and put her face in her hands for a moment. "Sorry," she said eventually, taking her hands away from her face and pushing her shoulders back. "Sorry, I think I'm completely overwhelmed."

Andrew smiled and then took his seat again. "I know how you feel," he said. "This whole return to the island has been overwhelming for me."

"What brought you back after all this time?" Anne asked, studying his face.

"I'm not totally sure," Andrew replied. "I guess you could call it a desire to reconnect with home."

"When did you arrive?"

"Wednesday morning."

"So, after Moirrey's unfortunate passing?"

"Indeed," Andrew frowned. "I'm still in shock about that,

really."

"I'll bet," Anne said dryly. "Well, I'd better clear your plates or I won't have this job for long." She quickly piled up the dirty dishes. "Did anyone want coffee or anything else?" she asked.

"I think we're good," Bessie answered. "Perhaps you could ask our waiter to bring the cheque?"

Anne nodded and then disappeared out of the room without a backwards glance. Bessie watched her go, puzzling at her behaviour.

"She didn't seem at all grateful to you," Doona complained to Andrew as soon as Anne was out of earshot. "I mean, you offered to give her a house and she just gathered up the dishes and left."

"I'm sure it's all been a huge shock for her," Andrew said. "She might thank me later, once she's had time to think things through. Or maybe she won't. I meant what I said, that house should have been given to her family when my father passed away. I'm sure she resents how she was treated by my sister and I don't blame her one bit."

Bessie suddenly felt completely worn out by everyone else's problems. She was grateful when Doona drove her home a short time later.

"What are your plans for the weekend?" Doona asked, after she had checked Bessie's cottage for intruders.

"I don't really have any," Bessie replied. "I think I'll take it easy and work on the first draft of my paper, unless you wanted to do something."

Doona shrugged. "Andrew said something about maybe doing some sight-seeing this weekend. He hasn't been here in so long; he said he feels like a tourist. I thought we might visit Castle Rushen and Peel Castle, that sort of thing. You're more than welcome to join us, of course."

Bessie laughed. "I'm sure Andrew would just love having me tag along," she said. "You go and have fun with Andrew and I'll see you on Monday night. Do you want me to cook dinner before class?"

"That would be great," Doona answered. "I'll come here straight from work at half five and we can have dinner and practise before class."

"Oh goody," Bessie said unenthusiastically. "More practise."

"Oh come on," Doona laughed. "We didn't say anything in Manx all night tonight."

"Well, oie vie, then," Bessie said in a grumpy voice.

Doona just laughed again. "Oie vie, my dear."

CHAPTER SIX

The weekend seemed to fly past for Bessie. She got a workable first draft of her paper done, but not without a visit into Douglas to check a few things out at the museum library. Bessie also read both of her new paperbacks, adding one to her collection and putting the other in a box to take to a charity shop when she next went into Ramsey. It was important that she be selective about what she added to her shelves, only keeping books that she thought she might want to read again. Otherwise her small cottage would soon begin to overflow with books.

Monday dawned bright and sunny, and Bessie was pleased when she was able to get a long walk in after breakfast. She walked past the new cottages, all the way to the beach below the Pierce family cottage, Thie yn Traie. She stood on the beach for a few minutes, looking up at the house that had been at the centre of events the previous month. She knew that the house was soon going on the market and she hoped that a nice family would buy it and live in it year-round rather than use it as a summer home as the Pierces had done.

With a sigh, she turned and made her way back down the beach. Whatever happened, it was yet another change. It seemed like things were constantly changing on the island. She let her mind wander, thinking about how different her life had been when she had first purchased her little home. None of the other small cottages that had dotted the beach in those days were still standing. Hers was the only one that had withstood redevelopment. And one day, she supposed, her heirs would sell her cottage to someone who would be eager to tear it down and replace it with something more profitable.

Of course, her heirs were all in America. The last thing they needed was a tiny cottage on an isolated beach on a remote island in the Irish Sea. Bessie sighed again. She was working herself into a really bad mood. And she knew that the root cause of the bad mood was nothing to do with her cottage or even the island generally. She was worried about the evening ahead. For the first time since she had met Doona, she was anxious about spending time with her. When Bessie first met her friend, a few years earlier, Doona had just come out of a somewhat bitter divorce. Now she was seemingly falling for Andrew Teare and Bessie felt anxious and unhappy about that.

By the time Doona arrived that evening, Bessie had had a very stern conversation with herself. Whatever happened between Andrew and Doona was their business and not hers, she had told herself. She almost believed it as well.

"Fastyr mie," Doona greeted Bessie.

"Fastyr mie," Bessie replied.

Bessie was quick to serve the shepherd's pie she had made, not wanting to be late for class.

"This is delicious," Doona enthused after a few bites. "Perhaps we should get Marjorie to teach us how to say that tonight."

"Please," Bessie moaned. "I can't remember everything we've already learned. I'm hoping tonight will be a review session. Marjorie crammed in a lot last week."

"That was just to shut Moirrey up," Doona said. "I'm sure she'll slow things down now."

"I feel bad about being happy that Moirrey won't be there tonight," Bessie admitted after a short and slightly awkward silence.

"I know what you mean," Doona agreed. "I had a great time with Andrew this weekend, but I felt like I had to be really careful with what I said. I didn't want him to know just how nasty his sister really was."

"Yes, I found that hard enough over dinner on Friday."

Doona shrugged. "Not everyone is feeling the need to tread carefully around him," she told Bessie. "More than one person came up to Andrew while we were out and about and told him quite unpleasant things about Moirrey."

"How did he take it?"

"Better than I think I would have under the circumstances," Doona told her. "He was unfailingly polite to everyone. He just kept telling them all how sorry he was and that he would do his best to fix former wrongs once he was in a position to do so."

"I hope that satisfied everyone."

"Pretty much," Doona shrugged again. "Moirrey hurt a lot of people's feelings, which is something that Andrew can't really do anything about. He really shouldn't have to apologise for her either. Her behaviour wasn't his fault."

"It sounds like you're feeling rather protective of him," Bessie said shrewdly.

Doona blushed. "He's such a terrific guy," she said defensively. "And he's nothing like his horrible sister. I just feel badly that so many people on this island can't seem to see that. More than one person told him that he should be ashamed of himself for turning up now, just to claim his inheritance. He should have been here, running things and keeping Moirrey under control, apparently."

Bessie sighed. "I can sort of see their point," she said.

"I can't," Doona said sharply. "Although apparently Andrew can. He's being ever so nice to everyone no matter how horrible they are to him."

"Well, good for him," Bessie replied. "I'm sure most people will come around, given enough time. His reappearance has been something of a shock for everyone, and coming on the heels of Moirrey's unexpected death, I'm not surprised that people don't quite know what to say to him."

Doona nodded reluctantly. "I suppose so. Andrew says the same, that given time, everyone will accept him. I guess I'm just not that patient."

Bessie laughed. "I knew that about you," she teased.

Bessie served the jam roly-poly with custard while Doona told her about her weekend. "We did the castles mostly, although on Sunday afternoon we visited the wildlife park. I love the capybaras and Andrew enjoyed seeing the wallabies. He said it reminded him of Australia, where he spent many happy years."

Bessie gathered up her supplies for class as Doona cleared the table. They didn't have far to go, but Bessie made sure they gave themselves plenty of time.

"I forgot to mention, Hugh's in big trouble," Doona told Bessie as they climbed into her car.

"Oh dear, what's he done now?" Bessie asked with an amused smile.

"Do you remember him telling us about using Moirrey's bedroom as a practice crime scene?" Doona asked.

"Yes, he was quite excited about all the things they did," Bessie recalled.

"Well, he got so excited that he went a little overboard," Doona told her. "He actually sent a few of the prescription bottles over to the lab in the UK to be analysed. Inspector Rockwell got the bill from the lab today and he wasn't pleased."

"Oh dear," Bessie laughed. "I suppose such things aren't cheap, either, are they?""

"Not at all," Doona replied. "My eyes popped when I opened the bill. At least he only sent two of the bottles and not all nine. He would have been in real trouble if he'd done that."

"So will the inspector make him pay for it out of his salary or what?" Bessie asked.

"I doubt it," Doona answered. "John gave him a good talking-to and reminded him that everything that we do is paid for by hardworking taxpayers, and Hugh's promised to be more careful in the future."

"John?" Bessie asked.

"That's Inspector Rockwell's first name," Doona told her. "Now that we work together every day, he has us all call him John."

"I see," Bessie said. "And did you call Inspector Kelly by his first name when he was in charge of the station?"

Doona laughed. "No way. He was, and still is, Inspector Kelly at all times. I suspect even his wife calls him that."

Now Bessie laughed. "Surely not."

Doona shrugged. "I have to say that I much prefer working with John. He's much more relaxed and he really includes everyone in the things that happen at the station. He's having the break room redone and he's asked all of us what we want to see in there, for example. And he's ever so patient with the younger constables. He's keen on helping them learn and move up. I can tell you that if Hugh made a mistake like that on Inspector Kelly's watch it wouldn't have been dealt with so easily."

Bessie and Doona were quiet as they climbed the stairs this week. In the classroom, they took the same seats they had a week earlier. The table where Moirrey had sat seemed emptier than the rest, even though no one else had arrived yet. Marjorie was only a minute behind them, though.

"Ah, you two are nice and early," she said as she swept into the room. "Fastyr mie."

Bessie and Doona echoed the greeting and then exchanged polite chatter in the limited Manx they could remember from the previous week. They had just about run out of vocabulary when Liz arrived.

"Oh, I'm even early," she laughed as she rushed in. "I was smart and got the kids through their baths and into their jammies. Hubby just has to read them a story or two and tuck them up to bed this week."

Joney and Henry weren't far behind, and Marjorie had them practising everything from the previous week before anyone had time for more than quick greetings. Because they had covered so much in the first session, the review took them until time for a tea break.

"I really need this break," Bessie said, feeling as if her head were spinning slightly from the volume of information she was trying to cram into it.

"Don't we all?" Joney asked with a laugh. "I haven't worked

this hard since university and that was more than a few years ago."

"What happened to the other lady?" Liz asked. "I'm sure we're one short tonight."

Bessie finally broke the difficult silence that followed the question. "Of course, you don't live in Laxey, do you, dear?" she said. "Moirrey passed away last Monday evening. I'm sure it was in the local paper, but you probably wouldn't have recognised the name, even if you saw it."

"We don't usually get the local paper," Liz said, blushing. "Hubby gets some of the London papers at work, but otherwise we just watch the news when we want to know what's going on. I never really thought about it. But what happened to her?"

"She had a heart condition," Bessie explained. "Apparently it finally caught up to her."

"Oh dear, that's so sad," Liz said. "I mean, she seemed like such an unhappy woman, but her family must be devastated."

"She didn't have much in the way of family," Henry told her. "She was the last of the Teares as such. Although her long-lost brother isn't so lost anymore, I hear."

Bessie glanced at Doona, who took a huge sip of tea and kept quiet.

"I'd love to get my hands on some of the books in the Teare family collection," Marjorie said.

"Really? I didn't know Ewan collected books," Bessie said.

"Ewan started the collection, but Moirrey was the one who really built it up."

"Moirrey? I never saw her with a book in my life," Bessie replied.

"She didn't buy them to read," Marjorie answered. "I'm not sure why she bought them, actually. Ewan started collecting books on Manx history when he moved back to the island in the nineteen-fifties. For a while it was suggested that he would leave his collection to the museum when he died, but apparently that clause never made it into his will. Anyway, Moirrey wouldn't hear of parting with any of the books her father had acquired and she seemed determined to build the collection as well. Whenever anything especially rare or interesting appeared at auction anywhere, the museum could be sure that it would be bidding against at least one other person, Matthew Barnes. Of course, he was only ever acting as Moirrey's agent, and they outbid the museum on just about everything."

"That's terrible," Bessie said. "The museum would put the books in their library and let the whole country have access to them. I didn't even realise that Moirrey had them and she certainly wasn't interested in reading them herself."

"I'll talk to Andrew," Doona offered. "I'm sure he'll be willing to donate them to the museum."

"We'd be happy to offer him a fair sum of money for them," Marjorie told her. "Although a donation would be very much appreciated."

Doona nodded. "Let me talk to him and see what he thinks," she suggested. "I'm sure you'll be able to come to some sort of agreement with him. He may want to read a few of them before he gives them to you, though. Now that he's back, he wants to immerse himself in the island."

"There's a lot of great history for him to study," Marjorie said with a smile. "Maybe he should try out this class as well."

"I did suggest it," Doona laughed. "But he said he'd feel funny joining in after the first class, especially since his sister was in the class. He may well give it a try the next time you run it, though."

"So he's planning on sticking around for a while?" Joney asked. "I heard he was just here to get everything sold off and then he was going back to Australia or something."

Doona frowned. "As far as I know he's planning on being here for the foreseeable future," she answered. "If nothing else, he's busy trying to arrange a suitable memorial service for Moirrey."

"When is that likely to be?" Henry asked. "I mean, I expect I'll want to go."

"He isn't sure yet," Doona answered. "Technically, Andrew isn't allowed to do anything official until the authorities are fully satisfied that he is who he claims to be. They are working to verify his identity now, but it's taking some time. He'll sort out what he's calling a celebration of Moirrey's life just as soon as he's able."

"How can he prove his identity?" Liz asked. "Is it like on telly, where they use DNA and fingerprints?"

"I'm not sure exactly what they're doing," Doona answered. "He has his passport and a bunch of driving licenses from all over the world as well as papers and other artefacts from his childhood, but until they can confirm everything, he's sort of in limbo."

"He's going to struggle to get many to turn up for the service anyway, isn't he?" Joney asked. "I mean, no one liked the woman. I suppose a few might turn up just to make sure she's really dead, but beyond that, who'd go?"

Liz looked shocked. "But surely everyone who knew her will go to pay their respects," she said. "I mean, even if she wasn't especially nice, she had to have friends, right?"

"I'm afraid Moirrey didn't have friends," Bessie chimed in. "And it wasn't that she wasn't nice, she was deliberately unpleasant and difficult. She had nasty falling-outs with many people on the island. I can imagine that her service will be rather poorly attended. I will go, but more as a mark of respect for her father and her brother than for her."

"I said I plan to go," Henry said. "But mostly because she was in this class with us and I feel bad that I wasn't nicer to her on the night she died."

"You couldn't possibly have known that she was going to die," Bessie said soothingly as Henry looked sadly into his cup of tea.

"I'll probably go as well," Marjorie said. "Because she was in the class and also because we had many conversations about Manx history. Mostly I was just trying to get my hands on her book collection, but she could be interesting to talk with sometimes. She had her own unique views on the world, anyway."

"Well, I won't be there," Joney said emphatically. "The woman was just plain mean and I don't feel any obligation to help celebrate her life, whatever her brother has planned."

"I'm only planning on going for her brother's sake," Doona told Joney. "If I hadn't met him and really liked him, I wouldn't go either."

"I've heard he's really cute," Joney replied.

"Oh, aye, he is at that," Doona laughed.

"And just about the right age for you, isn't he?" Joney asked.

"Well, I guess so," Doona blushed. "Actually, I think he's a bit younger than me, but we're just friends, so it's okay."

"I never blush like that when I'm talking about my friends," Joney said, giving Doona a wink.

Doona blushed even more but didn't answer.

After the tea break Marjorie put them all to work on learning more food and drink words. When they grew bored with them, they switched to discussing the weather. By nine o'clock Bessie was exhausted and felt like she was never going to be able to actually learn any of it. The class made their way into the car park as a group. Anne Caine was just arriving as they left.

"Would you like a hand tonight?" Marjorie asked Anne as she came towards them.

"Oh no," Anne replied quickly. "I feel guilty enough about you helping me last week. I'll have the place shipshape in no time."

"Why are you still working so hard?" Bessie asked. "I thought, with everything on hold at the moment, that you could at least quit one job."

Anne shook her head. "I'm not sure what's going on with anything," she told Bessie. "And I'm not taking any chances. I'm going to keep earning every penny I can in case I need them."

"Andrew isn't going to make you pay any more money towards your cottage," Doona told Anne. "He told me that cancelling your debt was one of his first priorities once things were sorted out."

"He says that now," Anne said darkly. "But I don't trust him and I really don't trust Matthew Barnes. Andrew might think there's plenty of money and that he can be generous with me, but I bet Matthew Barnes has other ideas. He isn't going to let his share of a quarter of a million pounds slip through his fingers without a fight."

Doona opened her mouth to protest, but Bessie held up a hand. "Anne's right," she said grimly. "Matthew Barnes may well fight Andrew on just about everything. I bet he won't be in favour of donating the book collection either. I'm sure he'll want a fair price for it."

"No doubt," Marjorie agreed. "Do you know he's already sent me a demand for repayment of the balance of what Moirrey paid for this class?" she asked.

Bessie shook her head. "He's chasing down every penny," she said. "Things could get quite ugly before they are settled."

"Exactly," Anne said angrily. "And I'm not losing my home, not after everything that's happened."

Everyone was surprised when a car suddenly turned into the car park. The driver pulled up as closely as he could to the small group, parking sloppily across multiple spaces. After a moment, he rolled down the driver's side window.

"Hey mum, I thought you said I could have a twenty," a voice called out from the car's interior.

Anne's lips pressed together and her jaw tightened. She drew a deep breath and then took a few steps towards the car. Bessie held up a hand to stop her.

"Who's there?" she demanded, turning towards the car. With the car's headlamps shining in her eyes, she was effectively blinded.

"Aunt Bessie? Is that you, you old cow?" Bessie heard the car door open and then slam shut. The dark shape came towards her at speed and she just had time to brace herself before she was engulfed in a hug.

"Aunt Bessie? I can't believe you're still around," the young man told her as he let her go. "I thought you'd have popped your clogs ages ago. You were like a hundred and ten when I were a kid."

Bessie took a step away from the man and studied him in the light from the headlamps. She immediately recognised Anne's son, Andy. Although he was a few years older than when she had last seen him, he looked almost the same. He had the same brown hair and eyes as his mother, although they were somehow more attractive on him. Bessie had never been able to see anything of his father in his appearance. He was taller than she remembered, and he'd put on a few pounds, but it appeared to be mostly muscle.

His smile was bright and Bessie found herself forgiving his unkind comments about her age when she saw how genuinely pleased he was to see her. He'd spent more than a few nights in her spare room during his teen years. Andy had a difficult relationship with his father and Anne never seemed quite sure how to mother a boy only sixteen or so years younger than herself. Bessie had provided a strange sort of stability for him, letting him stay with her for over a month at one point when Jack was drinking heavily and Anne was too busy working to pay attention.

"It's good to see you as well," she told him now. "You've grown both taller and broader."

"I've been doing lots of manual labour," he told Bessie. "Lots of heavy lifting builds up muscles without you even trying."

"Well, it suits you," she said. "But when did you get back to the island?"

Andy exchanged a look with his mother. "Not long ago, a few days," he said vaguely. "Mum called and said she was in a spot of bother, like, with Ms. Teare demanding all that money, like, so I came back."

"That was good of you," Bessie said. "I hope you've been doing well across."

"Not bad," Andy told her, not quite meeting her eyes. "I've been thinking about going back to school, like, though. I could get ahead faster if I had some good qualifications."

Bessie grinned. "That sounds like a great idea."

Andy flushed and gave her a sheepish smile. "Thanks for not saying I told you so," he said. "I know you always told me that I wouldn't get far without any qualifications and I thought I knew more than you. Hel..., heck, I just wanted to get away, you know? But you were right, all along. The problem is, school is expensive."

"I told you we'd figure something out," Anne told her son. "You find the course you want to take and I'll worry about paying for it."

"Anyway, I shouldn't be keeping all of you out here. It isn't all that warm tonight, is it?" Andrew asked.

"Did you come to give your mum a hand with the cleaning, then?" Bessie asked sweetly.

Andy flushed again. "Well, I was supposed to be meeting some old friends down at the pub," he said. "But I guess I could give you a quick hand, mum, if you want." The last remark was addressed to Anne, who was busy shooting nasty looks at Bessie. Bessie simply pretended to be completely unaware of the looks.

"I suppose I'll finish quicker with a bit of help," Anne said grudgingly.

"Great," Andy said with a marked lack of enthusiasm. He walked back over to the car and climbed back inside to turn off the lights and engine.

"I'd better get going." Liz used the interruption as an excuse to get away.

"Yes, me too." Henry was quick to follow.

Joney grinned at Bessie. "I'm not in any rush," she laughed. "Andy's return home will be tomorrow's big news."

Anne sighed. "I really hate being talked about," she told Joney in a tired voice.

"At least having your son visiting is a nice thing, much nicer than when everyone was talking about your fight with Moirrey." Joney was blunt but honest with the other woman.

Anne sighed again. "Maybe Jack and Andy both have the right idea, getting off this rock and starting over across."

"Jack is still across?" Bessie asked.

"Not that it's any of your business," Anne snapped, "but yeah, he is."

Andy rejoined the group now, giving Bessie another hug. "I'm going to stop by one day soon for shortbread and tea," he told Bessie.

"I'll look forward to it," she replied.

Anne and Andy headed into the building and left the others in the car park.

"Well, that was interesting," Joney said. "I guess I should get home now."

Marjorie said her goodbyes in Manx and that left Bessie and

Doona to climb into Doona's car and head for Bessie's cottage.

"What a strange evening it's been," Bessie remarked.

"I hope every class doesn't end with odd car park confrontations," Doona told her.

"I think we've had enough strange car park conversations to last us a good long time," Bessie agreed.

Back at Bessie's cottage, Doona insisted on carrying out her quick check of the space before she left Bessie to get to bed.

Bessie locked up her doors and then checked her kitchen cupboards. She could just about manage another batch of shortbread, but she was running low on flour. She added it to the shopping list she kept by the phone, checked that its ringer was switched off and headed to bed.

She had another beautiful spring morning for her walk the next day and she thoroughly enjoyed strolling past the new cottages to the Pierce property and beyond. Back at home, she frowned at the blinking message light on her answering machine. What could anyone possibly want this early in the morning?

She switched the ringer back on and the phone rang almost immediately.

"Hello?"

"Bessie? It's Doona. This time you really need to sit down. Are you sitting down yet?"

Bessie slid into a chair and frowned at the receiver. There was no way that this was going to be good news, was there? "I'm sitting down," she told her friend.

"Moirrey was murdered," Doona hissed.

CHAPTER SEVEN

Bessie sighed. If she could have, she would have rewound time and let the call go to the answering machine. Having just about recovered physically from everything that had happened the previous month, she didn't even want to think about another real-life murder. After the second attempt on her life, she hadn't even wanted to read about fictional murder for several weeks.

"What's happened?" she asked Doona.

"You know those tablets that Hugh sent away by mistake? It turns out they weren't what they were supposed to be. Someone switched Moirrey's medication for some other drug."

"Really? I guess that means Hugh isn't in trouble anymore?" Bessie suggested.

"He isn't, but Inspector Rockwell and Dr. Quayle both are," Doona told her. "Hey, look, I have to go, but how about if I stop over at lunchtime and bring you up to date? At least I can tell you the things that the police are sharing with the press. That's about all I get to find out about anyway."

Bessie laughed. "I'm sure you know everyone's secrets in that station," she told her friend. "But I'll take whatever information you can share safely and I promise not to push you for more. I'd hate for you to lose your job because of something you told me."

Bessie's phone kept ringing all morning, as somehow the news had already leaked out. Everyone on the island seemed to want Bessie's thoughts on who the murderer might be.

"I've absolutely no idea," she told everyone who asked. "I don't know enough about what happened to even begin to form an opinion. Ask me again once the police have released more information."

By lunchtime, Bessie had turned the phone's ringer back off and shut herself up in her sitting room with a good book. Unusually for her, though, she found she simply couldn't lose herself in the story. Instead, her mind was racing as she tried to imagine who could have killed Moirrey. She was relieved when Doona finally knocked on the door and took her away from the same page she had read at least a dozen times without comprehension.

"I brought bacon butties from the shop across from the station," Doona told Bessie as the delicious smell of bacon filled her small kitchen. "And chips, of course."

Bessie grinned. "I suppose I shall have to eat extra veggies at dinner, then."

Doona laughed. "Okay, maybe I didn't pick the healthiest of options, but I wanted to get something quick. I don't dare take a long lunch today. The rumour is that the chief constable himself is coming up this afternoon to talk to John about, quote, 'the mistakes made in the investigation,' end of quote."

"Oh dear, how's Inspector Rockwell coping with all of this?" Bessie asked, worried about her new friend.

"He's surprisingly fine," Doona said. "What I mean is that he's much more calm than I would be under the circumstances. Dr. Quayle was the one who ruled it a natural death, so John was perfectly justified in not doing any formal investigating. I suppose we're just lucky that he decided to use it as a training exercise and that Hugh did what he did. If it weren't for that, Moirrrey would have been dead and buried and no one would ever know that she had been murdered."

"Okay, tell me exactly what happened then," Bessie demanded.

"I told you how Hugh sent the bottles across. Apparently, when they analysed them they found the wrong drugs in the one bottle," Doona answered.

"What do you mean, the wrong drugs?" Bessie asked.

"Instead of something that was supposed to be good for her heart, there was some strong painkiller, I guess. Something strong enough to be fatal to someone with a heart condition, although I gather that simply missing the tablet she was supposed to have taken could have been enough to make her pretty sick or even kill her."

"How hard would it have been for someone to get access to that type of painkiller?"

"Apparently the drug was pretty common for many years, both in the UK and the US."

Bessie frowned. "So, in theory, just about anyone could have acquired the tablets to switch with Moirrey's regular drugs?"

"Pretty much," Doona answered. "And once they got them, they just to find which of her real tablets looked most like the substitute ones. They had nine different bottles to choose from, after all. Now the police just have to figure out exactly how the tablets got switched."

"I hope no one is blaming poor old John Corkill for mixing things up." Bessie said. "He's got enough to worry about, having been dragged back from his retirement to fill in while the shop owners look for a new chemist."

"Oh no," Doona assured her. "John Rockwell is as sure as he can be that this wasn't a simple mix-up."

"All of the tablets that were left in the bottle were the wrong thing?" Bessie asked.

"Yes, although there were only two left, apparently, and it originally held a month's supply. She only took them once a day, at bedtime, and actually, from the dates, it was probably Jack White who last refilled the bottle."

"Could he have had something to do with the switch?" Bessie asked, eager to believe that the man, already in gaol for drug offenses, might also be a murderer.

Doona shrugged. "I suppose the inspector will take a good look at him, but I can't imagine what his motive could have been."

Bessie shrugged. "I'd rather think it was him than anyone

else. I already don't like him."

Doona laughed. "I don't think that will stand up in court," she told Bessie. "But I sort of agree. All of the other suspects are rather closer to home, aren't they?"

"Indeed," Bessie frowned. "If whoever did it only changed a few of the tablets, they could have done so any time in the last month. That makes for an awful lot of possible suspects. Moirrey would insist on carrying her bottles of tablets with her everywhere she went," Bessie sighed.

"But if they were in her handbag, surely that would limit access," Doona suggested.

"Maybe," Bessie said. "But really, she was always leaving her bag somewhere. If you remember the first class, when we did our first round of talking to one another, she left her bag on her table and went all around the room talking to everyone. I think she might have even gone off to the loo without it. I'm sure I saw her do that more than once in restaurants and cafés, anyway. Getting access would have been pretty simple for anyone who knew her habits."

"So I guess we need to focus on motive and means rather than opportunity," Doona said.

Bessie smiled. "Surely just about everyone who knew Moirrey had a motive," she said dryly.

Doona laughed. "Certainly just about everyone disliked her," Doona agreed. "But it's a long way from dislike to murder."

"I'm not sure it's that long," Bessie told her. "But some people definitely had stronger motives than others."

"And I need to get back to work," Doona sighed.

"Never mind, you go. Maybe we can continue this chat tonight?"

Doona blushed. "I wish we could," she told Bessie. "But I promised Andrew I'd have dinner with him tonight. As you can well imagine, he's taking the news quite hard. It was bad enough that his sister died before he saw her, but to discover that she was murdered? It's just about broken his heart."

"Indeed," Bessie murmured.

"And of course, now they may have to exhume the body. This

whole conversation is totally premature, actually. Just because they found that her medication had been tampered with doesn't actually prove anything. It's possible that only the tablets still in the bottle were switched and that she really did die of natural causes."

"That seems unlikely," Bessie remarked.

"It does, but it is possible. Anyway, Andrew is devastated that they're talking about re-examining Moirrey. He was pushing to have her cremated. He insisted that she always said that was what she wanted, but Matthew Barnes wouldn't hear of it."

"It's hard to believe that Andrew talked to his sister about cremation. She was only two when he started at boarding school," Bessie said.

"He said they had the conversation when he was back here before his gap year, when she was more like eight. Apparently she'd had been having nightmares about her mother being trapped underground and she made Andrew promise that he'd never let her be buried alive, that he'd have her cremated and sprinkle her ashes somewhere sunny and warm."

"Moirrey's mother died when she was only four or five," Bessie argued. "I can't believe that she'd remember her and dream about her several years later."

Doona sighed. "I don't know why we're arguing," she told Bessie. "I'm just telling you what Andrew said. I think it felt important to him because it was one of the few things he remembered talking about with Moirrey. Anyway, it's just as well he didn't get his way, because if she'd been cremated they would have a more difficult time proving it was murder."

Bessie shook her head. "I'm not sure I understand how they're going to prove it anyway," she told Doona.

Doona frowned. "John said something about testing some of the samples that were taken before she was embalmed. Apparently the coroner took samples before Dr. Quayle signed the death certificate. John said that the painkiller should be easy to pick up, especially because it was quite a high dose. If they can do that, they might not have to exhume the body."

"Poor Moirrey," Bessie said sadly. "I hope she didn't realise that she was dying."

"From what I've heard, she would have just taken her tablets and gone to bed as normal. She simply never woke up."

"While that's sad enough, it's better than the alternative."

"It isn't such a bad way to go," Doona said. "I don't mind if that's how I go, in about sixty years."

Bessie laughed. "I wouldn't mind another sixty years myself," she told Doona.

Doona smiled at her. "I hope you get them," she told her friend.

Once Doona left, Bessie tidied up the kitchen, and then she felt restless. The news about Moirrey had left her feeling unusually unsettled. A trip into Ramsey didn't appeal and as it was nearly two o'clock it felt too late to think about going any further afield. She thought about ringing a friend and arranging to meet for dinner, but she really didn't want to talk about Moirrey and no one in Laxey would be talking about anything else.

She'd just decided to take a long walk on the beach, regardless of how busy it might be, when someone knocked on her door.

"Andy Caine, what a lovely surprise," she said when she pulled the door open.

"I tried to ring," the young man told her, "but you haven't been answering your phone. I figured I would try just dropping in since I was going past."

"Oh that's right," Bessie laughed. "I turned the ringer off on the phone. I was tired of talking about Moirrey," she explained.

"Well, that suits me," Andy answered. "If I never hear her name again, that would be just fine by me."

Bessie gave him a sympathetic smile. "I know she was making your mother's life miserable lately," Bessie said. "But she didn't deserve to be murdered."

"She was murdered?" Andy exclaimed, shock flashing across his face.

"Sorry," Bessie said. "I just assumed you'd heard. It's all anyone is talking about."

"I hadn't heard," Andy replied. "And I don't think my mother will have heard either." He gave Bessie a questioning look. "Do you think I should ring her?" he asked.

"Is she at home?" Bessie asked.

"No, she's at the restaurant. She goes in early to help with the prep work."

"Maybe you shouldn't bother her at work," Bessie suggested.

"I'm just worried that someone will say something to her about it and upset her. Everyone knows she was fighting with Moirrey. What if someone asks her if she did it?"

"I don't think anyone would be that rude," Bessie said. "But it would probably be better if she knew, I suppose."

Andy took out his mobile. "I'll send her a text and tell her to ring me when she can," he said.

Bessie watched as his fingers flew across the tiny number pad, presumably making words and a sensible message from what seemed to be random tapping.

"So what happened to Moirrey?" he asked when he'd finished. "I mean, I thought her heart just gave out. I assume she wasn't shot or stabbed or something. It wouldn't have taken the doctor until now to spot that, surely."

"They think some of her medication was swapped for something that killed her," Bessie explained.

"That probably wouldn't be hard," Andy remarked. "She was always leaving her handbag full of bottles all over the place. When I was pretty little I remember her coming to visit my mum one day. She left her bag on a table and I got into it and started playing with all the pretty tablets. Luckily mum caught me before I swallowed any, but I messed them all up and Moirrey was furious."

"I'll bet she was, but she was totally irresponsible leaving them where a small child could get to them."

"She told my mum that childproof tops were too tricky for her to open," Andy remembered.

Bessie thought back to the last time she'd seen Moirrey. She visualized Moirrey's row of bottles. "You're right," she said after a moment. "She didn't have safety caps on her bottles. I don't know if that's significant or not, but it's interesting."

Andy's phone let out a burst of cacophonous noise. "That'll be mum," he told Bessie. He punched a button on the phone and then turned away slightly. That did nothing to prevent Bessie from hearing his end of the conversation, though.

"Hey," Bessie heard.

"I'm at Aunt Bessie's." There was a pause, and then, "I told you I was going to visit her and get some shortbread."

Andy listened for a moment and then sighed. "Can you save the lecture for tonight, please? I asked you to ring for a reason."

This pause was a long one and Bessie could see the tension increasing in Andy's shoulders as his mother spoke. Finally, he sighed deeply. "Look," he said, "I was just ringing to warn you that people might be talking. It turns out Moirrey was murdered and I didn't want you to find out when someone said something weird to you about it."

Another long pause had Andy shaking his head. "Yeah, whatever," he muttered. "I've gotta go."

Bessie smiled encouragingly at him as he disconnected the call and sank down at the kitchen table. For a moment Bessie thought he might cry and she was reminded of the young boy who had haunted her spare room that one hot summer. She moved towards him, but he took a deep breath and then looked up at her.

"I'm okay," he told her. "It just seems like mum and I can't talk without arguing at the moment. I know she's really worried about money and upset about Moirrey as well, but she won't talk to me about that. All she'll talk to me about is how disappointed she is that I haven't made a fortune yet." He sighed.

"I thought you were planning to go back to school," Bessie questioned.

Andy shrugged. "I don't know. Everything costs so much money, and I'm not sure what I really want to do."

"I know what you should do," Bessie said.

"You do?"

"I do. You should help me make some shortbread."

Andy laughed. "That sounds like a plan."

Bessie got out the measuring scales and utensils while Andy gathered the necessary ingredients. He'd helped in the kitchen a lot during his frequent stays with Bessie, always happier cooking or baking than talking about his problems. Now he expertly combined flour, butter and sugar in a large mixing bowl.

Bessie preheated the oven and then set the kettle on while Andy shaped the shortbread on a metal tray. Once it was safely in the oven, he and Bessie sat down and enjoyed their tea.

"This will taste even better with the shortbread," Andy said as he sipped his drink.

"Patience," Bessie laughed. "It will be ready soon."

"It already smells fabulous."

"It really does," Bessie agreed. "You did a great job."

Andy flushed. "I love to bake," he said sheepishly. "It always reminds me of staying here with you. Those were the happiest days of my childhood, you know?"

Bessie sighed. "I'm sorry things were so difficult at home. I wish I could have done more to help."

"More?" Andy asked. "You let me stay as often as I liked. You taught me to cook and bake and you helped me pass my GSCE algebra exam."

Bessie laughed again as she remember long nights at the table struggling to explain math that she'd never actually learned to a frustrated teenager. "I'm glad I could help," she told Andy. "I thoroughly enjoyed all of it, except the algebra."

Now Andy laughed. "Aye, I am sorry about that," he told her. "I'm just not that good with numbers, like. And mum and dad were no help. Mum was too busy trying to keep a roof over our heads and dad, well, he was just drinking."

Bessie sighed. "Things haven't changed much for your mum and dad, have they?"

"Well, from what I can see, dad's moved out, so that's a change."

"Really?" Bessie asked in surprise. "Your mum said he'd gone across, but she didn't say he'd moved out."

"Um, I guess I'd rather you didn't mention it to anyone," Andy said, looking embarrassed. "I reckon mum doesn't want folks to know."

"Don't you worry," Bessie told him. "I won't tell anyone

anything."

"Thanks," Andy replied.

A few minutes later Bessie's oven timer rang. Andy quickly grabbed an oven glove and carefully removed the tray of shortbread from the oven.

"Can we eat it hot?" he asked Bessie.

"We should let it cool, at least a little," Bessie answered. "And we should have something healthy to eat before we fill up on shortbread."

"How about if I pop to the chippy?" Andy suggested. "I can grab dinner for us both and be back before the shortbread has cooled."

"That sounds delicious," Bessie told him. "It's been ages since I've had fish and chips."

While Andy was gone, Bessie quickly ate an apple. Her lunch had been indulgent, but having fish and chips tonight was almost too much. She hoped the apple would provide a few of the nutrients her meals that day had been missing.

As much as she enjoyed her dinner, Bessie was eager to get to pudding. The cooling shortbread made the cottage smell buttery and sweet.

She served generous portions on her very best china, smiling as Andy took a huge first bite. Her own bite was only slightly more delicate. "This is delicious," she told Andy. "I think it's better than mine."

Andy laughed. "It is yours," he told her. "It's the one recipe I never change when I bake. I love to experiment with different ingredients and the like, but I never do that with your shortbread recipe."

"I'm sure it tastes better than mine ever did," Bessie insisted. "You could open a bakery with this."

Andy shrugged. "I thought about going back to school to study baking, like, but dad reckons real men don't make their living baking cakes. Mum wants to help, but dad won't let her pay for anything like that."

Bessie sighed and chose her words carefully. "Your father is entitled to his opinion," she said. "But I think you're really talented."

"Thanks," Andy smiled. "Mum's going to see if she can get me a job where she's working, actually. Just bussing tables, like, and washing dishes. I'm hoping that eventually I might get to move up to like prep work and whatever. If I can manage it, maybe I can take a few classes on the side as well, learn about catering and things like that."

"That sounds like a plan," Bessie said.

"Yeah, I'd much rather bake than cook, but cooking is better than loading and unloading container lorries all day, anyway."

"I'm sure," Bessie laughed.

Bessie divided the remaining shortbread into two containers, one for herself and one for Andy to take home. "It was so wonderful to see you," she told the man, wrapping him in a huge hug before he left.

"It was wonderful to see you as well." Andy hugged her back tightly. "If I decide to stay on the island, I'll come and visit again soon."

"And if you decide to head back across, you'll come and say goodbye," Bessie said sternly.

"Yes, ma'am, I will," Andy promised.

Bessie's little cottage felt lonely for a moment or two after Andy left. She'd forgotten how much she'd enjoyed his company when he used to stay with her. And he seemed to have grown into a lovely young man in spite of his difficult childhood. She tidied up the kitchen and then grabbed her latest novel. Tonight she felt like reading in bed, she decided.

Upstairs, she washed her face and brushed her teeth. She propped herself up in bed with a pile of pillows and read until she couldn't keep her eyes open any longer. Then she turned off her light and snuggled under the covers, falling into her usual deep sleep.

CHAPTER EIGHT

Wednesday was sunny yet again, but Bessie kept her walk fairly short. She had a lot she wanted to get done.

Dave picked her up at nine as planned and drove her into Douglas. She spent a happy half hour poking around the various charity shops there while she waited for the Manx Museum to open. Her paper was coming along nicely, but as usual, once she'd started writing it she found little odds and ends that she needed to double-check. An hour in the museum's library proved hugely productive. Then, since she was there, she decided to pay Marjorie a quick visit.

"Moghrey mie," she greeted her friend.

Marjorie looked up from behind a desk covered in papers, books and odd pieces of rock. "Moghrey mie," she responded. "Kys t'ou?"

"Ta mee braew, kys t'ou?"

"Ta mee braew, gura mie ayd," Marjorie replied with a smile. "But what brings you here?"

"I needed to do some extra research for next month," Bessie admitted. "No matter how careful I think I am when I take notes, I always seem to miss one or two little things. I guess they didn't seem important originally, but then, when I'm writing, they suddenly seem to matter a great deal."

Marjorie grinned. "I know exactly what you mean."

"Anyway," Bessie smiled, "at least if I'm here and not at home I'm not fielding endless phone calls about Moirrey."

"Are people still talking about her death?" Marjorie asked. "I would have thought something else interesting would have happened by now."

"Murder is always pretty interesting," Bessie replied.

"Murder?" Marjorie gasped. "I thought she died of natural causes."

Bessie shook her head. "The police think it might have been murder. Some of her medication was tampered with."

Marjorie frowned. "I'm having trouble getting my head around this," she said. "People get murdered in books, not real life."

"If only that were true," Bessie sighed.

Marjorie flushed. "Sorry, Bessie," she said. "I forgot about last month."

"No worries," Bessie told her. "The experience hasn't done any lasting damage, except that I'm even less surprised at how people behave now."

Marjorie nodded. "I guess I can understand that."

"Anyway, I came into town as much to do research as to get away from my telephone. It's been ringing constantly and I've simply nothing to tell people. I can't imagine anyone killing Moirrey, no matter how much they might have wanted her dead."

"She was rude and nasty, but that usually isn't enough of a reason to kill someone," Marjorie remarked.

"She was rich, though, and money often is more than enough of a motive."

Marjorie's phone rang. Bessie waited patiently while she answered it and had a brief conversation. Once she hung up, she got to her feet.

"I'm awfully sorry, but I have to go," she told Bessie apologetically. "A group of researchers are over from Scotland and I'm scheduled to spend the afternoon taking them through the archives. You'll have to fill me in on the rest on Monday night, okay?"

Bessie nodded. "Of course," she replied. "As long as I can do it in English."

Marjorie laughed. "If you insist. Slane lhiat."

"Slane lhait," Bessie answered.

As it was just about lunchtime, Bessie took herself down to the promenade and bought herself lunch at one of her favourite Italian restaurants. She ate crunchy flatbread dripping with garlic and olive oil and then a huge plate of spaghetti bolognese. She felt full to bursting when she met Dave for the journey home.

"Oh, I love it there," Dave told her when she mentioned her lunch. "But I always eat too much. It's always so delicious that I can't seem to stop myself."

"Exactly," Bessie laughed. "But now I feel like I won't want to eat for a week."

Back at home, Bessie spent an hour adding her new research notes into the draft of her paper. Then, feeling guilty about her lunch, she took a long walk along the beach, enjoying how different it felt in the late afternoon compared to her usual early morning excursions.

She smiled and shared casual greetings with several families who were sprinkled across the sand, dodging sandcastles and badly organised games of catch as she went. As she passed the new cottages, she was startled to see someone walking down the cliff side path behind the Pierce cottage. The path was set with multiple short sets of stairs and the person seemed to be negotiating them cautiously. Bessie couldn't resist getting a better look.

She reached the bottom of the last flight of stairs at almost the exact same time as the man she'd seen. "Matthew Barnes?" she said in surprise. "What on earth are you doing at Thie yn Traie?"

The advocate looked startled and not terribly pleased to see Bessie. He smiled uneasily and then tugged at his suit jacket, pulling it back into place after the descent. He frowned at Bessie, his grey complexion giving his thin face an almost cadaverous appearance in the light of the slowly setting sun. Everything about the man was grey: his hair, his eyes, his suit and tie, and his personality.

"Yes, well, good afternoon Mrs., er, Ms., um, I'm sorry, I seem to have forgotten your name."

Bessie bit her lip to keep from laughing out loud. The man had no more forgotten her name than she had forgotten his. She could only assume that his pretense was meant to be a snub of some kind. As if she cared in the slightest what he thought of her.

"What are you doing at Thie yn Traie?" she repeated herself.

"If you really must know," he replied haughtily, "I'm getting it ready for sale. I'm acting as Daniel Pierce's advocate here on the island, handling the sale on his behalf."

Bessie raised an eyebrow. "Will the house be going on the market soon, then?" she asked.

"It won't be long," he told her. "Now, if you'll excuse me?"

Bessie watched as the man turned and slowly made his way back up the steps. When he got to the top of the final staircase, he turned and looked back down at her. Bessie felt like she could feel the frown on his face, even though he was too far away for her to actually see it.

Feeling devilish, she waved merrily at him, laughing when he, seemingly reluctantly, gave her a small wave in return. She turned and made her way home, around the sandcastles and the families packing and unpacking picnics. Once back at her cottage, she made a phone call.

"Is it possible that Doncan has time for a quick chat?" she asked Breesha Quilliam, who'd been Doncan's secretary for many years.

"I'm sure he does, for you, Miss Cubbon," Breesha replied. A moment later Doncan's voice was booming in her ear.

"Bessie, what can I do for you today?" he asked.

"I just have a quick question for you," Bessie told him. "I was out walking and I ran into Matthew Barnes. He was coming down the stairs behind Thie yn Traie. He told me he's acting for Daniel Pierce in selling the property. I just wondered if you'd heard anything about it."

Doncan sighed. "Actually, I was rung this morning by Mr. Pierce's solicitor in the UK," he told Bessie. "He wanted to know if I'd be interested in handling the sale and, if so, what sort of fee I would charge. I'm guessing he contacted Matthew Barnes as well, with the same questions."

"And Mr. Barnes was happy to undercut your fee," Bessie concluded.

"Maybe," Doncan told her. "I've not heard back from the man one way or the other as yet. I would expect him to ring and let me know whatever was decided, as a professional courtesy."

"So maybe Mr. Barnes is jumping the gun by stomping around the property uninvited," Bessie suggested.

"He might be," Doncan told her. "But equally he might have been given the job and be there for good reason."

Bessie sighed. "I really hope you get the job," she told her friend.

"It's always good to have more work," Doncan replied. "But to be honest, I'm quite busy right now. I won't mind if Mr. Barnes gets the job. I can't see it leading to more work, at least not for the Pierce family. I can't believe they'll ever come back to the island."

After the call Bessie pottered around her kitchen, making herself a simple evening meal. She reheated some vegetable soup from the freezer, reminding herself that it was a much healthier option than her admittedly tastier choices from the previous day and today's lunch.

She'd just tidied up and taken herself into her sitting room to read when someone knocked on her door.

"Inspector Rockwell? What brings you here?" Bessie said in surprise when she saw the man on her doorstep.

The tall man with the gorgeous green eyes grinned at her. "It's nice to see you again, too," he teased.

"Oh, sorry," Bessie blushed. "I was just so surprised to see you. I wasn't expecting anyone this late at night."

The inspector smiled at her. "I was just driving by and I thought you might be able to spare a biscuit for an old friend," he said.

"Really?" Bessie said incredulously. "I thought you lived in Ramsey? Never mind, come in and have some tea and shortbread and tell me what's really on your mind."

Rockwell smiled as he followed Bessie into the kitchen. "What makes you think I've something on my mind?" he asked.

"You haven't dropped in to see me in a month," Bessie pointed out. "I find it hard to believe that my shortbread is suddenly irresistible coincidently when you're in the middle of another murder investigation."

Rockwell laughed. "This is why I come to see you," he told Bessie. "You understand people."

Bessie laughed and then got out plates and cups and set the kettle to boil. "While we wait for our tea, you can tell me how you've been," she instructed the man.

"Oh, I'm fine," he replied airily. "It's been interesting running the station here. Lots of neighborhood policing, but not a lot of CID work."

"I hope you're not getting bored."

"Oh no, I've really been enjoying having the time to get to know the community. Laxey is wonderful and Lonan is very special as well. But I'm sure you can imagine why, when Moirrey Teare died, I was eager to use her home as a practice crime scene."

"Indeed, and young Hugh seems to have learned a lot from the exercise."

"Yes, and his mistake was just about the only thing that saved my job for me as well," he told Bessie.

"Really?" Bessie was appalled.

"Well," Rockwell shrugged, "I don't know what might have happened if it came out later that Moirrey was murdered and we hadn't suspected. I'm not sure that they would have fired me, but I might have been reassigned. Even the chief constable has admitted that there was no reason to suspect murder. Her own physician was happy to sign the certificate as natural causes." The inspector sighed. "Turns out it was anything but natural."

"You've had the test results?" Bessie asked. The kettle whistled and Bessie quickly made up a pot of tea, offering milk and sugar to the inspector. Then she piled pieces of the delicious leftover shortbread on a serving plate and offered it to him as well.

He took a large piece and ate half of it, washed down with tea, before he answered her question.

"Ah, that's terrific," he told Bessie. "And yes, we've had some test results back and it seems clear the Moirrey took one of the switched tablets, which makes it murder in my book. Now we just have to figure out why someone wanted to kill her."

"And that's why you're here?" Bessie guessed. "You think I can help supply a motive or two?"

Rockwell grinned. "I'm really hoping you can," he told her. "From what I've heard, anyone who spent any time with Moirrey in the past month could have switched the tablets."

"Which probably includes pretty much the entire population of the island," Bessie told him. "In spite of her insisting that she rarely went anywhere because of her ill health, she was prone to popping up at just about any event going. She'd arrive, make a bunch of incredibly rude comments to the hosts and the guests of honour and then rush away, claiming she felt unwell." Bessie sighed. "She really was most unlikeable."

Now the inspector sighed. "I was rather hoping you might narrow it down a bit more than that," he told Bessie.

Bessie shrugged. "What about means?" she asked. "Can't you trace the origins of the tablets?"

"I wish we could," Rockwell sighed. "Right now it looks like they were standard prescription tablets that just about anyone could have had access to over the years. Apparently this particular drug fell out of favour in the UK a few years back and the company that was producing it stopped making it, but at its most popular it was being prescribed daily to help people deal with chronic pain and difficulty sleeping."

"But Moirrey wasn't prescribed it?"

Rockwell shrugged. "Her doctor tried to explain it all to me, but I'm sure I didn't understand. Basically, though, no, this drug would never have been given to Moirrey. Dr. Quayle said that, in spite of all the medication she was taking, he'd never had to prescribe something to help her with pain or sleep. And if he did, it certainly wouldn't have been this particular drug because of the negative ways it interacts with some of the other medications she was taking."

Bessie sighed. "But lots of other people might have been prescribed it over the years?"

"That's what I'm told," Rockwell agreed. "And so far we've found thirty-seven people on the island who were prescribed this drug in the last ten years. We've spoken to several of them, but they all say the same thing."

Bessie smiled. "Let me guess, they all reckon they took them when they needed them and then threw out any left over, but it's been so long now, they aren't sure."

Rockwell laughed. "That's it," he told her. "And to make matters worse, it's still being manufactured and widely prescribed in the United States, and I've found two Internet pharmacies that carry it as well. I suspect I could get my hands on some with very little effort."

"But you'd still have to know enough about medicine to know that it would kill Moirrey," Bessie said.

"Or simply be desperate enough to try," Rockwell suggested. "The killer might not have had any idea what the drugs would do to Moirrey," he said. "He or she might have thought that Moirrey would die if she didn't get her normally scheduled medication and simply switched her normal tablets for whatever he or she had lying around."

Bessie shook her head. "This is impossible," she complained.

"No, it's never impossible," Rockwell insisted. "We just have to focus on motive."

"I guess," Bessie said doubtfully as she refilled tea cups and took another piece of shortbread. Well, she'd had rather a lot of vegetables that evening, hadn't she?

The inspector took his own second piece and then smiled encouragingly at Bessie. "I need you to tell me who had a motive," he said. "And I need every possibility you can come up with, no matter how slight. Sometimes it can be the littlest thing that tips someone over the edge, and with this sort of remote method, that might be more likely than usual. It seems to me that switching tablets, especially if you aren't sure what the result might be, hardly feels like murder, more like helping fate along."

"This is hard," Bessie complained. "Many of the people I could name are friends of mine."

"So let me start you off," Rockwell suggested. "Tell me about

Moirrey's fight with Anne Caine."

Bessie sighed deeply. "I don't know how much I can tell you," she prevaricated.

The inspector sighed. "Bessie, this is all strictly off the record," he assured her. "I'm not going to arrest anyone because of what you tell me. I just need some hints that might point me in the right direction. I need to know who might benefit from Moirrey's sudden death, and from what I've been told, Anne Caine definitely falls into that category."

"She didn't need to kill Moirrey," Bessie argued. "I gave her enough money to get Moirrey off her back."

"When?"

"When what?"

"When did you give the money to Anne?"

"Oh, sorry," Bessie shook her head. "On the Monday night, the night that Moirrey died."

"And the tablets could have been switched any time in the last month," Rockwell pointed out. "Anne couldn't have known you were going to help her out. She could have switched the drugs weeks ago."

Bessie wanted to argue, but the inspector was right. Anne couldn't possibly have guessed that Bessie would help her out. "It sounds like you already know all about Anne's problems," she said.

"I've heard the story, but I'd like to hear it from you as well."

Bessie nodded. "Basically, Anne's father, Robert, worked for Moirrey's father, Ewan. Robert managed the estate and in return he was given a small cottage to live in. Anne was born in the back bedroom of the cottage, but, unfortunately, her mother died in childbirth. It was about ten years later that Ewan Teare finally offered to sell the cottage outright to Robert Hall, rather than just let him live in it while he was working for the estate."

"Any idea why he made the offer at that point rather than earlier or later?"

Bessie shrugged. "The rumour at the time was that Robert was offered a job across at some stately home. Ewan had to find something to make it worth his while to stay here. The initial agreement for the sale of the property made it almost more of a gift than a sale."

"So then what happened?"

"Ewan and Robert had a falling out about five years later. Robert started drinking heavily, and apparently there were other issues as well," Bessie sighed. "You have to remember that the Teare family has always been very private, and Robert wasn't any more forthcoming about family matters. Everything I'm telling you is second- or third-hand and unsubstantiated."

"That's fine," the inspector told her. "I'm just gathering information at this point. Everything you can add to the general picture is a help."

Bessie nodded and continued reluctantly. "From what I heard, eventually Robert and Ewan made up, but by that time Robert was about six months behind in his monthly payments. Ewan had his new advocate, Matthew Barnes, draw up a new agreement. From what I'm told, the new agreement had higher payments and very strict penalties for missing any. I still think that Doncan could have challenged the agreement if Moirrey had really tried to push Anne out of her home."

"But as far as Anne knew, she was about to get thrown out of the only home she'd ever known?"

"Yes, but that doesn't mean that she killed Moirrey," Bessie said stoutly.

"I didn't say that it did," Rockwell said smoothly. "But it certainly gives her a motive."

"I suppose," Bessie replied.

"And it gives her son a motive as well," the man added.

"Andy? He wasn't even here," Bessie argued. "I would look at her husband before I'd consider her son."

"Sorry to disappoint you, but her husband, Jack, has been off the island for nearly two months. We've checked flight and ferry records and they match what he's told us. He left the island in February and hasn't been back."

Bessie frowned. "Anne made it sound like he'd only just left."

"Well, maybe she was embarrassed to admit that he's been gone so long."

"He could have snuck back and switched the tablets, though, couldn't he? The ferry and flight records aren't perfectly kept, are they?"

"I'm sure they aren't perfect, but they are reasonably good," Rockwell told her. "Both the ferry and the airlines require photo identification now. I've spoken to Jack Caine several times on the phone and I don't think he's capable of planning something as complicated as faking his identification, coming over and swapping the tablets and then leaving the island again without anyone who knows him spotting him. I could be wrong, but for now I'm ruling him out."

"You can rule out Andy as well," Bessie told him. "He wasn't here, either."

"Actually, he arrived back on the island on Easter Sunday," Rockwell corrected her. "He didn't let his mother know he was back until Tuesday afternoon, which was after Moirrey had been found. But he was definitely on the island in time to do the swap."

Bessie frowned. "Did he tell you why he didn't contact his mum until Tuesday?" she asked.

"He says he was with a girl from Sunday afternoon until Tuesday lunchtime, but he won't tell us who she is to verify the alibi. I'm guessing she's either married or otherwise committed, but I don't know for sure."

"Andy is a lovely young man," Bessie told Rockwell. "I'm sure he would never have done anything to harm Moirrey."

"Even if Moirrey was threatening to destroy his mother's life?" Rockwell asked. "Even lovely young men have been known to resort to murder for their mother's sake."

Bessie shook her head. "You're never going to convince me that Andy had anything to do with the murder," she told Rockwell firmly. "You need to look elsewhere."

The inspector looked like he might argue, but then he shook his head. "We don't have any evidence that Andy spent any time with Moirrey in the short time he was on the island before she died. Of course, he didn't have to spend time with her to switch her tablets, but it would have been difficult for him. Okay, tell me about Matthew Barnes instead," he suggested.

"What does he have to do with Moirrey's murder?" Bessie asked.

Rockwell frowned. "When I said that everything we discuss is off the record, I need you to promise you won't repeat anything I say as well, okay?"

"Of course," Bessie told him. "You shouldn't have to ask."

"I know, but this is an especially tricky one," he told her. "We have reason to believe that Moirrey wasn't happy with how Mr. Barnes was handling her affairs."

"Really?" Bessie asked, intrigued.

"Yes, really," Rockwell frowned. "Not long before she died, she asked for a full accounting of all of her assets. Mr. Barnes insists that it was simply a routine request for information, but our initial enquiries suggest that she was suspicious that she was being cheated in some way. It's entirely possible, of course, that she was wrong, in which case it seems unlikely that Mr. Barnes killed her."

"But she might have been right," Bessie said. "I've always wondered why she moved out of the big house and into that cottage. Can Mr. Barnes explain that? Ewan always seemed to have plenty of money, but since he died Moirrey seemed to be far less well off than I would have expected her to be."

"That's something I'll have our financial experts take a look at," Rockwell told her. "Knowing Matthew Barnes, do you think it's possible that he was cheating a client?"

Bessie laughed. "Absolutely," she told him. "He's as unscrupulous and dishonest as they come. It wouldn't surprise me to learn that he's cheating every single one of his clients. There must be a myriad of ways that an advocate can sneak money away from a client and into his own pocket, and I'd bet that Matthew Barnes knows every one and uses most of them."

The inspector laughed. "I didn't realise how much you dislike the man," he told Bessie. "I take it you wouldn't mind if he was Moirrey's killer?"

"I'd be delighted," Bessie replied. "Nothing would make me happier than seeing that man behind bars."

Rockwell nodded. "Okay, I'll definitely take a closer look at him. There's no doubt he had more than ample opportunity to switch the tablets. Moirrey was at his office at least once a week, and apparently they met socially quite regularly as well."

"It's a small island," Bessie shrugged. "Everyone meets everyone socially at least once in a while."

Rockwell nodded. "And not so socially," he told her. He laughed as she gave him a confused look. "What I mean is that I seem to run into everyone all the time. No matter where I go, I seem to bump into people I know. I was grocery shopping the other day and ran into Doona and, um, a friend of hers."

"Which friend?" Bessie asked, curious about the odd expression on the inspector's face.

"Andrew Teare," he answered.

"Moirrey's brother," Bessie said. "Doona seems to be spending a great deal of time with him at the moment."

"Yes, she does, doesn't she?" Rockwell sighed. "At least, as far as I can tell, he has an alibi for Moirrey's murder. He didn't arrive on the island until the day after the body was found."

"Why would he want to kill his own sister?" Bessie asked. "He seemed really upset about her death when I met him."

Rockwell shrugged. "We have to consider anyone with a connection to Moirrey, and you don't get much closer than brother and sister. Maybe he is still bitter because he thought his mum liked her best."

"He might be," Bessie remarked. "There was no doubt that Jane Teare doted on her daughter. I always thought poor Andrew was rather pushed aside once Moirrey arrived. Of course he was shipped off to boarding school not long after. Still, I can't see childhood rivalries triggering murder this many years later. By all accounts Andrew's had a great life, seeing the world and such, and now he gets his inheritance which he was entitled to even when Moirrey was alive. I can't see why he'd want her dead."

"And if she were still alive, she could help speed things up for him," Rockwell remarked. "He's still struggling to prove his identity, and Matthew Barnes seems to be going out of his way to make it difficult. I can't help but wonder if Mr. Barnes is trying to hide things from the Teare family heir."

Bessie grinned. "Can't you just lock Mr. Barnes up now and find the evidence later?" she teased.

The inspector laughed. "If only it were that easy," he told her.

"There must be other people who had motives for killing Moirrey," Bessie suggested.

"We have a list started down at the station," Rockwell laughed. "She didn't have a lot of friends, and she seemed to have made a lot of enemies in her relatively short life."

"Most of the folks on your list will just be people who disliked her," Bessie said. "But that isn't usually enough reason to kill someone."

"True," Rockwell nodded. "Let me run through a few of the names and see if you have any more information about them than I do."

In the next half hour they got through an entire pot of tea and all of the rest of the shortbread. Bessie wasn't surprised at any of the names on the list. She'd heard about every single one of the fights and disagreements that Moirrey had started with the various people the inspector named.

Eventually Bessie sighed. "I know her neighbours have been fighting with her about the fences for years, and I know that Joney Kelly has never forgiven her for getting her fired from her tutoring job, and I know all the others that you mentioned had legitimate reasons for disliking the woman, but not one of the quarrels or disagreements you mentioned seemed anywhere near enough to be a motive for murder."

"I'm inclined to agree with you, since you haven't added anything to any of the stories," Rockwell told her. "What about Janet Munroe?"

"Moirrey's housekeeper? What possible motive would she have had?"

"Apparently, Moirrey had recently terminated her employment and told her she had two weeks to get out of the cottage she was living in," Rockwell told Bessie.

"Moirrey dismissed Janet?" Bessie repeated slowly. "But Janet has been working for Moirrey since just before Ewan died. She was the only person I know who could put up with Moirrey for any length of time."

"Well, apparently Moirrey decided she'd had enough of Janet."

"Surely being let go isn't a motive for murder, though?" Bessie asked.

"She was being kicked out of her home as well," Rockwell reminded her. "But she wasn't going without a fight, apparently. She'd been in touch with Doncan Quayle and was planning to take Moirrey to court."

"In that case, I would suspect Moirrey of trying to kill her, not the other way around," Bessie laughed. "I'm sure she didn't take kindly to the idea of her hired help taking her to court."

"Presumably not, but I'm surprised you didn't know anything about this," Rockwell told Bessie.

"I am as well," Bessie shrugged. "I would guess that Janet wasn't exactly bragging about losing her job and Moirrey wouldn't have said anything, at least not to me."

"Moirrey doesn't appear to have said anything to anyone," Rockwell sighed. "Right now I only have Janet's version of events to go on. Although I have no reason to doubt them, it's always nice to have independent confirmation."

"I'll give it some thought and ask around, if you like," Bessie suggested. "If you don't mind it becoming common knowledge?"

"Let me think about that one," Rockwell replied. "In the meantime, we have one other thing to discuss."

"What's that?"

"Who was Moirrey dating?" Rockwell asked.

Bessie felt her jaw drop. "Moirrey was dating?" she asked, shock evident in her tone.

Rockwell laughed. "Apparently that's news to you," he replied. "Although I shouldn't be laughing. I was really hoping you'd know the identity of her secret boyfriend."

"It's definitely news to me," Bessie answered. "I've not heard anything about it anywhere." She shook her head. "Are you sure she was dating?"

"Not entirely," he shrugged. "This has all come from Janet Munroe and, as I said, no one has been able to confirm anything she's told me. According to Janet, Moirrey recently bought a bunch of new clothes and started going out in the evening wearing them, with her hair all done up and with makeup all over her face. She claims that about a month ago or more she started seeing a car coming and going from Moirrey's cottage at odd hours as well. When she asked Moirrey about it, apparently Moirrey giggled and wouldn't talk about it."

"Well, that certainly sounds like a boyfriend," Bessie said slowly. "But no one I know ever mentioned seeing her out with anyone. And believe me, if she had been out on a date, everyone on the island would have been talking about it."

"Oh, that I do believe," Rockwell laughed. "Can you think of any reason why she would want to keep her boyfriend a secret?"

"I can only guess. Maybe he was married or otherwise involved somewhere? Or maybe he wasn't her social equal and she was embarrassed to be seen with him? Or maybe he was a she?"

"You think Moirrey was gay?" Rockwell asked.

"I didn't think Moirrey was interested in anyone except herself," Bessie answered. "I've no reason to think she was gay, but if she were, I would think she would want to keep it quiet."

"Okay, how about a list of possible suitors?"

Bessie shook her head. "I can't even begin to guess. I suppose she might have met someone in Douglas at some event. There are always new comeovers at events there. Maybe she met someone and it carried on from there."

"But you don't think it was anyone local?"

"I haven't heard of anyone local sneaking around or doing anything unexplained lately," Bessie shrugged. "How long ago did it start?"

"Janet wasn't sure, but she reckoned at least a month ago, maybe more."

"That's a long time to keep a secret on an island this small," Bessie remarked. "Whoever he was, he must have been really motivated to keep it quiet. And there must have been some very good reason why Moirrey kept it quiet as well. It wasn't like her to keep good secrets. I can see her not wanting to talk about getting rid of Janet, but she liked to tell everyone how wonderful her life was whenever anything good happened."

"And you can't think of anyone in Laxey that she wouldn't have wanted people to know she was involved with?"

"Well, perhaps if Jack Caine was still around, he might be a candidate," Bessie said thoughtfully. "There were all sorts of rumours years ago about Jack and Moirrey, but that was back when Moirrey was little more than a teenager. As soon as Anne heard the stories, she put a stop to Jack spending any time alone with Moirrey, and that was the end of that, as far as I know."

"And as I said earlier, Jack's been off the island for the last two months."

"Exactly," Bessie shrugged. "I mean, there are a lot of married men of the right sort of age in Laxey, but I can't see Moirrey getting involved with any of them. Sorry, but this is difficult. Aside from the rumours about her and Jack, there's never even been a hint that she was interested in anyone."

"Never mind," Rockwell sighed. "Maybe you can poke around a little bit and see if you can find out anything from any of your sources?" he suggested. "Ask about a boyfriend and also about Janet getting let go."

"Absolutely," Bessie promised. She glanced at the clock. It was too late to start ringing around tonight, but tomorrow would be an interesting day. If Moirrey had been dating, someone had to know about it.

The inspector finished off his last piece of shortbread. "I suppose I should get going," he said.

Bessie smiled at him. "You're welcome back anytime," she told him.

"I may stop by tomorrow night again, if you don't mind. I'm hoping you might have some hint as to the identity of the mysterious boyfriend by then."

"That doesn't give me much time," Bessie said, "but I'll do my best."

The inspector got to his feet. "Oh, one more thing," he said in an offhand manner. "Doona has been suspended with pay until the investigation is wrapped up."

Bessie's jaw dropped again. "What? Why?"

"It turns out her fingerprints are all over the prescription bottle that held the switched tablets."

Bessie just stared at him for a minute. "But, hang on, Moirrey dropped one of her bottles in class Easter Monday night," she told Rockwell. "Doona was kind enough to pick it up for her. It just figures that that was the bottle that was tampered with, poor Doona. But at least there's a perfectly logical explanation for her prints being on it."

Rockwell smiled at Bessie. "I'm ever so glad that your account matches Doona's," he told Bessie. "We still have to question the others in the class, but it seems like a logical enough explanation to me."

"So you can unsuspend Doona?"

"Unfortunately it isn't that easy," the inspector said in an apologetic tone. "Inspector Kelly and the chief constable both feel that it's better if we wait to reinstate her until after the killer is behind bars."

"But that could take ages," Bessie argued. "You just more or less told me that you've no idea who did it."

"Which is all the more reason why we have to be so careful. We were lucky we even found out it was murder; we have to tread very carefully. There has already been some suggestion that someone in the constabulary was being paid to ignore the evidence that it was murder, or even that Dr. Quayle was paid to certify natural causes when he knew it wasn't. If the press discover that one of our own staff left fingerprints all over what is essentially the murder weapon, the conspiracy theorists will go crazy."

"Who's making ridiculous suggestions like that?" Bessie demanded.

"Matthew Barnes, for one," Rockwell told her. "He may well just be trying to shift attention away from himself, but the press seem inclined to listen to him. Unfortunately, that means Doona is off the job until we get things sorted."

"You can't believe one thing that man says," Bessie argued. "Poor Doona must be very upset."

"Not so you can tell," Rockwell told her.

"What do you mean?"

"She seems to be taking advantage of the unexpected time off," he said grumpily. "As far as I can tell, she's spending all day every day with Andrew Teare."

Bessie opened her mouth to ask more questions, but the look on the inspector's face stopped her. It seemed that he didn't like Moirrey's brother, and while Bessie wanted to know why, she didn't want to upset the man any further.

"I'll have to ring Doona first thing in the morning and find out how she is doing," she told Rockwell.

"That's a great idea," the inspector replied. "You can update me on her as well when I see you tomorrow. I'm not allowed to contact her while she's on suspension."

Bessie frowned but bit her lip. She walked to the door with the inspector. "So I'll see you tomorrow night," she said.

"Why don't I bring pizza?" Rockwell suggested. "I'll try to be here a little bit earlier as well."

"That sounds great," Bessie agreed easily. "Feel free to bring Hugh if you think he can help as well," she suggested.

"I might," Rockwell shrugged. "He's pretty busy with his own romance at the moment, though."

Bessie smiled. "I heard he was dating, but no one seems to have any details. Who's the lucky lady?"

"Some girl from Douglas. I guess they met at a club there a couple of days ago and have been spending every spare minute together ever since. I can't remember her name, but if you really want to know, I'll make sure to find out before tomorrow."

"Oh, yes, please," Bessie replied. She opened the cottage door and waited for the man to walk out.

"Oh, one more thing," the inspector said casually. "Can you keep your eyes open for a little rental flat in the area? Just one bedroom will do."

"Who's looking for a flat?" Bessie asked.

"Me," Rockwell told her. "The drive back and forth to Ramsey late at night is getting old fast. Besides which, I seem to wake up the whole house when I come in. The wife and I figured it might be better for everyone if I rented a little space here in Laxey. That way, when I have to work late, I can just stay there instead of driving home."

Bessie considered him for a moment. "I don't know of anything right now," she said finally. "But I'll ask around. I'm sure you'd prefer a proper flat to just renting a room in someone's home."

Rockwell nodded. "Since it's especially for when I'm working late or irregular hours, I think I need something with its own entrance. I'm not sure how many flats there are in the area, though."

"I'm sure Thomas Clague would have given you a good deal on one of the new cottages over the winter," Bessie told him. "He can't rent them out. No one wants a beach holiday in January, and I bet he would have loved the idea of a resident police inspector staying there in case there were any problems. But now that spring is here, he's probably booked solid until October."

"Well, I guess if I haven't found anything else by October it might be worth considering," the inspector told Bessie. "In the meantime, let me know if you hear about anything else."

"I surely will," Bessie answered. "I'm going to be ringing everyone I know tomorrow to find out about Moirrey's boyfriend and Janet; I'll ask about flats as well."

"I'd appreciate that." The inspector smiled and thanked Bessie again for the tea and shortbread and then he was gone, into his car for the ten-minute commute back to Ramsey.

Bessie looked at the clock. It was nearly ten o'clock. The inspector's wife probably wasn't going to be pleased when he got home. Upstairs, she crawled into bed and almost immediately fell asleep.

CHAPTER NINE

After her walk the next morning, Bessie settled in to make some phone calls. The first three people she rang were all full of interesting skeet, but none of them had heard about Janet or had any idea who Moirrey might have been dating. None of them knew about any flats for rent, either.

She put the phone back down and filled the kettle. She'd rung Doona once she'd made a pot of tea. Before she had time to turn the kettle on, though, the phone rang.

"Hello?"

"Aunt Bessie? Er, um, sorry, but I couldn't think who to ring. It's Andy, Andy Caine."

"Hello, Andy, what can I do for you?" Bessie kept her voice calm, hearing tremendous strain in her caller's.

"It's mum, that is, the police just rang. Mum crashed in her car going over the mountain. They've taken her to Noble's, you see, and, well, my car won't start."

Bessie could hear the tears the young man was struggling to hold back. "I'll ring my taxi company and we'll be around to pick you up just as soon as we can," Bessie told him. "You are at your mum's cottage, right?"

"Yeah," Andy replied.

"While you're waiting for me, you should pack up a suitcase for your mum," Bessie suggested. "Pack her some pyjamas and slippers and her bathrobe. She'll want her hairbrush and her toothbrush and maybe a book or a magazine or something like that."

"Yeah, okay," Andy said. "I can do that."

"Well, you get busy and I'll see you as soon as I can."

Bessie hung up and rang her taxi service. She was lucky they had a car in the area, even if it was being driven by her least favourite driver.

Mark Stone was always grumpy and dissatisfied with life. When Bessie told him where she was going, he began to grumble immediately.

"Anne Caine's cottage? Don't expect they've paved that road properly yet, have they? It'll play havoc with my suspension that road will. Don't suppose she could walk out to the main road to meet us, no?"

"We're actually picking up her son," Bessie answered coolly. "Anne's been in an accident."

"Oh, aye, well, women drivers, you know? Well, I don't reckon you do, but still."

Bessie briefly considered arguing with him, but decided there was no point. She wasn't going to change his mind and she preferred that he keep his focus on driving.

Andy was standing at door to the cottage with a small suitcase in his hand when they arrived. He looked totally bewildered and no more than ten years old.

Bessie climbed out of the taxi and gave him a huge hug. "Come on then, let's get to Noble's." With the suitcase stowed in the boot, Mark headed out of Laxey.

"All the way to Douglas," he began to complain. "I told the dispatcher I wanted to be on short trips today. My stomach's bothering me and...."

"I'm sorry, Mark," Bessie interrupted in her sweetest voice. "But as this is rather an emergency, do you think you could just drive?"

The driver gave her a look she couldn't read, but she was far more interested in talking to Andy than she was worried about what Mark Stone thought of her.

"So, who rang and what exactly did they say?" she asked the young man.

Andy sighed. "Hugh Watterson rang. We were at school together, you know. Anyway, someone from the Douglas constabulary rang the Laxey station and Hugh took the call. Someone saw mum go off the road and called 999. The police checked the plates and called Laxey to find out about family. Hugh knew I was back on the island because he talked to me about Moirrey, so he rang me."

"Do they know what happened?"

"No," Andy said, rubbing his face with his hand. "Hugh said they got mum out and then they were going to tow the car into Douglas where the police and the insurance people could have a look. The car was so old; I guess it's not surprising that something went wrong. I don't think it would have passed an MOT if we were across, you know?"

Bessie sighed. "Did Hugh give you any indication of how badly hurt your mother is?" she asked, squeezing his hand.

"Not really; he just suggested that I make my way to Noble's at my earliest convenience."

"Well, that doesn't sound too bad," Bessie said, feeling slightly reassured.

"I don't know," Andy replied. "I mean he wouldn't exactly have encouraged me to speed to get there, would they?"

Bessie grinned in spite of her tension. "Probably not," she agreed.

They made the rest of the journey in silence, with Bessie holding on tightly to Andy's hand. When they arrived at the hospital, Andy climbed out of the car, just barely remembering to grab the suitcase and hold the door for Bessie.

"Put today on my account," Bessie instructed Mark, ignoring the flash of annoyance that passed over his face. He'd be worried about his tip, she supposed, but she'd make sure he got one. She didn't like him, but he had delivered her safely to her destination in reasonable time.

Inside the front doors, Bessie led Andy to the information desk. "We're here about Anne Caine," Bessie said in a hushed voice to the woman behind it.

She typed a request into her computer and peered at the screen. "Oh, aye, they've just sent her up from A & E to ward eleven. You can take the lift up to the second floor and then turn left and follow the signs."

Bessie smiled at Andy. "If they've sent her up to the ward, she must be doing okay."

"I guess," Andy muttered.

The pair rode the lift silently, and then followed the signs down the corridor until they reached the doors to ward eleven. Andy held the door open for Bessie and they made their way to the nursing station.

"Good morning," Bessie smiled at Helen Baxter, a thirty-something blonde with an interest in the medical history of the island. The two had met at a conference some months earlier and Bessie had immediately liked the intelligent and energetic woman.

"Bessie Cubbon? What brings you here? I don't think we've any of your historian friends tucked up in our beds today."

Bessie smiled. "I'm here to see Anne Caine," she explained. "This is her son, Andy."

"Isn't she popular?" Helen asked. "She's only been on the ward for five minutes and she's already building up a queue of visitors."

"Who else is here?" Bessie asked, surprised.

"Well, he didn't actually give his name," Helen told her. "But he's a very handsome man with dark hair. He said he grew up with Ms. Caine and I didn't see any reason to doubt him. And the police just rang to say that they're sending two men up to sit with her as well, although I guess they aren't really visitors."

"The police?" Andy's face went pale. "What do the police want?"

"I've no idea," Helen shrugged. "Why don't you ask your mum? She's in 1103."

Bessie led Andy down the hall. Anne was in a four-bed ward, but only two of the other beds were occupied. The curtain around Anne's bed was about three-quarters drawn but Bessie could see the bottom of her bed and, above the curtain, the top of someone's head.

As she approached the bed, she coughed loudly to warn Anne and her visitor that they weren't alone. The whispering voices she had heard as she approached stopped. Bessie peered cautiously around the curtain.

"Bessie? What are you doing here?" Anne greeted her unenthusiastically.

"I brought Andy," Bessie answered, gesturing for the man to join her from where he stood hesitating in the doorway to the ward.

"Andy?" Anne's eyes filled with tears as her son came into view. She reached out towards him and pulled him into a long embrace. Bessie turned away and met Andrew Teare's eyes across the bed.

"Mr. Teare? I wasn't expecting to find you here," Bessie said.

"You really must call me Andrew," the man said smoothly. He glanced down at Anne and then patted her arm. "You remember everything I said," he instructed her. "I'll be in touch very soon."

Anne muttered something without releasing her son. The other man nodded and then smiled at Bessie.

"I'll just be off then," he told her. "I'm meeting Doona for lunch down by the Promenade."

"But why were you here?" Bessie asked.

"I was only a few cars behind Anne on the mountain," the man explained as he circled around Anne's bed and came up beside Bessie. "Several of us stopped to help and once I realised who it was in the car, I followed the ambulance here. We might not have been allowed to play together often as children, but Anne is just about the only link to my past that I still have on the island. I wanted to make sure she was okay."

Bessie nodded. "Where were you going?" she asked curiously.

"What?"

"Where were you going this morning that you were crossing the mountain behind Anne?" Bessie explained the question.

"Oh, into Douglas for some shopping, and, as I said, to meet Doona for lunch," the man told her. "Obviously the shopping could wait, of course, in light of Anne's accident. But now I really do have to dash. I don't want to keep Doona waiting."

Bessie watched him leave the ward, wondering about his relationship with Doona. Doona already had two divorces to her credit, and Bessie felt protective of her friend. She shook her head and turned back to Anne and Andy. Doona wouldn't thank her for prying into her private life.

Bessie smiled as Andy finally managed to disentangle himself from his mother's embrace. "Okay, mum, I'm glad to see you as well," he told her with a shaky laugh.

Anne's face was wet with tears. "I've never been so frightened in my life," she told her son. "I thought for sure I was going to die."

"What happened?" Bessie asked as she studied the other woman. Anne was pale and had a bandage on one arm and another one her forehead, but she looked reasonably well for a woman who'd just crashed her car.

"I don't know," Anne answered. "I was running errands for work, into Ramsey and then into Douglas. I was just coming down the mountain and the brakes suddenly stopped working. I couldn't slow down and the road is so twisty that I lost control." She shuddered and Andy squeezed her hand tightly.

"You were lucky someone rang 999 right away," Bessie told her.

"The road was busy," Anne told her. "I suspect whoever rang did so out of guilt, though."

"Guilt? Bessie asked.

"The car right behind me was right on my bumper all the way across the top of the mountain. There was too much traffic for them to get around me, but they were clearly in a big hurry. My beat-up old clunker barely made it up the road; I was going as fast as I could."

"What did the doctor say?" Andy interrupted Bessie before she could ask for more details about the crash.

"That I'm badly shaken and I've squashed a few internal things with the seat belt, but it could have been much much worse. They want to keep me for twenty-four hours to keep an eye on everything, but then I should be good to go."

"Now I just have to find another car," Andy muttered. "Mine didn't want to start when I tried to come here," he explained to his mother.

"Actually, Andrew Teare said that he'd hire a car for me to use until the insurance pays out," Anne told her son. "You can use that while I'm stuck in here and we'll figure out something else once I'm home."

"Why would he do that?" Bessie asked in surprise.

"He says we're the closest thing he has to family now and he doesn't want to see us suffer," Anne answered, not meeting Bessie's eyes.

"That's great," Andy answered. "Did he say when he was going to get it sorted out?"

"He's going to stop back later with the keys and the paperwork," Anne answered.

Whatever Andy was going to say next was interrupted by the arrival of two uniformed constables.

"Good morning," the taller of the two men smiled at the little group. "We're just here to keep everyone company for a little while. Inspector Rockwell is on his way from the Laxey station. In the meantime, just ignore us."

Anne glared at them. "Ignore you? Why are you here?"

"I'm sorry, ma'am, I've absolutely no idea why we're here," the man smiled at her. "I'm just following orders."

"Well, I'm ordering you to go away," Anne said angrily. "I have enough problems in my life without having trouble with the law. You can't arrest me for crashing into a fence. I didn't hit any wildlife or any people, I'm sure of that."

"We're definitely not here to arrest you," the shorter man now spoke up. "Please, if you wait for Inspector Rockwell, I'm sure he'll explain everything."

Anne frowned. "But in the meantime, you're just going to stand there, in the way of everyone, and eavesdrop on my conversation with my son?"

"We're going to try our best to not get in anyone's way," the taller officer replied. "And we aren't going to deliberately listen to your conversation, either. We're just doing our job."

Anne opened her mouth to argue further, but Bessie held up a hand. "No point in taking your anger out on the officers," she pointed out. "They're just following orders. Save your anger for Inspector Rockwell. He's the one giving the orders."

Anne looked as if she might disagree, but finally she sighed and sank down under her covers. "I don't intend to say anything further," she announced. "You be sure and tell your boss you didn't overhear anything interesting."

Andy shook his head. "Mum," he began, "why don't you...."

Anne held up a hand to stop him. "Hush, we aren't talking about anything," she said stubbornly.

Bessie shook her head and then turned to the two constables. "So, tell me about yourselves," she suggested.

Twenty minutes later Bessie knew all about the two young men who were stationed at Anne's bedside. They were both very polite and came from good Manx families. Although Bessie didn't know either family well, she knew cousins and other more distant relations of both men. And both of them had heard stories about Aunt Bessie.

"I was always jealous of my cousin Jack," the tall man, who was called Pete, told her. "He used to talk about running away to your cottage and staying up eating cake until midnight."

Bessie laughed. "I'm afraid your cousin might have exaggerated slightly," she said. "My visitors always went to bed fairly early, when I did. No one was eating cake at midnight."

Pete made a face. "That figures. Jack always made the things I couldn't do sound like more fun than they were."

Inspector Rockwell's face was grim when he pulled back the curtain a few moments later. "Good morning," he said curtly to them all. "Although it's nearly midday, so good afternoon might be more appropriate."

"Hello, Inspector Rockwell," Bessie smiled at him.

"Miss Cubbon, Mr. Caine, Mrs. Caine," Rockwell nodded at each of them in turn. "I'm sorry it took me so long to get here."

"Oh, no worries," Anne said angrily. "We've had ever so much fun getting to know Pete and Doug. They've been such great company for us. I really must thank you for sending them over to spy on me."

Rockwell frowned. "I didn't send them to spy on you," he told her. "I sent them to protect you."

"Nonsense," she snapped at him. "Who did I need protecting from?"

"Whoever cut the brake lines on your car," the inspector answered tightly.

Bessie gasped as Andy grabbed his mother's hand. Anne just looked even angrier.

"That car is twenty-something years old. The brakes failed. I'm sorry I didn't look after it more carefully, but it ran well enough. I don't know why you're trying to scare me, but it won't work."

"I'm not trying to scare you," Rockwell said gently. "The brake lines were cut, there is no doubt about it. Our crime scene investigator is prepared to testify to that in court, once we find out who did it. You don't have to believe me, but I intend to do what I can to protect you until we figure out exactly what happened and why."

"Why would anyone want to kill me?" Anne demanded. An odd look flashed across her face and then she sighed and buried her head in her hands. "I'm sorry," she said in a muffled voice. "I'm just exhausted and in a lot of pain. Maybe you could talk to me later, once I'm feeling better."

"Pardon me?" The man peering around the curtain didn't look happy. "There are far too many of you in here," he said. "This is a hospital ward, not a coffee shop. If you want to hold a meeting, you'll need to take it downstairs. We actually have a decent café on the ground floor."

Inspector Rockwell nodded. "Sorry about this," he said. "I'm John Rockwell from the Isle of Man Constabulary, CID division. I'm usually stationed in Laxey. We have reason to believe that Mrs. Caine's crash wasn't an accident and may be linked to other events that took place in the Laxey area that I'm already involved with. The Douglas Constabulary is working with me, therefore. I've already requested that she be moved to a private room. We'll be less disruptive there."

"You might be less disruptive, but you'll still be keeping Mrs. Caine from rest and recovery," the other man replied irritably. "Wherever she is, I'm going to insist on no more than one visitor at a time."

"I just want my son," Anne said. "Everyone else can go home."

Rockwell shook his head. "That's not happening," he told her. He turned back to the other man. "I'm sure we can work this out," he told him.

The pair stepped out into the hallway. Bessie could hear the low murmur of voices but couldn't make out what was being said. Eventually the inspector returned.

"Dr. Harrison is going to make the arrangements for your move," he told Anne. "You should be more comfortable in a private room."

"How am I supposed to pay for that?" Anne demanded. "I know private rooms cost a fortune. I'm already going to have to find some money for another car."

Rockwell held up his hand to stop the complaints. "The Isle of Man Constabulary will be happy to pick up the tab for your private room. It will be far less bother than all of the paperwork I would have to complete if you were murdered."

"That isn't funny," Andy complained.

"Neither is attempted murder, but your mother isn't taking that seriously," Rockwell retorted.

Two hospital staff came in now to move Anne to her new room. They disconnected the various pieces of equipment that were monitoring her and then disengaged the wheel locks on the bed.

"Ready to go?" one of them asked Anne cheerfully. He didn't wait for a reply; instead, he began to pull the bed towards the doors that had been propped open. His companion pushed the bed from the other end and Bessie, Andy and the three policemen followed behind.

Anne's bed was pushed all the way to the end of the hallway, where a small private room sat alone amid supply cupboards and the staff break room.

"You can't get much safer than this," one of the hospital staff remarked loudly. "There aren't even any windows."

"Oh, great," Anne muttered from the bed.

Inspector Rockwell motioned for the others to wait in the corridor as he followed Anne into the room. After a moment, he beckoned everyone inside.

Bessie looked around the small room. There was just enough space for the large hospital bed and very little else. A small chest of drawers was tucked into one corner and a small tray table on wheels was flat against the wall. That left just enough room for one small visitor's chair. The two staff members had quickly reconnected everything and Bessie and Andy slid back into the hall to give them enough space to get out of the tiny room.

Back inside, Bessie could see the door opposite the entrance door that led to the teeny adjoining bathroom. Both the room itself and the bathroom seemed dark and dreary, possibly because of the lack of windows. It was clear that no real effort had been made towards decorating the space. The walls were beige, the floor was beige and everyone's skin looked beige in the harsh artificial light.

"Okay, it isn't the most attractive space," Inspector Rockwell admitted, "but it will be easy to keep you safe here." He motioned to the two uniformed constables and they followed him out of the room, shutting the door behind them. With the door shut, even with fewer people in it, the room felt positively claustrophobic.

Bessie tried to start a conversation with Anne, but every comment she made was greeted with the same icy silence. Andy looked from Bessie to his mother and back again, an embarrassed expression on his face.

"Mum, can't you just...." he began after Bessie's third attempt at engaging the injured woman.

Anne held up a hand. "I've got a terrible headache," she complained. "I think I need the doctor to give me something for the pain."

Andy leaned over and pressed the call button. Bessie edged towards the door.

"Maybe I should just leave," she suggested in a quiet voice.

"That might be best," Anne told her, sighing. "I don't mean to be rude, really I don't," she told Bessie. "But I'm in a lot of pain."

Bessie nodded. "I'll get out of the way, then. I hope you feel better soon."

She took the half step needed to reach the door, but it swung open before she touched it.

Inspector Rockwell stuck his head into the room. "Pete and Doug will be out here to screen your visitors," he told Anne. "Is there anyone you specifically do not want to see?"

Anne frowned. "I don't want to see anyone," she said. "Only my son should be allowed into the room."

The inspector nodded. "We can arrange that," he said. "We'll have the officers tell potential visitors that it's doctor's orders so that no one gets their feelings hurt."

Anne gave the inspector a thoughtful look, then she sighed. "That would be great," she said.

"Bessie, can I buy you a cup of tea in the café?" Rockwell asked.

Bessie smiled. "That sounds wonderful."

"Um, Bessie?" Andy said something to his mother and got a nod in return. "Um, if you don't mind waiting a little bit, I'll give you a ride home once Mr. Teare comes back. I mean, if he does hire a car for us, like."

"I'll wait in the café," Bessie told him. "If you aren't down in an hour or so, I'll just grab a taxi home."

"That sounds good," Andy replied.

"I hope you feel better soon," Bessie told Anne as she left the room.

"Thanks," Anne said grudgingly.

Bessie and Inspector Rockwell walked to the lift in silence. As it slowly descended, the inspector let out a long sigh.

Bessie glanced at him, but he shook his head. There were a few other people on the lift; they couldn't talk there.

Luckily the spacious café was all but deserted. Rockwell led Bessie to a table in the back corner of the room. No one else was anywhere near them. A waitress took their order, with Bessie getting soup and a sandwich to go with her tea. Inspector

Rockwell ordered a toasted teacake.

"It is lunchtime," Bessie pointed out.

Rockwell glanced at his watch. "So it is," he sighed. "The day has really run away from me." When the waitress brought their tea, he added soup and a sandwich to his order.

"So, what do you think of all of this?" the inspector asked Bessie as they sipped their tea.

"I don't know what to think," Bessie sighed. "I can't imagine why anyone would want to kill Anne. She doesn't have any money. Really, if I had to think of one person that would be happier with her dead, it would have been Moirrey."

"Why Moirrey?" The inspector asked.

"I don't know the ins and outs of the agreement between Ewan and Robert, but it's possible that Anne's death would have simplified things with regard to her cottage. If Anne died before she'd caught up on her payments, I'd bet Moirrey could have reclaimed the cottage as her own. I'm sure Andy would have fought it, but I suspect he could have been bought off fairly cheaply. He wouldn't have any idea of the true value of the property, of course."

"So maybe Moirrey cut the brake lines before she died," Rockwell suggested. "I'll have to talk to my experts and find out how far the car could have been driven before the brakes failed."

"It's a theory," Bessie said doubtfully.

"But?" the inspector laughed. "Come on, I hear the doubt in your tone."

"I simply can't imagine Moirrey having the first clue how to cut brake lines. And I really can't see her crawling under a car to do it, even if she could find out how from somewhere."

"Maybe her mysterious boyfriend did the dirty work for her."

Bessie shrugged. "I haven't had any luck tracking him down," she told the inspector. "No one seems to know anything about it. I thought I might go and have a chat with Janet Munroe. Maybe she can help me figure out who it was."

"I'm not sure I like the idea of you visiting suspects," the inspector frowned. "You know as well as I do how dangerous that can be."

"I'll arrange to meet her in a public place," Bessie suggested. "And you can have Hugh sitting at the next table if you really think it's necessary."

Rockwell grinned at her. "Definitely meet her in a public place. Let me know where and when, and I may just have Hugh, or someone, stationed nearby."

"Fair enough," Bessie agreed.

"Meanwhile, what can I do about Anne?" Rockwell asked.

"What do you mean?"

"She knows who cut her brake lines or at least she has a pretty strong suspicion. How can I get her to tell me?"

"What makes you think she knows?"

"Nothing specific," Rockwell shrugged. "Just lots of little things. She's refusing to have any visitors, for one thing. That suggests that there is someone she really doesn't want to see, but she doesn't want to single him or her out. She's hiding something and I want to know what it is."

"Well, I can see what I can get out of Andy while he's taking me home," Bessie told him.

"That would be good," Rockwell said. "Can you think of anyone, other than Moirrey, who might have had a motive for getting rid of Anne?"

Bessie opened her mouth to reply, but the soup, sandwiches and teacake all arrived at once. For several minutes the pair got on with the important job of refueling their bodies.

"This is good," Rockwell said as he scooped up the last of his soup.

Bessie laughed. "You sound surprised."

"Well, hospital food isn't usually known for being tasty."

"Oh, this isn't what they feed to the patients," Bessie told him. "That's as dire as you would expect. But they look after visitors and the staff quite well."

Rockwell shook his head. "You'd think people would get better faster if they were eating well."

"The problem, of course, is catering to everyone's very specialised diet. Everyone in hospital is on a low-salt or low-cholesterol or low-something diet. Here in the café, they can add salt and fats and all the things that make everything so delicious but so bad for us."

Rockwell laughed. "Well, they've done a good job with this." He popped the last bite of his sandwich into his mouth and then buttered his teacake. Bessie washed down her last bite with the last of her tea.

"It was very good," she agreed. "But you asked me who else might want to get rid of Anne, and I've been thinking about that while I ate. If Moirrey is a possible candidate, what about her brother?"

"I'd love to take a closer look at him," Rockwell told her. "But I was afraid that I was letting my dislike of the man cloud my judgment. What would he gain by Anne's death?"

"Well, presumably the same thing Moirrey would have gained. I'm guessing the title to Anne's cottage. He does seem to have been going out of his way to be helpful to Anne and Andy, though."

"Yeah, very helpful," Rockwell muttered. "It makes me wonder why."

"He says it's because they're all that's left of his family," Bessie told him. "I doubt that he and Anne knew each other well as children, but at least they grew up in the same place at the same time."

Rockwell shrugged. "I'm trying to get Matthew Barnes to let me see the trust document that was set up before Ewan Teare died. It established everything that Moirrey was fighting with him about."

"Presumably Andrew Teare has seen it?" Bessie asked.

"I'm not sure," Rockwell told her. "Matthew Barnes was insisting on Andrew proving his identity before he would talk to him about the estate, but the last I heard Barnes and Andrew were having lots of long meetings. Neither of them wants to tell me anything, of course."

"Maybe I should have a chat with Mr. Teare as well," Bessie suggested.

Rockwell frowned. "I don't like him and I don't trust him. Make sure, if you do talk to him, that you do it in a public place."

Bessie nodded. "But he couldn't have switched Moirrey's tablets, right? He wasn't even on the island until after her death."

Inspector Rockwell didn't get a chance to comment; he was interrupted by Andy Caine's arrival.

"Aunt Bessie? Mr. Teare's just dropped off the keys to our rental car. I can run you home now," the young man said as he joined them at the table.

"How's your mum?" Bessie asked.

"She's resting," Andy shrugged. "She told me to go and get some lunch and gave me a long list of stuff she wants from home. I didn't grab any of the right things, apparently. She's going to try to get some sleep. I told her I'd be back before dinner time."

"So you should have some lunch," Bessie suggested. "The food here is quite good."

Andy shook his head. "That's okay, there's loads to eat at home. Mum hit the grocery store yesterday before she went to work and she filled the cupboards. I'll drop you off and then go home and make myself something. Then I'll pack up mum's stuff and bring it to her. I'm going to bring her a sandwich or something as well. She said the food here's inedible."

Bessie laughed. "It sounds as if you're going to have a busy afternoon. We'd better get moving. I don't want to hold you up."

"Thanks." Andy smiled gratefully at Bessie. She rose from the table and reached into her handbag for her wallet.

"Lunch is on me," Inspector Rockwell said before Bessie had managed to find it.

"Oh, that isn't necessary," Bessie replied.

"Maybe not," Rockwell shrugged. "But I insist."

Bessie smiled at him. "That's very kind of you."

"We'll be leaving at least one uniformed constable on duty outside of your mother's room while she's here," Rockwell told Andy. "You're the only person who will be allowed in to visit, although I intend to try to have a word with her at some point. We'll need a formal statement from her before too long, as well."

Andy frowned. "I'd really appreciate it if you'd just leave her alone for today," he said after a moment's thought. "She really needs rest and to not be thinking that maybe someone tried to kill her."

"I can appreciate that," Rockwell replied. "But the sooner I can get a statement from her, the sooner I can start trying to figure out who did it. Surely she'll sleep better knowing that that person is behind bars?"

Andy shook his head. "I just don't know," he said quietly. "It all seems impossible. None of this seems like real life, you know? I suppose you don't because you're police and you probably deal with this sort of thing every day. But in my life, in my mum's life, no one tries to kill other people. This is the stuff of fiction, you know?"

Inspector Rockwell smiled at the young man. "I get that, really I do, but unfortunately it is real life at the moment and I need all of the cooperation I can get."

"I guess. When I come back I'll talk to mum, see if I can persuade her to talk to you. Maybe she'll feel better after a nap, anyway."

"I certainly hope so," the inspector told him. "Bessie, I'll see you tonight," he reminded her.

"Indeed," Bessie grinned. "I'm looking forward to it."

Bessie and Andy left the café and walked back through the hospital.

"Mr. Teare said that he left the car on the next street," Andy told Bessie.

The hospital was located near downtown Douglas. It had its own small car park, but there was never enough room in it for all of the staff and visitors who needed it. There were numerous parking restrictions on the streets that surrounded the hospital and Bessie suspected that the highways administration made a fortune issuing parking tickets to the many hospital visitors who parked on the streets without paying attention to the restrictions or time limits.

Bessie followed Andy around the corner. He stopped in front of an almost brand-new saloon car that had a hire car sticker on its rear bumper.

"This must be it," Andy said as he pushed the remote entry button on the keypad. The car beeped once. Andy tried the passenger door and it opened. "Here you go," he said, holding the door for Bessie.

Once Bessie was safely tucked up inside the car, Andy moved around to the driver's door and climbed in. Bessie sat patiently while he adjusted his seat and moved the mirrors to and fro. Finally, he checked that he could find the indicators and the windscreen wipers.

"Okay, I guess we're good to go," he said to Bessie, sliding the key into the ignition.

The car roared to life and Andy carefully eased it out of its parking space. "I'm not used to anything this fancy," Andy muttered as he manoeuvred the car down the narrow road.

Bessie kept quiet until he'd made his way out of Douglas and onto the coast road. He kept his speed reasonable and seemed to relax as he settled in to the journey.

"I'm glad your mum seems to be okay," Bessie said as they began their trip.

"Yeah, the doctor says she should be fine as long as she takes it easy for a few days. She wants to go home, of course, but the doctor said she has to stay until Monday. He wants to keep an eye on the bump on her head, apparently."

"It certainly seems to have made her grumpy," Bessie laughed.

Andy laughed with her. "Yeah, she's not usually that bad."

"Did she say anything to you about who might have done it?" Bessie asked.

Andy sighed. "She refused to even discuss that," he told Bessie. "I was hoping she might have some idea, but she won't even consider the possibilities."

"Do you have any ideas yourself?"

"Not really," Andy sighed. "I've been away for ages and I haven't been good about keeping in touch. If it was dad that crashed, I would have suspected mum, but I can't imagine anyone wanting to kill mum."

"You father is still across, isn't he?"

"I guess," Andy said vaguely. "Mum's better at keeping track of him than I am. I haven't talked to him."

Bessie frowned. "Surely if he were here, he would be staying at the cottage with you and your mum?"

"Don't know," Andy shrugged. "I'm not sure what's going on with mum and dad. And I am not going to ask my mum about it, either. She has enough to worry about right now without worrying about dad."

Bessie swallowed a dozen questions. "For what it's worth, I can't imagine anyone wanting to hurt your mother either," she said eventually.

"It must have been an accident. The brakes probably just wore out. Mum was terrible about looking after that car."

"The police seem pretty certain that the lines were cut," Bessie said doubtfully.

"Maybe someone cut the wrong brake lines," Andy said. "Mum left her car at the restaurant last night and got a ride home with the head chef. Maybe someone was after the owner or someone else who leaves their car there."

"I suppose that's possible," Bessie said. "I'm sure Inspector Rockwell will check into every possibility."

Andy nodded. "I guess. It all just feels so unreal, you know?"

Now Bessie nodded. "I know exactly what you mean," she told him. "But if your mum does know anything or suspect anyone, she needs to tell Inspector Rockwell. The person behind this, whomever his or her target was, is dangerous."

"I'll talk to her when I get back, really I will," Andy told her. "And I'll find out where dad is, too."

The rest of the journey was a quiet one. Andy focussed on driving the unfamiliar car safely along the coast, while Bessie made a mental list of all the things she needed to do. At her cottage, she was quick to thank the young man for taking time to drive her home.

"It's no problem, I had to come back to Laxey to get mum's stuff, anyway. And I really appreciated your helping me out this morning." He paused, blushing. "I know I sort of panicked. Thank you for everything."

"It wasn't any trouble," Bessie told him. "I was happy to help."

Andy nodded. "Well, I appreciated it a lot. I'll bake you

something nice as a thank-you once mum is settled."

"No one ever bakes for me," Bessie laughed. "That would be a real treat."

"Soon, I promise," Andy told her. Then he was gone, off to pack his mum's bags and get back to Douglas.

Bessie let herself into her cottage and set her bag down with a sigh. The day was over half over and she didn't feel as if she'd accomplished anywhere near what she had meant to do.

CHAPTER TEN

Bessie's message light was flashing frantically at her, so she grabbed a pen and paper and pressed play. She took note of each caller and then rewrote the list in the order in which she wanted to ring everyone back. That made Doona her first priority. Doona's home phone rang several times and then the answering machine picked up.

"Oh, hello, it's Bessie, just ringing you back." Bessie frowned into the phone. She'd really wanted to talk to Doona. She started to replace the receiver when she heard Doona's voice.

"Bessie? Are you still there? I'm here."

"Oh, there you are," Bessie laughed into the phone. "Did I catch you at a bad time?"

"No," Doona laughed. "You caught me at a great time. I just got back from lunch in Douglas. I could hear the phone ringing when I got to the door. You know how you tell yourself it doesn't matter? That the machine will take a message? Well, I kept telling myself that, all while trying to hurry like an idiot. I dropped my keys twice and then I couldn't get the key to turn properly and, ah, never mind. I'm glad I got to you in time, anyway."

Bessie laughed again. "Of course you could have just rung me back," she pointed out.

"But it's so much more fun to nearly kill myself trying to get to the phone in time."

"So, how are you?" Bessie asked.

"I'm okay," Doona replied. "I mean, I hate being suspended, but I'm still getting paid so I won't have to start selling off all of my possessions just yet."

"Well, I am glad to hear that," Bessie chuckled. "Would you like to have lunch with me tomorrow? My treat, somewhere nice."

"Oh, Bessie, ordinarily I'd love to, but I've already made plans with Andrew. Since I'm not working, we're spending a lot if time together. I'm showing him the island."

"As long as you're not sitting home, being bored, I'm happy," Bessie replied untruthfully.

"Oh no, I'm having a wonderful time with Andrew. It's been years since I've been to most of the heritage sites. I think I'm enjoying it all at least as much as he is."

"Well, that's good to hear," Bessie said, with forced cheer.

"Tomorrow we're heading to the House of Manannan. I've actually never been there before, so we can enjoy the experience together."

"It's only been open a short time. I was lucky to get an early tour. It's very good," Bessie told her. "Manx National Heritage did a great job bringing the island's history to life and there are lots of interactive displays as well. You should enjoy it."

"I'm sure we will," Doona answered. "Although I think I'd have fun doing just about anything with Andrew."

"Oh?"

"Bessie, he's just wonderful. He's been all over the world. He keeps talking about all of the places he wants to take me, once the estate is all settled. I'm trying to remember to take it slowly, but he's just about the most interesting and worldly man I've ever met."

Bessie struggled to find the right words for her reply. "I'm glad he's making you happy," she said eventually, just before the silence grew uncomfortable. "But I am worried about things moving too quickly. There's so much you don't know about him."

"He's told me pretty much his whole life story," Doona replied. "Even the details he knows I probably don't want to hear about, information about old girlfriends and that sort of thing."

"I still don't understand why he stayed away so long," Bessie said.

"I don't think he really knows the answer to that either. I think, after a while, coming back just seemed too hard. He was making good money, living a good life. I guess he figured he didn't need anything from anyone here."

"Surely he must have wondered about his parents and his little sister," Bessie argued.

"You, of all people, should understand that things can drive families apart," Doona told her friend.

Bessie was silent for a moment. Doona knew her life story, of course, even the parts Bessie wasn't proud of. Bessie's parents had forced her to return to the island when she was seventeen, leaving the man she loved in America. When he attempted to follow her across the ocean, he hadn't survived the crossing. Bessie had never forgiven her parents for making her leave and for inadvertently causing Matthew's death. Now, many years after her parents had passed away, she would have appreciated a chance to reconcile with them.

"I suppose that's true," she said after the pause. "I just don't want to see you get hurt, that's all."

"I know. I don't want to see me get hurt, either," Doona laughed. "But I do rather feel that I'm being swept off my feet, and it's quite a pleasant feeling."

"Does Andrew talk about Moirrey at all?" Bessie asked. "I'm wondering if he has any idea who might have wanted to kill her."

"Don't tell me your getting involved in the investigation?" Doona demanded. "Didn't you learn anything from what happened last time?"

"I learned a lot," Bessie told her. "I shall only ever be meeting potential suspects in public places, for one thing. Anyway, I'm not really getting involved; I'm just being nosy. I can't imagine anyone killing Moirrey, even though she was an unpleasant person."

Doona chuckled. "She was definitely that, although I've tried hard to say nice things about her to Andrew."

"That must be a struggle," Bessie laughed.

"It isn't too bad," Doona replied. "I barely knew the woman, after all. We only spoke twice, once at the station and then at the first language class. She was rude and nasty to me on both occasions, but we get all kinds at the station and she was horrible to everyone in class."

"You didn't answer my question," Bessie reminded her. "Does Andrew have any idea who might have killed his sister?"

"He doesn't really," Doona replied. "We've discussed it once or twice, but he wasn't able to come up with anyone that he thought would have wanted Moirrey dead. Oh, he knows she was fighting with Anne about the cottage and I guess she wasn't the only one Moirrey was battling, but none of that seems worth killing someone over."

"I was hoping he might be able to suggest someone we hadn't thought of," Bessie said with a sigh. "I can't see anyone I know being responsible."

"I can't see anyone I know being responsible, either. It was obviously carefully planned, right down to making sure they didn't leave any fingerprints on the tablets or on the bottle. Maybe it was all just an accident of some sort."

"I'm not sure how, but never mind," Bessie said. "What about Anne's car? Does Andrew have any ideas on who might have damaged her brakes?"

"Andrew and I both reckon that whoever did it was targeting someone else," Doona replied. "I heard a rumour that the assistant manager is having an affair. Maybe his wife found out and wanted to kill him."

"Surely his wife would know which car was his?" Bessie argued.

"Okay, maybe his wife thought that he was having the affair with Anne?"

"Anne wouldn't do that."

"But the wife might not know that," Doona replied. "Why else would anyone want to kill Anne?"

"I have no idea, but I can't help but think that the attack on her is connected to Moirrey's murder somehow."

"Maybe that developer that Moirrey was talking about is behind it all," Doona said. "You know, the one who offered

Moirrey loads of money for Anne's cottage? Maybe he got tired of waiting for Moirrey to get the property back, so he decided to kill both Moirrey and Anne."

"What good would their deaths do him?"

"I'll bet he's got some deal going with Matthew Barnes. If Andrew hadn't turned up when he did, Mr. Barnes would have been left in charge of everything. Mr. Barnes probably promised the developer that he could buy the property at a great price once the estate was settled."

"But Andrew did turn up," Bessie reminded her friend. "And before Anne's brake lines were cut. With Andrew here, any deals that anyone made with Mr. Barnes won't go through."

"I don't know," Doona laughed. "Maybe Matthew Barnes is trying to kill everyone associated with the Teare estate. Maybe Andrew is next; I'd better warn him."

"I don't like Matthew Barnes," Bessie stated the obvious. "But I'm not sure that he's a murderer."

"Well, Andrew doesn't like him either. He's really pushing hard for DNA testing before he'll let Andrew have anything to do with the estate. Meanwhile, everything is in limbo, which means Andrew is running low on funds."

"Don't lend him any money," Bessie said sharply.

Doona laughed. "My goodness, you are suspicious of everyone, aren't you? I'm not going to lend him any money. At least not yet. But if they don't get things settled quickly, he's going to have to liquidate some assets in the UK and that means a trip across. He's suggesting that I should go with him when he goes. He's promising a romantic weekend somewhere fabulous."

Bessie swallowed a dozen replies before she managed a neutral answer. "You should think about that very carefully."

Doona laughed again. "Aye, I certainly will. But now I have to dash. Andrew's picking me up in just a few hours for dinner and I want to do my nails and have a long soak in the bath first. I thought we'd drive down to Port Erin and try that new Japanese restaurant everyone's talking about."

"I've heard good things about the food," Bessie told her. "And from what I've heard, the views from the dining room are gorgeous as well."

"I've heard the same. I can't wait."

Bessie spent the rest of the afternoon returning the rest of the calls from her answering machine and then getting back to her list of people to talk to about Moirrey's possible boyfriend. While she always loved having a chance to chat with her friends, it was frustrating today because she didn't feel as if she was getting anywhere.

Finally she rang Janet Munroe, a woman she knew more by reputation than in reality.

"Yes?" The voice on phone was clipped and sharp, even on that single syllable.

"Ms. Munroe? This is Bessie Cubbon. I was just ringing to see how you were doing now that Moirrey is no longer with us."

"She's dead, Ms. Cubbon. I've never understood why people feel the need to tip-toe around death, finding all sorts of ridiculous euphemisms for it, when it's a perfectly natural occurrence that we shall all experience one day."

Bessie wasn't sure how to respond to that, so she changed the subject. "I hope you aren't feeling too lonely?"

"I'm never lonely," was the emphatic reply. "People who are miserable in their own company are never good company for other people, either."

"I was wondering if you'd like to meet up for a cup of tea and a chat?" Bessie pressed on in spite of her desire to hang up.

"I suppose you want to question me about Moirrey," the woman said tartly. "I'm sure you fancy yourself an amateur detective after your experiences last month. Luckily for you, I've nothing better to do at the moment. If you want to spend your money buying me tea and cake, I can't complain."

Bessie thought about arguing that she hadn't said anything about cake, but decided she wanted to talk to the other woman too much. "Good," she said. "Where would you like to meet and when?"

"We can meet at the coffee shop at the Manx Museum tomorrow at two," the other woman told her. "I'll see you there."

The phone was hung up, none too gently, before Bessie had

a chance to reply. "Well, okay then," she muttered into the dead receiver, feeling grumpy and out of sorts. Janet and Moirrey deserved each other, she thought to herself as she tidied up the cottage.

She expressed the same opinion to Inspector Rockwell a few hours later when he arrived with the pizza. Hugh wasn't far behind, and two large pizzas seemed to disappear at an astonishing rate. The inspector had also brought apple pie and custard and that didn't last long, either.

"What do you mean?" Rockwell asked her.

"I mean Janet Munroe sounds as nasty and unlikeable as her former employer," Bessie explained. "She was quite sharp with me on the phone."

"She was quite sharp with me when I interviewed her," the inspector replied. "She's, um, difficult, but perhaps not as deliberately rude and unkind as Moirrey was."

"She accused me of playing amateur detective," Bessie complained.

Hugh nearly choked on a sip of soda. "Sorry," he sputtered as he coughed and tried to get his breath. "Your comment just struck me funny."

"I don't see anything funny about it," Bessie sniffed. She and Rockwell exchanged glances and then they both laughed. "Okay, maybe she has a point, but she didn't have to be so rude about it."

Inspector Rockwell chuckled as he finished his last bite of pie. "I'm just hoping you can get more from her than I did," he told Bessie. "I have a feeling the missing boyfriend is significant."

"Unless Janet made him up to shift suspicion from herself," Bessie suggested.

"You really didn't like her, did you?" Hugh laughed.

"No, but even so, has anyone else said anything about a boyfriend?"

"No," Rockwell admitted. "But there is some evidence to suggest that she's telling the truth. Moirrey had hangers full of new dresses in her wardrobe and a bunch of bottles and containers of makeup on her dresser. She also had a bottle of very expensive perfume in her bathroom. I've been told that she usually lived in trousers and never wore makeup or perfume."

"I'd have to agree with that," Bessie said, thoughtfully. "I don't think I ever saw her wear makeup in all the years I knew her, not even as a teenager when all the other girls her age were experimenting with it. In fact I seem to remember her saying something about having an allergy to quote, 'all that goo,' end of quote."

"According to Dr. Quayle she didn't have any allergies," Rockwell remarked. "But he remembered her once saying something about makeup not being worth the expense or bother."

"That sounds like Moirrey," Bessie agreed.

"So why did she have a bunch of containers of makeup on her dresser?" Rockwell asked. "Some of them hadn't even been opened yet."

"Maybe they were planted there by the housekeeper to give more believability to her story," Bessie suggested.

"Wow, I almost hope she's guilty of something, given how much you dislike her," Rockwell said. "If she did plant them, she did a great job. The only recoverable fingerprints on any of the containers were Moirrey's own. And I'm told the prints were positioned where she would've held the containers if she was using their contents."

"Well, I talked to every nosy woman in Laxey and not one of them had any idea that Moirrey was dating anyone. If she was dating, she and her partner were both very discreet."

"That's hard to imagine on this island," Hugh said.

"Indeed," Rockwell replied. "Moirrey, or possibly her suitor, had to have a very strong reason for keeping the relationship a secret. Any idea what it might have been?"

Bessie shook her head. "The family was always very private, but this does seem to go beyond that. I would guess that the man must have been unsuitable in some way."

"Unsuitable?" Rockwell asked.

"Married? Working class? Much younger or much older? Take your pick or add another category."

"Okay, let's start with married. Any married men rumoured to be cheating at the moment?"

"Not really," Bessie said. "There are a few men that people have been speculating about, including the assistant manager at *La Terrazza*, where Anne works, but from what I've heard, he's cheating with one of the waitresses."

"No chance he dated Moirrey and then moved on to the waitress after her death?" Rockwell asked.

"Unlikely," Bessie replied. "Apparently they've been a not terribly secret couple for a few months now."

"What about Anne's husband, Jack?" Hugh asked. "I've had him in the back of my car more than once, getting him home after a long night in *The Cat and Longtail*. Usually, he'd been keeping company with a woman before he passed out. I reckon he'd have gone after anything female."

"You may be right, but it appears he was off island for the last few months. It's possible, but not confirmed, that he came back to the island in the last couple of days." Rockwell told him.

"So he could have cut his wife's brake lines," Hugh suggested.

"He could," Rockwell agreed. "And I guess he might have had a motive as well. It wasn't exactly a happy marriage."

"I can't see Moirrey getting involved with Jack Caine, anyway," Bessie interjected. "She knew exactly what sort of man he was and I can't see her being anything other than insulted if he ever tried to flirt with her."

"You said Moirrey would have hidden a relationship with anyone working class," Rockwell said. "Was she really that much of a snob?"

"Oh, absolutely," Bessie answered. "But before you ask, I don't have any suggestions for possible candidates in that category. Moirrey wasn't exactly hanging around at the pub or doing her own shopping. I'm not sure where she'd meet anyone of any class, really."

"Maybe she had some work done at the house?" Hugh suggested. "Or maybe she took up with the window cleaner or something."

"That's something else I'll ask Ms. Munroe about tomorrow," Bessie replied. "From what is heard, Moirrey wasn't having anything done anywhere. I think money was tight, although she'd never admit to it."

"What about Matthew Barnes?" Hugh asked.

"What about him?" Bessie replied. "You're not suggesting that he was the mystery boyfriend?"

"Why not?" Rockwell chimed in. "They certainly had an excuse to spend time together."

"He must be nearly twice her age," Bessie argued. "And she'd known him since she was a teenager. I can't imagine them starting a relationship now. Why would they?"

"What if Barnes has been stealing from her all these years? Maybe he figured if he could get her to fall in love with him she wouldn't sue him," Hugh suggested.

"As much as I'd like to believe every bad thing I can about the man, that seems too awful, even for him. Besides, I can imagine that Moirrey would be really excited about dating him. He was considered quite a catch when she was younger and I think she'd still see him that way. I can't believe she'd be able to resist bragging to someone if she were dating him."

"To whom would she have bragged?" Rockwell asked. "She must have had a friend and confidante that she would have shared all the details with."

Bessie shrugged. "I don't know that she did. As I said, the family was quite reserved and almost secretive. I never gave it much thought in the past, but now that I look back, they kept both children very close to home and kept their secrets to themselves. I don't know that Moirrey has ever had a close friend."

"So maybe she wasn't hiding the boyfriend, maybe she just didn't have anyone to tell," Rockwell speculated.

"No, Moirrey bragged to everyone she met when she had something exciting to tell people about," Bessie answered. "And finding a boyfriend after all these years would have been very exciting for her. She would have mentioned it in class if she wanted anyone to know."

"Well, I guess we'll just have to wait and see what you can find out from Ms. Munroe," Rockwell shrugged.

"This seems weird without Doona here," Bessie remarked as

she made a pot of tea for everyone.

"It does," Rockwell agreed. "But I doubt she'd have come, even if we could have invited her. She's far too busy with Andrew Teare to worry about anything else."

"I think she's very worried about the murder and about the attack on Anne Caine," Bessie disagreed. "But there isn't really anything she can do, is there?"

"I guess not," the inspector shrugged.

"What's going on with Mr. Teare?" Bessie asked. "Doona said Mr. Barnes was pushing for a DNA test, but he wasn't cooperating?"

"Actually, Mr. Barnes rang me this afternoon," Rockwell told her. "He's now acting for Andrew Teare and his client has supplied a hair sample for us to use for DNA testing."

"Doona didn't know that," Bessie remarked. "But I thought it was Mr. Barnes who was insisting on the DNA sample. Surely if Andrew Teare has proper identification, a DNA sample isn't needed?"

"When Mr. Teare first turned up, Matthew Barnes insisted that he was an imposter and demanded that we DNA test him before he would proceed with settling Moirrey's estate. Now that the two appear to have made up, Mr. Teare has apparently offered the sample so as to, as Mr. Barnes put it, 'remove any stain of doubt' from his claim."

"So how long will it take to get the results?" Bessie asked.

"At least a week," the inspector sighed. "I'm doing everything I can to encourage the lab to work faster, though."

"So where does all of this leave us?" Bessie asked. It was getting late and they seemed to have just been talking in circles all night.

"I don't know," Rockwell replied. "We have a handful of suspects for Moirrey's murder. I would put Anne and Janet Munroe at the top of that list. I'd love to add Jack Caine to it, but he wasn't on the island to do the swap. Matthew Barnes is on the list as well, but my favourite suspect, by far, is the mystery boyfriend."

"If only we knew his identity," Bessie said.

"And then we have a handful of suspects for slashing Anne's brakes. I can't imagine Ms. Munroe wanting to kill Anne for any reason. I guess Mr. Barnes is a possibility on that one, but then, so is Jack Caine, or even Andy. Realistically, just about anyone on the island had the means and the opportunity to do it, but the motive is a mystery."

"And the two things might not be connected," Hugh added.

"That's always possible," Rockwell conceded. "But it would be an awfully big coincidence if they aren't."

"I guess that's it for tonight then?" Bessie asked. "I'll talk to Ms. Munroe tomorrow and see what I can find out from her. Are we meeting again tomorrow night?"

"If you don't mind," the inspector replied. "I'll bring Chinese if you want."

"That sounds good to me," Hugh smiled. "But actually, I sort of have a date tomorrow night." Hugh blushed a deep red and looked down at the floor.

"Good for you," Bessie said. "You go and have fun. Inspector Rockwell and I can have our meeting without you."

"I thought I told you to call me John?" The inspector shook his head. "Anyway, as Bessie says, you go on your date. I'm sure there will be plenty of times in the future when you'll have to cancel because of work. My wife could tell you stories you wouldn't believe. If you can get away from work tomorrow on time, go have fun."

"Thanks," Hugh grinned.

"So just enough food for two normal people," Rockwell continued. "I won't have to get enough for a small army."

"I'll make a bread and butter pudding," Bessie told him. "I haven't had one in ages and it sounds good. I'll make homemade custard as well. It's ever so much better than the store-bought kind."

Hugh frowned. "Maybe I can reschedule my date," he said.

Bessie laughed. "Don't you dare. The poor girl won't know what to think. I'll make you a bread and butter pudding another time, I promise."

Hugh chuckled. "I suppose I'd rather spend time with Grace,

anyway. You just made it sound so good."

Once the pair left, Bessie finished tidying the kitchen and then settled into her favourite chair in the sitting room for a while. She read a few chapters in her latest book, but it wasn't grabbing her attention like it should have been. Irritated, she shut the book, not sure if the problem was with the book or with her.

She wasn't tired enough to go to bed yet, so she made herself a cup of hot chocolate and used it to wash down a few custard creams. She really didn't need the sugary treats after apple pie, but she was just grumpy enough to not care. The biscuits did nothing to improve her mood, however.

It was late now and quite dark outside. A few months earlier Bessie would have happily gone for a late-night stroll on the beach, but now she was more cautious. She looked out the window at the water. The beach looked deserted. With a sigh, she grabbed a light jacket and headed for her back door. Within minutes she was strolling down the beach that was illuminated by an almost full moon.

A large rock was situated not far from her cottage. At high tide several inches of water surrounded it, but now the tide was out and the rock was on dry land. Bessie seated herself on it with a sigh. It was a perfect night to sit outside and enjoy the sounds of the waves washing up on the shore. A light breeze meant she kept her jacket on, but it wasn't unpleasant.

Bessie sat and watched the waves for a while. The night became darker as clouds began to roll in and obscure the moon. She frowned at the black clouds that seemed to be gathering right over her head. As if in response, they sent a light shower of rain down over her.

A little rain doesn't bother me, Bessie thought to herself as she turned her attention back to the sea. Moments later the wind picked up and the light rain turned into a heavy shower. Bessie couldn't help but laugh as she made her way back to her cottage as quickly as she could.

She pulled off her sodden jacket and grabbed a towel from the downstairs loo. After drying herself as well as she could, she made her way upstairs and got ready for bed. In her office, she scanned her bookshelves, looking for something different to read. She finally settled on a book about the Tudor dynasty, a period in history that fascinated her.

She took the book into bed with her. She'd only read as far as Arthur's marriage to Catherine of Aragon when she realised how tired she suddenly felt. As usual, she slept soundly, any dreams forgotten when her internal alarm woke her around six the next morning.

CHAPTER ELEVEN

The rain seemed to have worn itself out overnight. Friday dawned overcast but dry. Bessie took a short stroll and then got ready for Dave to pick her up for her run to the grocery store. Again, he dropped her at the bookstore in Ramsey, one of her favourite places in the world.

"Hello, Claire," Bessie greeted one of the most helpful assistants in the store. "I need something new and maybe a little bit different, please. I'm halfway through one of the books I got here last week and for some reason my mind keeps wandering when I'm reading it."

"Have you ever read this one?" the girl asked, holding up a book with a brightly coloured cover. Bessie shook her head.

"The heroine is a lingerie buyer who becomes a bounty hunter. They're set in New Jersey in the States. They aren't your usual cozy mysteries, but I think they're fun."

Claire handed Bessie the first book in the series and Bessie read the blurb on the back. "It definitely isn't my usual thing," she told the girl. "But as it's available in paperback for a reasonable price, I'll try it."

She added another of Claire's recommendations to the pile, as well as a new cookbook full of American-style cake and pudding recipes, before moving on. The charity shops were disappointing, though. Bessie didn't find anything that tempted her in any of them. She was at the grocery store in good time, therefore, to shop in a leisurely fashion.

She was standing in front of the baking supplies, gathering everything she needed for both the bread and butter pudding for that evening and some American-style chocolate brownies for another day, from a recipe that caught her eye in her new book, when someone said hello.

"Bessie? How nice to see you," Andrew Teare's voice was full of enthusiasm. "And serendipitous as well. I promised Doona I would cook dinner for us tonight, and I haven't the first clue what to make."

"I'd suggest you make something that you've made many times before," Bessie told him. "Something easy and uncomplicated so you can socialise while you're preparing it. You don't want to be so worried about the food coming out right that you don't get to enjoy yourself."

Andrew laughed. "That's great advice," he told Bessie. "But not at all what I was expecting."

Bessie laughed as well. "Sorry, how about: Doona isn't a huge fan of seafood or beef, except in spaghetti bolognese. She'll eat chicken just about any way you can think to prepare it. She loves pasta dishes, as well. And make sure you have something nice for pudding. Something chocolate would probably be best."

Andrew laughed again. "Perfect, thank you so much. One of these nights we will have to have you join us for dinner," he told Bessie.

"I'd like that," Bessie replied.

She finished her shopping and made it out to the taxi rank with minutes to spare. Andrew was still wandering the aisles when she was at the checkout, and as Bessie climbed into her taxi she wondered what he'd decided to prepare. She'd have to ask Doona the next time she talked to her.

The journey home was a quick one. Putting the groceries away took only a few minutes and then Bessie fixed a light lunch and ate hurriedly. She'd asked Dave to pick her back up at one o'clock to give them plenty of time to get to Douglas.

As it happened, the journey into Douglas was uneventful and

took less time than she had allowed. Bessie found herself with over half an hour to while away before she was due to meet Moirrey's housekeeper. She wandered around a few shops and then, when it began to rain lightly, she walked up to the museum and spent a few happy minutes revisiting exhibits she'd seen dozens of times before.

At exactly two o'clock she walked through the doors to the small café. Janet Munroe was already seated at a small table by the window. Bessie quickly joined her, smiling and nodding at the waiter who knew her well enough to call "Pot of tea, Bessie?" as she walked in.

"I had to wait ages for service," Janet sniffed as Bessie said hello.

"I do a lot of research in the museum and, inevitably, drink a lot of tea here as well," Bessie told her.

The waiter hurried over with tea for both Bessie and Janet. "Did you want anything else?" he asked.

"Yes," Janet answered. "I'd like a cup of today's soup and a chicken sandwich. I'll have jam roly-poly for pudding."

And I'm going to get stuck with the bill, Bessie thought sourly. "I'll have a toasted teacake," she told the waiter.

Bessie watched silently as her companion poured tea into her cup and then added what seemed like exactly half of a packet of sugar to it. There was something about the way the woman poured the sugar, slowly and carefully, just a few grains at a time, that made Bessie wonder if the other woman was actually counting each grain as it tumbled gently into her cup. Janet added milk in exactly the same way, slowly and exactingly as if a single drop too much would spoil the drink.

Once Janet was satisfied with her beverage, Bessie casually added a healthy dollop of milk and a packet of sugar to her own cup. She took a sip and then smiled across the table. "I appreciate your taking time to meet with me," she told Janet.

"I haven't much else to do at the moment," the other woman responded. "Besides, I had a job interview in Douglas this morning and fancied lunch out. This way we both get something we want."

"So tell me about Moirrey's boyfriend," Bessie replied. If the woman was getting lunch out of this, Bessie wasn't going to waste time with social niceties.

"Hurump," Janet said with a frown. "A woman Moirrey's age ought to have known better than to get involved with a married man."

"What makes you think he was married?" Bessie asked.

"There had to be a reason why she was sneaking around," Janet said. "And believe me, she'd have been way too happy to have hooked a man to be sneaking around if she didn't have to be. There was something weird about the relationship, I guarantee it."

"And you think he was married?"

"Or too old or too young," Janet shrugged.

"Or not of her social class?" Bessie suggested.

"I can't see Moirrey dating anyone who didn't fit into her social class," Janet replied stiffly. "She was very old-fashioned in her ideas about class. I can't imagine her lowering her standards in that way."

"She was getting older," Bessie pointed out. "Maybe she was lonely and just happy to have someone."

"I suppose it's remotely possible," Janet conceded. "But I think it would be much more likely that the gentleman in question was married."

"What about too young or too old? You suggested those as possibilities. What ages would Moirrey have considered as falling into those categories?"

Janet frowned. "I would guess that Morriey would have considered anyone younger than herself as too young. As I said, she had some old-fashioned ideas. She felt that men should always be older than their partners. I'm not sure that she would consider anyone too old, really, perhaps a man in his seventies?"

"You think she would have dated a man in his sixties? More than twice her age?" Bessie asked.

"I think she would consider it, depending on who he was," Janet answered. "If he were someone important, she wouldn't have hesitated, and she would have bragged about it."

"What about Matthew Barnes?" Bessie suggested.

The arrival of Janet's lunch and Bessie's snack interrupted the reply. Bessie buttered her teacake and watched in silence as Janet rearranged the contents of her sandwich until it was layered exactly as she preferred. Using her soup spoon as a measuring device, Janet poured out small portions of salt and pepper, watching carefully until she had exactly the amount she wanted. She stirred the condiments into her soup and then tasted it gingerly. Bessie held her breath as Janet looked thoughtfully at the soup. After another small taste, Janet gravely shook out a tiny number of additional pepper flakes and added them to the bowl. She stirred it again and then took another bite. Bessie felt relieved when Janet nodded, apparently finally satisfied with the meal.

The pair ate silently for a few minutes. Bessie's teacake disappeared quickly, but Janet's soup and sandwich took a little bit longer. When the waiter cleared the dishes and promised to have Janet's pudding right out, Bessie added her own request for a slice of Victoria sponge. She felt like she needed something sweet to balance out her less than pleasant company.

"So, what about Matthew Barnes?" Bessie asked again while they waited for their puddings.

"I hadn't forgotten the question," Janet snapped. "I was just considering it while we ate. A few months ago I might have given it even more thought, but Moirrey and Mr. Barnes were not getting along well just before Moirrey died. She was pushing for a full accounting of her estate and Mr. Barnes was prevaricating. I think that Moirrey's boyfriend was behind the push and also behind Moirrey's attempts to have her brother declared dead."

"And the boyfriend's motive for those things?"

"Money," Janet laughed. "What else is there? I think he was after Moirrey's money and he wanted every penny he could get. If Andrew was declared dead, the estate would, presumably, all belong to Moirrey. That is if there is anything left with Matthew Barnes in charge of it."

"You think Mr. Barnes has been stealing from the Teare estate?"

"Oh, I'm sure everything he's done has been legal," Janet

waved a hand. "I'm sure he's allowed to charge fees for his services and the like. But I know money got tighter and tighter every single year that I was with Moirrey. Last year her new fancy car was leased rather than purchased outright and she was doing a lot more of her own driving. When she wanted to impress people, she hired a driver from an agency. The driver she used to keep on staff was let go about eighteen months ago. I'm pretty sure she only got rid of me because she couldn't afford to keep me on any longer."

The waiter returned with full plates. Bessie was relieved to see that apparently Janet's pudding had been delivered exactly the way she liked it. Janet dug in while Bessie considered what she had said about her former employer. Ewan Teare was supposed to have been a very wealthy man. Everyone had suspicions about Moirrey having money troubles when she moved into the small cottage several years ago, but Janet was suggesting that things were even worse than Bessie had thought.

"And yet she was buying new clothes and makeup and perfume?" Bessie questioned.

"The boyfriend probably told her that he'd help her get her money from Mr. Barnes," Janet sighed. "Look, Moirrey had a very sheltered upbringing. Her father did everything for her, and when he died Mr. Barnes took over the financial side of things. Moirrey never questioned anything that he told her do, from moving into the little cottage to selling off parcels of land. If Mr. Barnes thought it was a good idea, Moirrey went along. It never would have occurred to her, on her own, to start questioning Mr. Barnes. Someone put the idea in her head and I think that someone was her new boyfriend."

"But you don't have any idea who he was?"

Janet shrugged. "I can't imagine that it was anyone local," she said. "She knew everyone in Laxey far too well. I'm guessing it was someone she met in Douglas, maybe someone who has just moved here from across. I'm guessing he's married. That makes the most sense to me."

"Someone from Douglas?" Bessie echoed, her mind racing. "I can see that. There are so many bankers and the like coming over at the moment to work. I don't suppose the police can investigate them all."

"I can't see why they'd want to," Janet told her. "Surely, Moirrey's mysterious boyfriend would have been the last person to want her dead."

"So who do you think switched her tablets?" Bessie asked.

"Matthew Barnes has to be on the top of my list," Janet answered. "I've never liked the man."

Bessie bit her tongue. Many years ago, when Janet had first started working for Moirrey, there had been quite a lot of talk about Matthew Barnes and Janet Munroe. The general consensus among Laxey residents at the time had been that Janet had developed a crush on the advocate and that she had made quite a fool of herself in chasing after him. As far as Bessie knew, nothing had ever come of it, but now it made her question Janet's honesty.

"Do you have any ideas beyond Mr. Barnes?" Bessie asked.

"Not really," Janet shrugged. "No one liked Moirrey, but I can't see why anyone wanted her dead, either."

"What about possible suitors? I know you said he was probably from Douglas, and I'm inclined to agree, but if he was local, is there anyone you can think it might have been?"

"No one," Janet answered definitely. "There wasn't a man in Laxey that she'd have considered dating."

"What about Jack Caine?"

Janet laughed. "That old drunk? Even if Moirrey was starting to feel like an old maid, and I've no reason to believe that she was, she wouldn't have given that man the time of day. He's an old drunkard and she wouldn't have condescended to speak to him."

"What about Andy Caine?" Bessie hated herself for suggesting him, but she was curious what the other woman would say.

Janet gave her an odd look. "It's an interesting idea," she conceded. "Moirrey might have been flattered by his youth. But I don't think she would have been able to see past who his parents were. In fact, I'm sure she wouldn't have."

The waiter cleared away the last of the plates. Janet seemed to see that as her cue to leave. "Well, thank you for lunch," she told Bessie. "I suppose I must be off."

"You never saw the boyfriend?" Bessie asked, desperate for more information.

"Never," Janet shrugged. "I saw his car from time to time, going in and out of the lane, but I was never close enough to get a look at the driver."

"Did you notice what sort of car it was?"

"Pretty much different every time," Janet answered. "They all had hire car stickers on them; you can see them from miles away."

Bessie nodded. The island only had two hire car companies and one of them insisted on plastering bright yellow stickers on the back bumpers of every car in their fleet. "It would have been more discreet for him to use the other hire car company," Bessie remarked.

"What other hire car company?" Janet demanded. "MannCar has started using bright green stickers now. Haven't you seen them? They are just as ugly and unmistakable as the yellow ones that CarManx has had for years."

Bessie had to admit she hadn't spotted one yet. "Which car place did the mystery man use, then?" she asked.

"Both," Janet replied. "I saw cars with stickers from both companies at different times."

"How often did the man visit?"

"It all started about two months ago," Janet answered. "At first I saw a car maybe once a week, then it started to get more frequent. Two weeks before Moirrey died, I think I saw a car go past at least three times, maybe four. The last week before Moirrey's death, though, I didn't see him at all."

"Is it possible that more than one person was visiting Moirrey?"

"Of course it's possible," Janet snapped. "I told you I never saw the driver. I'd be surprised if it was more than one person, though. Moirrey never had visitors except for her advocate before this person started dropping by. I can't imagine where she'd suddenly find two new friends."

"And you only knew he was there because you saw the car?"

"Sometimes there were other clues," Janet told her. "A pair of wine glasses left on the deck or two dinner plates left in the sink, that sort of thing. I think Moirrey wanted me to find clues and ask her about him. I think she thought keeping him a secret was huge fun."

"Could her guest have been a woman?" Bessie asked.

"Ms. Teare didn't have those sorts of inclinations," Janet said primly.

"I didn't mean it in that way," Bessie replied. "I mean could it just have been a female friend coming to visit?"

"Why all the secrecy, then?" Janet demanded.

"I don't know," Bessie admitted.

"Anyway, I doubt it," Janet told her. "There was something about the way Moirrey refused to answer any questions. She was being coy and girly about it, like you would about a man. If she was just having a friend around, she would have told me."

"And you can't remember anything that she said while she was being coy that might be a clue?"

"No," Janet said and then sighed. "She said something when she was telling me to go that you might be interested in, though."

"What was that?"

"She said she was letting me go and that I needed to vacate the cottage where I was staying, and then she said something about needing to get everything sold and settled before she left."

"Left for where?" Bessie asked excitedly.

"I asked her where she was going and she went all coy on me. She said it wasn't any of my business, but that she was going to take her fortune and do some travelling. She said she'd decided that it was time for her start enjoying her life and living a little bit."

"When was this?"

"About two weeks before she died," Janet answered.

"And yet, when I saw her the night before she died, she didn't say anything about leaving. She'd just signed up for a six-week class in Manx as well. That isn't the sort of thing she would do if she were leaving, is it?"

"No," Janet shrugged. "She was too cheap to sign up for something if she didn't expect to finish it. Maybe her plans changed or maybe she was just telling me that as an excuse to get rid of me. As I said, no one had been visiting her lately, so maybe the boyfriend dumped her and she decided that she wasn't going anywhere."

"But she was still pushing Anne Caine about her cottage," Bessie mused.

"That was about money. She could be quite obsessive about money."

"I thought you said Matthew Barnes handled everything for her on that front."

"That didn't stop her from getting involved sometimes," Janet replied. "Especially where Anne Caine was concerned. Moirrey had a definite dislike for her and I never really understood why."

"I always thought that Ewan Teare had quite a soft spot for Anne," Bessie answered. "Maybe Moirrey resented that."

"That all happened before my time," Janet shrugged. "Whatever, I really do have to go."

This time Bessie let her go without any further questions. She looked at her watch. It felt like it had been hours since she walked into the café, and she was surprised to find that it was only just three o'clock. After she settled the bill she made her way out of the museum, walking past Marjorie's office along the way. Marjorie's door was shut and the lights were off. Never mind, she'd see Marjorie on Monday.

Bessie hadn't arranged for a ride home, not knowing how long the chat with Janet would take, so now she found herself wondering what to do with herself. A quick stop at Noble's Hospital to see Anne seemed tempting. The taxi rank in front of the museum was full of available cars, so Bessie climbed into a cab and was on her way.

In the hospital lobby Bessie paused and bought a small bouquet of flowers and a couple of paperback books for Anne. Then she made her way to the lift and then down the corridor to ward eleven. The young uniformed constable sitting in front of the door to Anne's room jumped to his feet as Bessie approached.

"Good afternoon, ma'am," he said politely. "Who are you here to see?"

"I was hoping to visit Anne Caine," Bessie replied. "But if I can't see her, maybe you could take the flowers and books in to her and tell her that Bessie Cubbon was here?"

The man smiled. "I am sorry," he said. "But I can't let you in. It's, er, doctor's orders, you see. No one is allowed in to visit Ms. Caine except her son."

"That's fine," Bessie assured him. "Just give her these and tell her I'm thinking of her, please."

"Yes, ma'am," the man smiled. "And thank you for not arguing with me."

Bessie grinned. "It's a tough job, is it?"

The young man shrugged. "It sounded like a terrific and easy assignment when the boss told me about it, but it's dead dull and when it isn't dull that's because someone is arguing with me that I need to make an exception for them. I'll be happy to get back out on the street."

Bessie thanked him for his willingness to take on such a thankless job and turned to go. She could feel the constable's eyes on her as she turned down the corridor towards the lift.

Was there anything more boring than waiting for a lift, she wondered idly after pressing the call button. It was that feeling that she could be going somewhere, if only the lift would hurry up and arrive. She pushed the button again, knowing it was pointless, but unable to resist. There had to be stairs somewhere, but the hospital apparently didn't want anyone to find them. She tapped the illuminated disc another time, telling herself to be patient.

"Aunt Bessie?" The voice from behind her startled her. She pulled her hand back from the button guiltily and spun around.

"Oh, I'm so glad I caught up with you," Andy Caine beamed at her. "Let me walk out with you."

Behind her, the lift doors opened slowly. Bessie and Andy walked inside and Bessie selected the ground level. Bessie was surprised to find that they had the lift to themselves.

"I just wanted to thank you, on mum's behalf, for the flowers and the books," Andy said. "She's hugely grateful."

"I'm glad," Bessie replied. "I was hoping to see her, but I wasn't surprised to see the guard still in place."

Andy frowned. "I don't understand it," he told Bessie as they exited the lift and began to make their way towards the lobby. "The doctor offered to let mum go home today and she said no. The police said no as well. What's going on?"

Bessie patted Andy's arm. "I think everyone just wants to do whatever they can to keep your mum safe," she told the man.

"Safe from what?" Andy demanded.

"Safe from whoever cut her brake lines," Bessie suggested.

"Inspector Rockwell has been to see her a bunch of times. He thinks she knows who did it."

Bessie shrugged. "It's his job to question people," she told him.

"I think she knows, too," Andy admitted quietly. "That's why she won't go home and that's why I'm so worried about her."

"She's safe here," Bessie said consolingly. "Give the police some time. I'm sure they'll figure it out."

At the hospital's front door, Andy looked deeply into Bessie's eyes. "I'm scared," he told her, looking exactly like the six-year-old boy she'd first met so many years earlier.

"Come and stay with me tonight," she suggested. "You can sleep in the spare room. It's always ready for guests."

Andy smiled. "I love your spare room," he told Bessie. "It feels like the safest place in the world. But I can't come tonight. I'm staying here, in an unoccupied room, to be close to mum. She's insisting on it."

Bessie nodded. "I'm sure she feels better knowing you're close by."

"I guess," Andy shrugged. "Anyway, when this is all over I'm going to take you up on that offer," he told Bessie. "I'm going to have my night in your spare room and I'm going to bake shortbread with you before bedtime."

"That sounds wonderful," Bessie told him. She gave him a big hug and then looked into his eyes. "It's going to be okay," she assured him.

"I hope so," Andy replied. He helped Bessie into a taxi. "Oh, and mum says to tell you that she will pay you back, with interest, next week, assuming she can get out of here."

Bessie shook her head. "Tell your mother that there is no rush. She needs to look after herself for now. That's all that matters."

"I will," Andy smiled. "Thank you, for everything."

Andy shut the taxi door and Bessie watched him as he stared after her taxi as it pulled away. A short while later she arrived back home with a couple of hours still to fill before Inspector Rockwell was due.

She mixed up the custard for the bread and butter pudding and then assembled everything. She put the dish in the refrigerator when she'd finished. She'd pop it in the oven when the inspector arrived and it would be lovely and hot once they'd finished eating.

Her new cookbook was calling to her, so Bessie grabbed it and settled at the kitchen table with a pad of paper and a pencil. She usually bought cookbooks for the joy of looking at the pictures more than for trying the recipes, but this one was an exception. Page after page of glorious sweet recipes were too tempting to resist. She'd already bought what she needed for the brownies. Now she made note of what to buy in order to create American-style chocolate chip cookies. They would be a perfect treat for her unexpected visitors next week.

A knock on the door startled her. The inspector wasn't due for another hour. She got to her feet and headed for the door, ignoring the little voice that wanted to remind her that there was a murderer loose on the island.

CHAPTER TWELVE

There weren't any windows near the door that would allow Bessie to see her visitors before opening the door to them. And the old wooden door and sturdily built walls were too thick for anyone to hear a shouted "Who is it?" through. This had never bothered Bessie in the past, but tonight she had a moment's pause before she pulled open the door.

"Jason? What are you doing here?"

The teenager burst into Bessie's kitchen full of barely repressed energy. "I just can't take it anymore," he told Bessie. "I'm nearly seventeen. I shouldn't have to account for every second of every day. It isn't even like I'm out causing trouble or the like. I just want to spend some time with my friends without having to give every detail to mum and dad. Is that too much to ask?"

Bessie laughed. "Your parents are giving you a hard time again, I gather?"

Jason shook his head, his long light-brown hair bouncing around and his blue eyes blazing. "I was late one night, just the once, and now they've grounded me for the rest of the month."

"If you're grounded, maybe you shouldn't be here?" Bessie suggested.

"Oh, coming to see you doesn't count," Jason told her. "They'll be happy I'm here and not with my friends."

Bessie chuckled. "I suppose I should be glad that I'm more acceptable company than your friends."

Jason smiled back at her. "Sorry for all the shouting as I came in," he said apologetically. "I just feel so frustrated, you know? All my friends are allowed to come and go as they please, and my parents just keep making up new rules all the time. It's like they don't want me to have a life of my own or they want to keep me as a baby or something."

Bessie nodded. "Parents always seem to struggle with their children getting older," she told the boy. "I think it's hard for them to think of someone who was once totally reliant on them for everything as a responsible adult. It will probably take you years to prove to them that you are all grown up now."

Jason frowned. "I haven't got years," he complained. "The concert I want to go to is tomorrow night and they've said I can't go, even though all my friends get to go and I sorted out a ride and everything all by myself."

"What concert is that?" Bessie asked.

"The Screamin' Manxmen," Jason replied. "They are really good. They're like a covers band mostly, but they do a few originals as well. Everyone on the whole island will be there, well, everyone my age."

Bessie nodded. "And your parents said you can't go? That is a shame."

"I was late just once, well, maybe twice," Jason told her. "I'm thinking about getting my own place, then I won't have to answer to them anymore."

"How about some tea and a few biscuits?" she asked the teen.

"That would be great," Jason answered.

Bessie took her time making tea and pulling out biscuits. She wanted to give the youngster time to calm down before continuing the conversation. She smiled to herself as he poured nearly half a cup of milk into his mug before adding the tea to it; four heaping scoops of sugar went in as well. Hopefully, the sweet milky drink would improve his mood.

"So, if you get your own place, will you stay here in Laxey or are you thinking about moving into Douglas or elsewhere?"

Jason gave her a surprised look. "Well, um, I guess, that is, I hadn't really thought about it," he told her. "I guess I'd want to stay in Laxey. I've got school to finish and all my friends are here."

"I'm only asking because I have a friend who is looking for a flat right now and he's having a hard time finding one. I didn't know if you knew of any that you could suggest to him?"

"Sorry, I don't know anything about flats," Jason shrugged. "I was thinking I'd just stay with some friends or something, I guess."

Bessie nodded. "It's great that you have friends that you can stay with," she told him. "That way you can share all the expenses and all the housekeeping."

"Yeah," Jason muttered. "Anyway, I was just saying I might move out. I'd rather not, at least not yet. I've got school and whatever. I just really want to go to the concert tomorrow night, that's all."

"I can't imagine how disappointed you must be," Bessie told him soothingly. "I mean, these sorts of concerts probably don't happen very often, do they?"

"Well, they're supposed to be playing every other Saturday all through spring and summer, but you never know, the club might decide to cancel or something."

"Still, if all your friends are going this time, it does seem a harsh punishment," Bessie told him. "Of course, I don't know all of the particulars."

"Like I said, I was just late a few times, nothing major or anything. Mum and dad act like they were never kids."

Bessie laughed. "I remember both of your parents as children," she told Jason. "And they both got up to their fair share of things they shouldn't have. And I remember them both being grounded on more than one occasion as well."

Jason shrugged. "You'd think they'd be more understanding then," he complained.

"Or maybe they understand too well," Bessie commented. "Who did you say was going tomorrow night?"

"Robbie and Beth and Suzy," he answered. "I know it sounds

like a date thing, but really it isn't. I've sort of got a girlfriend already."

"And she doesn't mind your going without her?"

"She isn't real happy about it, but her parents are even worse than mine. When they heard that Robbie was driving, they said she couldn't go."

Bessie pressed her lips together for a moment. "Is that Robert Kneale?" she asked eventually. "I thought his license was suspended at the moment."

"He just got it back," Jason told her. "No one got hurt anyway, he just hit a stone wall."

"He'd been drinking, and it wasn't the first time," Bessie reminded him.

"Yeah, but...."

Bessie held up a hand. "There is nothing you can say to defend him," she told Jason. "Driving while drunk is incredibly stupid and unbelievably dangerous. You know I never take sides when children come here after fights with their parents, but this time I'm going to make an exception. If you were my child, there is no way you would be going anywhere with Robert Kneale driving, especially not all the way to Douglas and back."

Jason jumped to his feet, eyes blazing again. "You can't talk about my friend like that," he told Bessie. "I'm leaving."

"Off you go then," Bessie replied. "You'll not be welcome again if you take that attitude."

Jason stared at her. He had to know that Bessie's threat was genuine. And being banned from Aunt Bessie's was a serious punishment. His mouth opened and closed repeatedly several times before words managed to come out.

"I'm sorry," he muttered. He sank back down in his chair and snapped a digestive biscuit into pieces, shoving a large portion into his mouth in one bite.

Bessie reached out and patted his arm. "Jason, I don't want to argue with you," she told him. "You know you've always been one of my favourites."

"I have?" The boy's eyes lit up.

"Of course," Bessie assured him with the same words she

used for nearly every guest. "You're smart and funny and kind and caring and I have high hopes for you. I always thought you'd finish school and go off and make your family, and me, very proud. Your parents are just trying to keep you safe, and I'm on their side. I would be devastated if anything happened to you."

The boy blushed under Bessie's gaze. "Ah, thanks, I mean, well, ah," he cleared his throat. "Maybe missing the concert isn't the worst thing ever," he said. "Can I stay here tonight anyway? I could use a break from my folks."

"Of course you can," Bessie told him. "I'll just ring your mum and let her know."

Bessie had a hard and fast rule about overnight guests. She always rang the relevant parents to let them know where their offspring were staying. And all the parents in Laxey were well aware of the rule. No child ever got away with telling their folks that they had stayed at Aunt Bessie's when they were actually somewhere else.

Jason's mum was pleased to hear that her son was going to be staying in Bessie's spare room. "See if you can talk some sense into him, will you?" she asked. "I don't like him hanging around with that Robert Kneale and the kind of girls he attracts. My Jason has a nice girlfriend in that Jennifer he's seeing, but his head might be turned by a really short skirt and you can bet that's what they'll be wearing at that concert tomorrow."

After the phone call she filled Jason in on her plans for the evening. "Inspector Rockwell from the Isle of Man Constabulary is coming over for dinner," she told him. "You are welcome to join us for dinner, but then I expect you to head upstairs and entertain yourself for a short while so that the inspector and I can talk."

"You're going to talk about Moirrey Teare's death, aren't you?" Jason asked.

"Among other things," Bessie told him.

"It was really neat how you helped solve that murder last month," he replied. "Are you going to help solve this one as well?"

"All I'm trying to do is provide background information for the police," Bessie told him. "I'm trying to find out all I can about Moirrey and her friends and things like that."

Jason opened his mouth and then snapped it shut. "Okay," he said, without meeting Bessie's eyes.

She filed the reaction away to think about later and rang Inspector Rockwell to ask him to add a few extra dishes to the dinner order. "We need to talk privately," Rockwell argued.

"That won't be a problem," Bessie assured him. "After dinner he can go upstairs and sit in the office. He won't be able to hear us from up there."

She knew that the inspector wasn't happy with the arrangements, but she wasn't about to tell Jason that he had to go home, especially now that she'd talked to his mother. Bessie was responsible for him for the evening and Inspector Rockwell was just going to have to live with that.

She and Jason spent a quiet half hour reading. Bessie lent him a classic Agatha Christie novel. He'd started it reluctantly, but by the time the inspector knocked on the cottage door he appeared to be engrossed.

"Should I get that?" he asked Bessie as he lifted his eyes from the page.

"I've got it, thanks," Bessie answered. "I need to pop the pudding in the oven anyway."

"I'll just finish this chapter, if that's okay?"

"Of course it is," Bessie agreed.

"It looks like you brought enough to feed an army again," Bessie remarked as she helped Inspector Rockwell carry the bags full of food into the kitchen.

"You said you had a teenaged boy as a guest," the inspector said. "We'll be lucky if he leaves anything for us."

"Maybe we should grab our share now, before he gets in here," Bessie laughed.

Jason was wary of the inspector for a few minutes, but Rockwell had a son of his own and he soon put the boy at ease. The pair talked about football while they ate, leaving Bessie with nothing to do but listen. She didn't mind; she quite enjoyed seeing a different side of the inspector who was usually all business with her. And she was happy watching Jason argue about which teams had the best chance of getting into some competition or other. Both men seemed to take it all very seriously.

After an astonishing amount of food had been eaten, Bessie pulled the bread and butter pudding out of the oven. The top was golden brown and crunchy-looking under its generous sprinkling of sugar. Bessie received an enthusiastically affirmative answer from both of her guests when she offered the pudding, so she piled steaming hot squares onto plates and carried them to the table.

The men waited with ill-concealed impatience as Bessie cut her own smaller piece and joined them. No one argued about sports while they were enjoying their treat.

The inspector insisted that Bessie relax while he and Jason washed the dishes, and Bessie wasn't about to complain. Once the kitchen was restored to order, the inspector smiled at Jason.

"It's been a pleasure meeting you," he told the young man. "I hope you'll excuse us now. I really need to talk to Bessie."

"Sure," Jason grinned. "I'll take my book upstairs and read in the office."

"Before you go, I just have one quick question," Bessie smiled at him. "Do you know anything about Moirrey that might help us figure out who killed her?"

Jason blushed and shook his head. "What could I know?" he muttered. "I didn't even know the woman."

"And yet," Bessie said, staring into his eyes, "there is something you're not telling me."

Jason shook his head again and looked down at the ground. "It's nothing," he muttered.

Inspector Rockwell cleared his throat. "Jason, if you have any information, even if it doesn't seem all that important, I'd appreciate it if you'd share it. I'm not interested in how you got the information. If you were doing something you shouldn't have been doing that doesn't concern me. I'm CID, we deal with murder, and it's important we find out who killed Moirrey."

"I really don't know anything," Jason insisted. "It was just something kind of strange, that's all."

"What was?" Rockwell asked.

"Some of us like to hang out on the beach near the Teare

mansion. I guess it's sort of trespassing, but since no one lives there, no one ever complains," he flushed and looked down at his feet.

"I'm not interested in busting up your beach parties," Rockwell told the teen. "I'm sure you always leave the beach clean and tidy."

"Oh, yes, sir," Jason nodded. "We just go and sit and talk, maybe take a few beers, nothing stronger, and we all walk from home so no one is driving or anything."

"Fair enough," the inspector told him. "But what did you see that was strange?"

"Well, I guess it wasn't that strange. I mean, it's her property, right? There wasn't any reason why Ms. Teare shouldn't have been walking on the beach there. It was just that I'd never seen her with a guy before, and she was acting all kind of weird with him as well."

"Weird how?" The inspector's tone stayed even, while Bessie pressed her lips tightly together. She didn't want Jason to know how important the information he had might be.

"She was acting sort of giddy and silly, laughing and, well, flirting I guess," Jason shrugged. "I know she was kind of old, but she was acting like a teenaged girl with a crush or something."

"When was this?" the inspector asked.

"About a month ago, maybe?" Jason sounded uncertain. "It was still quite cold once the sun went down and sunset was still really early. I didn't break my curfew that night for sure."

"But you don't remember the exact date?"

"Sorry, we hang out there a lot. The nights kind of all run together."

"Can you describe the man?" Rockwell asked.

Jason looked at him blankly. "He was just some guy. I mean, I think he had brown hair, but I wasn't really paying attention. We were like, um, hiding, sort of, because we really weren't supposed to be there, you know? I was more worried about them seeing us than anything else."

"You're sure it was Moirrey Teare?"

"Well yeah, I mean, everyone knew her. We all tried to avoid her whenever we saw her anywhere. She didn't like children or teenagers. Maybe she didn't like anyone, but she certainly seemed to like this guy."

"But you can't tell me anything more about the man?" Rockwell asked.

"I didn't really notice," Jason said apologetically. "But I can ring Jennifer. I bet she noticed more than I did. Girls always pay more attention to that stuff than guys do."

Bessie considered arguing with him, but didn't. While the sweeping generalisation annoyed her, she hoped he was right in this instance.

"As you're meant to be grounded, I assume you aren't supposed to be ringing your girlfriend," Bessie suggested.

"Well, no, I guess not, but if it's police business, that's different, right?" Jason asked.

"How about if you ring her and explain what we're interested in and then I'll talk to her?" the inspector suggested.

"Um, no offense, sir, but I think she'd be happier talking to Aunt Bessie. You might make her nervous."

The inspector nodded. "I often have that effect on people," he admitted. "I'm happy for Bessie to talk to her."

Jason went to Bessie's phone and dialled a number he clearly knew by heart. Bessie and the inspector smiled at each other as Jason nervously asked for Jennifer when the phone was answered. A moment later, after Jason had explained the reason for the call, Bessie was talking to Jennifer.

"Hello, dear," she said. "How's your mother recovering from her surgery last week?"

"Oh, she's doing great, Aunt Bessie. I'll tell her you asked. She'll be pleased that you remembered."

"I've been thinking of stopping in to visit," Bessie told her. "But I don't want to be in the way."

"Oh, she's well ready for visitors," Jennifer told her. "She's about climbing the walls from boredom. She's used to working every day. Sitting at home is making her nuts."

Bessie laughed. "Tell her I'll be around tomorrow afternoon around two o'clock with some American-style brownies for her to try."

"Ooooo, I'll have to make sure I'm home as well," Jennifer said excitedly.

Bessie laughed. "In the meantime, what can you tell me about Moirrey Teare?"

"Well, it was sort of weird, seeing Ms. Teare with a guy, you know? Like, I didn't know she'd found a boyfriend and then there they were, walking on the beach hand in hand."

"They were holding hands?" Bessie checked.

"Yep, and, um, she kissed him, like."

"She kissed him, not the other way around?"

"No, that was kind of strange, too. They were walking along the water's edge and then she stopped and reached up and kissed him. I mean, he didn't push her away or anything, but he didn't look all that into it, either."

"Was he someone you knew?"

"No, in fact, I'd never seen him before anywhere," Jennifer told her.

"Can you describe him?" Bessie asked.

Inspector Rockwell passed Bessie a sheet of paper with a few questions scribbled on it. Bessie smiled when she saw that the first question on his list was the one she'd just asked.

"He was a few inches taller than Ms. Teare. He had light brown hair and I think his eyes were brown as well. He was wearing a business suit, or rather he was wearing a shirt and tie with the tie loosened and the top button undone and dark grey trousers. Ms. Teare had the matching jacket on."

"She did? Okay, maybe you'd better describe her as well."

Jennifer laughed. "She didn't look like herself," the girl told Bessie. "She had her hair pulled back and curled somehow and she was wearing a bunch of makeup, although it hadn't been put on very well. She was wearing a long skirt, or maybe a dress. I couldn't see the top because she had the man's suit jacket on, like I said."

"That's a lot of detail you picked up on a dark beach," Bessie commented.

"Oh, I couldn't see much on the beach," Jennifer answered. "I saw them earlier in the evening, when I was first walking towards the beach. I was coming from home and had to cross behind Ms. Teare's cottage. As I walked behind it, I heard voices on her patio and stopped to see what was going on. I've gone past her place dozens of times and there's never been anyone on the patio before."

"But this night Moirrey and her date were on the patio?"

"Yeah, they were sitting and talking and drinking wine. Ms. Teare was wearing the man's jacket, which made sense because it was pretty chilly. The sun was just going down and it was starting to get dark."

"I'm surprised you could see Moirrey's makeup if it was getting dark," Bessie remarked.

"I only spotted it when the lights suddenly came on," Jennifer told her. "Ms. Teare had these high-powered security lights at the back of her cottage. Jason and I know exactly where to walk to avoid setting them off; they have motion sensors on them, you know? Anyway, Ms. Teare and the guy were sitting and talking and then, when Ms. Teare got up for some reason, she set off her own security lights."

"And you were able to get a good look at both her and her companion?"

"Exactly. He didn't look best pleased, either," Jennifer told Bessie. "The lights were really bright and the whole back of the house was lit up. He looked around, as if he was worried someone might see him, and he said something nasty to Ms. Teare."

"How do you know it was something nasty?"

"I guess I don't, really, but he looked angry and then she looked really apologetic and sad and seemed to be talking a lot. After a minute she went in and switched off the lights. While she was doing that, I slipped past and headed for the beach."

"Did you notice any cars parked at the cottage?"

"Ms. Teare's car was there, it always was, and so was another car. It had a sticker from one of the hire car companies, but I can't remember which one."

"Did you notice what sort of car it was?"

"Sorry, cars aren't really my thing. I think it was blue?"

Bessie laughed. "I never notice cars, either. Anyway, you headed to the beach and then you saw Ms. Teare and her date there a little while later?"

"Yeah, we were really careful to stay away from the open area that night, just in case, but I was still really surprised when they came walking down to the beach. They came down from the mansion, as well. I'm not sure if they went inside or just walked past it, but that seemed like a long walk for Ms. Teare."

"Indeed," Bessie mused. "Moirrey never walked any further than she absolutely had to, because of her ill health."

"Well, she seemed to be feeling pretty good that night," Jennifer told her. "She was giggling and flirting and splashing in the water. It was like watching my thirteen-year-old sister with a boy she thinks is cute."

Bessie couldn't help but laugh, even as she felt sorry for Moirrey. "I don't suppose you remember exactly when this was?" she asked.

"Sometime in the middle of March," Jennifer said slowly. "I can look in my journal and get you the exact date if you want."

"That would be great," Bessie told her, wincing as Jennifer set the phone down on a hard surface with a bang.

"It was Friday, March 13th," she told Bessie when she returned.

"How unlucky," Bessie remarked. "Anyway, that's great information, thank you." Bessie wound up the conversation, reminding the girl that she would be visiting the next day. When she hung up, she grinned at the inspector. "Well, how very interesting."

The inspector shook his head at Bessie. "Jason, thanks for all of your help," he told the teen. "I think now would be a good time for you to head upstairs."

"Hang on one second," Bessie forestalled him. "I just have one quick question. The night you saw Moirrey and her friend, did you notice the cars in Moirrey's driveway?"

Jason shook his head. "I was coming from home," he explained. "I didn't go past Ms. Teare's cottage on my way to the beach."

"Never mind." Bessie said. Then she threw her own generalisation at him. "I just figured boys are more likely to notice cars than girls."

Jason nodded, missing the stereotyping in the remark as he agreed. "I love cars," he told Bessie. "But I can't remember what I didn't see."

"True," Bessie shrugged. "You get on upstairs and finish your book. I'll want to know if you guessed the murderer or not when you've finished."

"Oh, I know who did it," Jason said confidently. He named a character, and Bessie just barely held back a laugh.

"Wait and see," Bessie replied, almost wishing she could sit and watch his face as he finished the book and discovered the real culprit. He was in for a shock.

Inspector Rockwell was grinning as well. After Jason left Rockwell asked Bessie which book the young man was reading. "I actually guessed the murderer in that one in chapter three," he told Bessie. "I was convinced that I was wrong, though, until the very end. I couldn't have been much older than young Jason when I read it and I was unbelievably excited when I found out I was correct."

"And that's what set you on your way to becoming a police inspector," Bessie suggested.

Rockwell flushed. "Actually, I joined the police because there was this girl...." he trailed off and looked embarrassed. "Maybe that's a story for another day," he suggested.

"I'm going to hold you to that," Bessie threatened. The inspector just laughed.

Bessie quickly filled him in on everything that Jennifer had said. "I guess that means we have confirmation of what Janet Munroe told us," she concluded. "Moirrey had a boyfriend, even if I still can't quite believe it."

"They do say there's someone out there for everyone," Rockwell shrugged. "And Moirrey was quite wealthy. I'm surprised she didn't attract a man sooner, really."

"Moirrey wasn't stupid," Bessie said. "I think she would have been suspicious if anyone she knew started flirting. I think the mystery man almost had to be from across."

"You're ruling out Matthew Barnes now, then?"

"The kids would have recognised him," Bessie pointed out. "I'm not ruling him out for murder, but apparently he wasn't the boyfriend."

"It all helps build up the picture," Rockwell sighed. "But I'm not sure the new information brings us any closer to the murderer."

"From everything I've heard, I suspect the pair broke up some time before Moirrey died anyway," Bessie suggested.

"Based on what?"

"Well, Janet Munroe said that he had been coming around a couple of times a week, but that he didn't visit once in the last week before she died."

"Maybe his wife found out," Rockwell suggested.

"Whatever, I can't believe that I spent an evening with Moirrey and she never gave one hint that she was dating. I think if they were still dating she would have said something at class."

"You certainly knew her better than I did," Rockwell answered. "But broken up or not, I still want to find him."

"So how do you go about doing that?" Bessie asked.

"We'll have to request passenger lists from the airlines and the ferries," the inspector sighed. "And copies of rental contacts from the hire car firms. That's probably a better place to start. There should be fewer of them and we can narrow the list by age and gender as well."

Bessie nodded. "What happens once you find him?"

"Assuming he is across, we get one of our colleagues in his area to ask him a few questions and then go from there. It will all take time, but we should be able to locate him eventually."

"I can't imagine him having a motive for killing Moirrey, though," Bessie sighed. "And even if he did, where does Anne Caine fit into all of this?"

"Great questions," Rockwell told her. "I wish I had answers, but to be honest, something else is bothering me."

"Really? What?" Bessie asked.

"Andrew Teare," he replied. "I know he didn't kill Moirrey; he wasn't even on the island when she died. But there's something about him I don't like."

"Have the DNA test results come back yet?" Bessie asked.

"No, we won't have those for several more days."

"But you don't think he's who he claims to be?"

"I don't know," Rockwell said in a frustrated voice.

"If he isn't Andrew Teare, who could he be?" Bessie asked.

"I've absolutely no idea," Rockwell admitted. "He's has all the right identification and he talks quite easily about his childhood on the island. I can't imagine who else he could possibly be."

"But you don't trust him?"

"I don't like him and I don't like the way he's playing up to Doona," the inspector said. "I just think he's up to something."

"There's something I don't like about him either, but that might just be because he's suddenly Matthew Barnes' best friend and I don't trust Mr. Barnes."

Inspector Rockwell grinned. "Want to help me do some checking up on the man?" he asked Bessie.

"What did you have in mind?" Bessie replied.

"I want to get his fingerprints. I want to run them through the system and see if I get any hits. If they come back unknown, then I'll worry a bit less about Doona."

"Do you think he's a criminal?"

"I think he makes me uncomfortable," Rockwell shrugged. "Maybe it's just me, but I'd like to find out for sure whether he has a criminal record or not."

"So what's your plan?"

The inspector outlined his idea, which was fairly simple. Bessie would invite Andrew Teare over for tea and a chat. After the man left, the inspector would pick up his teacup and have the fingerprints checked.

"Is that strictly legal?" Bessie asked.

"Probably not," Rockwell admitted. "Anything I learn would be inadmissible in court. But I'm not worried about that for now. Let's find out who he is and then, if there's a problem, I'll figure out a way to get his fingerprints legally."

They spent a few minutes fine-tuning the plan before the inspector headed for home. "I don't suppose you've had any luck finding me a flat?" he asked at the door.

"Sorry, no," Bessie replied. "There are lots of holiday rentals, but I haven't been able to find anything long-term."

Rockwell nodded. "I may just have to buy myself a little flat," he told Bessie. "That might be the easiest option."

"They'll be plenty to rent in October," she told him. "Once all the holiday makers head home all the holiday rentals will be going cheap."

"October seems a long way off," the inspector sighed. "For tonight I guess I'd better get back to Ramsey."

It was too late to ring Andrew Teare, so Bessie headed up to bed after turning off the phone's ringer. Anyone who rang overnight could leave a message. Bessie had decided some time ago that she was too old to be running up and down stairs in the middle of the night. It was just about the only concession she was prepared to make to her age.

Upstairs, she checked in with Jason who was shaking his head over the book.

"I totally did not see that coming," he told Bessie. "It was very cleverly done. Are all of her books like that?"

Bessie laughed. "Pretty much," she told the boy. "Remind me in the morning and I'll dig out a few that I can lend you."

"Really? That would be awesome," Jason replied happily.

Bessie always kept a handful of extra copies of some of her favourite books that she bought up at charity shops. In that way she could lend them to friends and not worry if they never came back. In all of her years of lending, she'd only ever had two books not returned to her, which she didn't think was too bad considering she must have lent hundreds.

Bessie got ready for bed and then lay in her room listening to Jason as he washed his face and climbed into the bed in spare room. She loved having occasional visitors; they made her cottage feel cosier, somehow. And as long as young Jason only stayed the one night, she'd feel that way about him. It was visitors who stayed longer who often started getting on Bessie's nerves.

CHAPTER THIRTEEN

Jason left right after breakfast, eager to get home with the stack of novels that Bessie lent him. Bessie spent her morning walk mentally rehearsing what she was going to say to Andrew Teare when she rang him.

He was staying in Ramsey at the newly refurbished Seaview Hotel. Built in the 1930s, it had once been Ramsey's premier hotel, although Bessie had always lamented the lack of originality in the name. It had been sold in the 1970s to a consortium of investors from across and had been allowed to fall into disrepair. A year or so ago, a local developer had bought the property and he'd wasted no time before remodeling, repairing and updating the place.

It had hosted a grand reopening the week before Easter, and Bessie had already been hearing good things about the place. Certainly the reception desk seemed efficient, quickly patching Bessie through to Andrew Teare's room.

"Ah, Mr. Teare? It's Bessie Cubbon. How are you?"

"I'm fine." The voice on the phone seemed unnecessarily loud to Bessie, as if the man was shouting. "What can I do for you?" he asked.

"I was hoping I could do something for you," Bessie chuckled. "I'm making American-style brownies this afternoon and I thought you might like some."

"Now that sounds wonderful," the man replied. "What time should I be there, and shall I bring Doona, or are we not sharing?"

Bessie laughed. "Why don't you come around four o'clock?" she suggested. "And, actually, I'd rather you didn't bring Doona. I'd like a chance to have a chat with you on your own."

There was a long silence on the other end of the phone, and Bessie started to worry that the plan had failed before it had even started, when Andrew finally spoke.

"I should warn you," Andrew said after the awkward pause. "You aren't really my type. I prefer to date women with tattoos."

Bessie laughed uneasily, trying to react naturally. "What makes you think I don't have a tattoo?" she teased.

Andrew laughed. "I guess I'll see you at four," he told her.

Bessie hung up the phone and blew out a long breath. The silence had been weird, but hopefully, the rest of the plan would go smoothly. She rang Inspector Rockwell and filled him in.

"I'll see you at half three," he told Bessie. "We'll go back over everything then."

Bessie got busy then, making up several pans of brownies for all of the people to whom she had promised them. Jennifer's family only lived a short walk away, and Bessie made her visit there a short one. She delivered the brownies and thanked Jennifer for the information she had been able to provide and then had a short chat with Sandy, Jennifer's mum. Jennifer was right, her mother was recovering quickly, and Bessie felt bad that she had to keep her visit short.

"I'll come back and visit again next week," Bessie promised Sandy. "And I'll bring something else from my new cookbook with me."

Back at home, Bessie tidied up and paced around her cottage anxiously. When Andrew Teare knocked on Bessie's door at exactly four o'clock, Bessie was flustered.

"Oh, my, you're right on time and I'm not," she told the man as she opened the cottage door. "Please come in."

Bessie waved a gloved hand at him. "Sorry, I was just finishing the washing up," she explained, clapping the brightly coloured gloves she was wearing together. "I didn't realise how much mess a pan of brownies could make."

"They smell wonderful," Andrew told her as he shut the cottage door behind himself and walked into the kitchen.

"I hope so," Bessie said. "They were ever so much bother."

Andrew laughed. "Now I know why I don't bake."

"Anyway, please sit down," Bessie told him, gesturing towards the small kitchen table and chairs. "I'll just finish the last few bowls, if you don't mind?"

"Not at all," Andrew smiled amiably and settled into a chair.

"Now before you get too comfortable," Bessie laughed. "Can I put you to work?"

Andrew jumped up. "Of course you can," he assured her.

"I thought we'd stick to the American theme," she told him. "I picked up something called 'American-style lemonade' at ShopFast. Would you mind terribly pouring it into the glasses?"

Andrew nodded. "I think I can just about handle that."

Bessie laughed and turned back to the sink. She quickly finished washing the last of the dirty dishes and then rinsed them. With a sigh, she pulled off her gloves and joined Andrew at the table.

"How is it, then?" she asked as he put a glass to his lips.

"It's, um, interesting," he replied.

Bessie laughed. "Oh dear, maybe I don't even want to try it." She took a cautious sip from her own glass and laughed again. "Interesting was a good word for it," she told Andrew. "Should I make some tea?"

Andrew laughed. "I think I'd rather have tea, if you don't mind," he told her.

"I don't mind," Bessie replied. "I'd rather have tea as well." She carefully collected the glasses full of lemonade and set them on the counter. She'd poured the bottle of lemonade into a large glass pitcher and she removed that as well, putting it into the refrigerator.

"You never know," she shrugged at Andrew. "One of the neighbourhood kids might drop by and he or she might love it."

"As far as I'm concerned, they're welcome to it," Andrew told her.

Bessie had already filled the kettle just in case the lemonade was disappointing, and now she set out teacups and milk and sugar while she waited for the kettle to boil. She took the plate full of brownies from the counter to the table and handed Andrew a small plate. "Here you are," she told him. "You may as well get started while we wait for the kettle to boil. I hope these are less disappointing than the drink was."

Andrew took a brownie and bit into it. Bessie couldn't help but watch him closely as he chewed. After a moment he smiled at her. "They're delicious," he said. "Really chewy and chocolatey, the way a brownie should be."

"Oh good," Bessie sighed and sank down at the table next to the man. She picked up a brownie of her own and took a cautious bite. "You're right," she said a moment later. "These are really good."

Andrew laughed. A moment later the kettle boiled and Bessie quickly made a pot of tea. They both fixed their own drinks exactly as they liked them and then Bessie sat back down at the table with Andrew.

"I appreciate your stopping by," she said, a bit hesitantly.

"You promised me brownies," the man grinned. "I couldn't possibly have said no."

"That's good to know for the future," Bessie smiled back at him. "If ever I need to talk to you, I'll bake brownies."

"Oh, you needn't go to too much bother," he waved a hand. "I'll come visit you for a cuppa and just about anything sweet."

Bessie laughed. "I have to say, the brownies were more work than I thought they would be. The next time I want to chat with you, you might just get shortbread or something out of a packet from the shops."

Andrew grinned. "That works too," he assured her. "But what did you want to talk with me about?"

Bessie sighed. "This is awkward," she began. "I mean, I feel like a meddling old lady."

Andrew shook his head. "Just say whatever is on your mind," he suggested. "If I think you're meddling, I'll tell you so."

"It's just...." Bessie sighed again. "Okay, the thing is, I'm worried about Doona."

"Why? Is there something wrong?"

"I guess I should say that I'm worried about you and Doona," Bessie replied.

"Ah," the man frowned. "You don't think I'm good enough for her, is that it?"

Bessie shook her head. "It isn't that at all," she replied. "I just worry about my friend. Her last divorce was ugly and nasty and it took her a long time to get over it. I don't want to see her get hurt again."

"I'm not planning on hurting her," Andrew protested.

"I wasn't suggesting that you were," Bessie shrugged. "No one ever plans on hurting someone else, do they? I just worry that things are moving really fast between you two. You seem to be spending so much time together...." She trailed off, unsure of where to go next with the conversation.

"Is that it?" Andrew asked. "Am I taking her away from spending time with you?"

Bessie flushed. "I don't want you to think I'm jealous or anything," she stammered. "I don't begrudge you the time with her, really I don't." She sighed again. "I'm just worried, that's all. You've turned up after many years away and you've lived all over the world. I would hate for you to take Doona away, I guess."

"Bessie, I think it's sweet that you are so protective of Doona," Andrew told her, patting her hand. "And I can assure you that I don't have any plans for taking Doona away from the island in the foreseeable future. But please try to remember that Doona is a big girl and she can look after herself."

Bessie cast her eyes downward, feeling like a fool. "I'm sorry," she muttered. "Doona's become very important to me in the last couple of years. I guess I'm sticking my nose in where it doesn't belong."

Andrew patted her hand again. "Never mind," he said briskly. "Let's just enjoy our tea and brownies and not mention it again."

Bessie smiled at him. "That would be wonderful," she said. "Why don't you tell me about some of your adventures in America and Australia?" she suggested.

Andrew spent the next half hour entertaining Bessie with stories about his years in Australia. He happened to be an excellent storyteller, making Bessie laugh out loud repeatedly as he shared his many mishaps and missteps "down under."

"Oh my, look at the time," he said after a particularly long story involving a kangaroo, a can of beer and three unsuspecting German tourists. Bessie was still wiping away tears of laughter from her eyes as he jumped up.

"I'm taking Doona out for dinner," he told Bessie. "I really must go and get changed. I promised her dinner in the dining room at the Seaview and I need a jacket and tie."

Bessie nodded. "I hope all those brownies haven't spoiled your dinner," she told him.

"No chance," he replied. "Once I start looking at the menu I'll be starving."

"Menus can do that, can't they?" Bessie smiled. "I haven't been out for dinner in what feels like ages. One of theses days you must let me treat you and Doona to a meal."

"I'd like that," Andrew told her. "And I know Doona would as well."

He started picking up plates and teacups, but Bessie waved him away. "You get off and get ready for your big date," she told him. "I can clear up."

"Are you sure? I hate to leave you with a mess."

"It's only a couple of plates and a few teacups," Bessie laughed. "It's fine."

Andrew offered one final half-hearted protest before moving on to thanking Bessie for the tea and brownies.

"Nonsense," Bessie told him. "Thank you for coming over and for not thinking too badly of me for interfering in Doona's life. I'd be ever so grateful if you didn't mention that part of our conversation to Doona."

Andrew laughed. "You can consider my lips sealed by chocolate brownies," he said.

As she shut the cottage door behind the man, Bessie let out a sigh of relief. The visit had been even more of an ordeal than she had expected. After several minutes she looked out the window in the kitchen. She could see that the parking area beside her house was empty.

Cautiously she crept to the door and pulled it open. Andrew was nowhere in sight and his car was gone. She blew out another long breath, pushing the door shut as she did. She took a step backwards and screamed as she bumped into someone.

"Bessie?" Inspector Rockwell was clearly trying not to laugh. "Did you forget I was here?"

Bessie spun around and glared at him. "No, I didn't forget you were here," she said angrily. "I thought you said you were going to stay hidden until I told you the coast was clear."

"I was watching the road out of the sitting room window," the inspector explained. "I saw your friend drive away."

"He's not my friend," Bessie replied tersely.

"I thought you two were getting along rather well," Rockwell told her.

"Then I'm a better actress than I realised," Bessie replied. "There's something I don't trust about him. I can't quite figure out what it is, though."

"I thought it was interesting that he told you all about Australia but said nothing about his time in the United States," the inspector said.

"Why is that interesting?"

"I'm sure Doona has told him that you grew up in the US. Maybe I'm seeing things that aren't there, but maybe he didn't want to talk about a subject that you actually know something about."

"America is such a big place, and I left so long ago, he could tell me just about anything about his time there and I'd believe it."

"The key there is 'just about.' Maybe he did live in the US for years, but maybe he didn't."

While they were speaking the inspector had slipped on a pair of surgical gloves. Now he opened a large bag and removed several smaller bags. He carefully emptied the two lemonade glasses, dumping their contents down the sink. Each glass went into its own evidence bag that the inspector carefully labelled.

The glasses were carefully packed into a large box that

Rockwell had brought with him that afternoon. When he arrived it had contained the bottle of lemonade, the two glasses and the pitcher. Once emptied of those items, Rockwell had taken the empty box into the sitting room with him. Now he emptied the lemonade bottle and the pitcher down the sink as well. After bagging and labelling each one, he added them to the box.

"Do you want the brownie plates and the teacups as well?" Bessie asked.

Rockwell frowned. "I hate to take away your plates and cups," he told her. "The way the lab works, it could be years before you see them again."

"But what if you need them?" Bessie asked. "What if you can't get any good prints off the things you already have?"

"Do you have a cardboard box?" the inspector asked her.

"Sure," Bessie said. "What sort of size?"

"About the same as this one," he told her, gesturing to the box he had filled with the glassware.

Bessie popped up to her spare room and dug out an appropriate-sized box from a small selection she kept for no clear reason.

Back downstairs she watched as Inspector Rockwell carefully bagged and boxed the teacup and plate that Andrew Teare had used.

"I'll take these, but I'll keep them in my car. If we can't get useable prints from the lemonade glasses and the like then we can try these, but hopefully, we won't need them and I can return them to you soon," the inspector told Bessie.

She held the door open for him as he loaded the boxes into his boot. "I'm going to try to get these rushed through," he told Bessie. "I'll ring you when I hear anything."

Bessie felt at loose ends once the inspector left. She wasn't ready for dinner yet, and she didn't really feel like cooking, anyway. Instead, she paced around her cottage, wondering exactly what she should do with herself. Usually a walk on the beach settled her brain, but tonight it didn't appeal.

Finally, she decided to make herself a light dinner and then dig out something different to read. There was too much murder and mayhem in her life right now for a mystery to sound enjoyable. The courtly intrigues of a long-dead king and his succession of consorts didn't tempt her either.

She was still trying to figure out what she wanted for dinner when a knock on the door startled her. She headed for the door, telling herself not to be silly as she felt a sudden flash of nerves. She snapped on the outdoor light and pulled the door open.

"Hugh? What brings you here?" she asked in surprise.

"I just wanted to check in with you," Hugh said, flushing under Bessie's scrutiny. "I brought pizza," he added.

Bessie smiled. "Pizza sounds great," she told him.

Hugh grabbed the pizza from his car and followed Bessie into the house.

"I hope this doesn't mean that you and your new girlfriend are having problems?" Bessie asked, knowing it was nosy, but asking out of genuine concern for the young man.

"No," Hugh answered slowly. "Not really, I mean, I guess not." He sighed deeply. "She's okay, but maybe I don't like her as much as I thought. I mean, we have fun together, but I'm not sure it's going anywhere. I figured we've been spending a lot of time together lately, so maybe we needed a break from each other."

"Well, you're always welcome to take a break here," Bessie smiled at him as she passed him a plate. She handed him a fizzy drink and then sat down at the table with him. The pizza disappeared in short order.

"I have brownies for pudding," Bessie offered. Hugh's face lit up.

"That sounds wonderful," he told her.

Bessie cut a huge piece of brownie from the last tray. They were certainly disappearing quickly.

"Aren't you having any?" Hugh asked, his fork poised over his plate.

"I had a couple earlier," Bessie explained. "I've sort of overdosed on them."

Hugh nodded and then dug in, offering little more than a "yum" as conversation until the chocolatey square was gone.

"That was delicious," he told Bessie as he carried his plate to the sink. He quickly washed it in the water that Bessie had left after washing the pizza plates. Leaving it dripping in the dish drainer, he returned to the table.

"So, what's your theory on our latest murder?" he asked Bessie as he sank into his chair.

"I wish I had a theory," Bessie sighed. "I don't even know where to start."

"Means, motive, and opportunity," Hugh told her. "Those are always the keys."

"It seems like there were an awful lot of people with the means and the opportunity for Moirrey's murder," Bessie sighed. "Apparently the tablets that were substituted for her tablets were fairly common, at least a few years ago. And Moirrey was careless with her bag. Just about everyone had access to it."

"Inspector Rockwell is convinced that the missing boyfriend is the key to solving the murder," Hugh told her.

"I don't know about that," Bessie replied. "But I sure would love to meet the guy."

Hugh laughed. "I would too," he agreed. "I can't imagine anyone being interested in Moirrey, only Moirrey's money."

"Sadly, I'm inclined to agree with you," Bessie sighed.

"Inspector Rockwell is also pretty hung up on Andrew Teare," Hugh told her. "The inspector doesn't like him for some reason."

"I don't like him, either," Bessie admitted. "But he didn't kill Moirrey. He wasn't even on the island until after she died."

"So let's focus on who might have killed her. If means and opportunity are fairly open, what about motive?" Hugh asked.

Bessie shrugged. "No one liked the woman, but I can't imagine anyone wanting her dead."

"She was fighting with several people just before her death," Hugh suggested.

"She was fighting with Anne Caine, Janet Munroe and Matthew Barnes. Of the three, Mr. Barnes is the only one I can see as a murderer."

"Anne Caine probably had the best motive," Hugh argued.

"But she's not a killer," Bessie replied. "Besides, someone tried to kill her, remember?"

"Unless she cut her own brake lines to divert suspicion towards someone else," Hugh suggested.

"And now she's hiding out under police guard so that no one thinks she did it?" Bessie shook her head. "I've known the woman for too long to believe all of that."

"What about her son?" Hugh asked.

"I can't see him having anything to do with Moirrey's death, and he certainly wouldn't do anything to hurt his mother," Bessie answered.

"So if you had to pick out the murderer tonight, who would you choose?" Hugh asked.

Bessie frowned. "I guess I'd pick Matthew Barnes, but I dislike him so much that I know I'm not being objective."

"Somehow this isn't the same without the inspector and Doona," Hugh complained. "I miss our conversations about murder."

Bessie shook her head. "I miss the little gatherings," she told Hugh. "But I'd be perfectly happy if the four of us just got together and discussed the weather and the football results."

Hugh laughed. "You don't follow the football," he said.

"I know," Bessie said. "But I'd much rather talk about that than murder."

Hugh nodded. "But since we're stuck in the middle of another murder investigation. I wish we were all together to discuss it."

"With Doona suspended, I can't see that happening," Bessie sighed.

"No, I guess not," Hugh shrugged. "I suppose I should be going. I don't want to overstay my welcome."

"Now you know there's no chance of that," Bessie told him, lying only a little bit. "But it is getting late and you do need your rest."

Hugh helped Bessie clear up the last of the cups and plates and tidy the kitchen. He gave her an affectionate hug before he headed out into the night.

Bessie locked the cottage door behind him and took herself up to bed. She still wasn't in the mood to read, so she decided to just go to sleep, hoping she'd feel less out of sorts in the morning.

CHAPTER FOURTEEN

Bessie wasn't sure she was in a better mood the next morning, but she got up at six anyway. Toast and an apple made for a quick breakfast and she followed that up with a longer than normal walk along the beach.

Back at home, she checked her answering machine as she turned the phone's ringer back on. A single message was waiting for her.

"Bessie, it's John Rockwell. I've had the fingerprint results and they're, um, interesting. I'll tell you more when I see you. I'll drop by tonight around six. In the meantime, if you bump into our mutual friend, just act natural."

Bessie stared at her answering machine, wondering exactly what the message meant. What was so interesting about the fingerprints? She replayed the message, but it didn't give her any more information the second time around. She sighed deeply. The message had done nothing to improve her mood.

When in doubt, shop, a little voice in her head suggested. Bessie decided it was as good advice as she was likely to get. Normally when she was in a foul mood she would ring Doona and her friend would find a way to cheer her up. That clearly wasn't an option at the moment.

Bessie rang her usual car service and ordered a taxi. She was frustrated but unsurprised to be told that none were immediately available. She agreed that she could wait an hour, since she had little choice.

She spent the hour she was forced to wait seriously considering learning how to drive. Many years earlier she had purchased a copy of the Highway Code and now she flipped through the pages, learning about road signs and stopping distances. If she'd had to wait even a few minutes longer she might just have signed herself up for some lessons.

Instead, she discovered that the taxi was at her door when she heard the loud blast of a horn. She hurried to the door and looked out at Mark, her least favourite taxi driver.

"Come on, Bessie," he shouted. "The metre's running."

Bessie frowned as she gathered up her handbag and rushed out the door. She locked up behind herself, feeling flustered. In the taxi she checked her handbag. At least she had her wallet.

Finally dropped off in Ramsey around half ten, Bessie was so annoyed with Mark that she didn't make arrangements with him to be picked back up. She'd grab a taxi at one of the taxi ranks instead, she decided.

Bessie spent a fruitless hour in her favourite bookstore. She failed to find a single book that captured her interest, which was hardly surprising as she had just shopped there a few days earlier. It was Sunday and the charity shops weren't open, which meant she could do no more than press her nose to their windows, convinced that they had undiscovered treasure inside. Turning away from the large window that showcased the biggest charity shop in town, Bessie frowned as it suddenly began to rain heavily.

Bessie dug into her bag. She'd forgotten to grab an umbrella. Cursing Mark Stone, she headed towards the taxi rank. She'd be better off being grumpy and miserable at home than out in public. As she stepped off the curb, a car horn startled her.

"Aunt Bessie," a voice called. "Let me give you a ride."

Bessie forced herself to smile as she met Andrew Teare's friendly grin. Inspector Rockwell's words rang in her ears and she struggled to "act natural" as she replied.

"Oh, I'm fine," she lied anxiously. "I need to hit a few more shops before I head home."

"At least let me give you a ride to your next stop then," Andrew insisted. "I wanted a word anyway, about Doona."

Those last two words were enough to overcome Bessie's reluctance to get into the car with the man. Act natural, she told herself as she buckled herself in.

"All set?" Andrew asked. When she nodded, he put the car into gear and pulled back into traffic.

"I was just heading to ShopFast," Bessie said, making things up as she went along. "You can drop me off there."

"Sorry, Bessie," Andrew gave her an apologetic grin as he tripped the automatic locks. "We need to talk and I have somewhere to get to as well. I'm afraid you'll just have to come along for the ride."

For a brief moment Bessie felt complete panic, then she inhaled deeply. She forced herself to calm down and focus. Inspector Rockwell hadn't suggested that the man was dangerous, after all.

"What did you want to talk to me about?" she asked in a voice that quavered only slightly.

"I need to go," Andrew told her. "I'm leaving the island, I mean. My ferry leaves in less than an hour."

"Doona must have been sad when you told her you were going," Bessie suggested.

"That's just it, I didn't tell her. I couldn't tell her. It's all too complicated to try to explain it to her."

"I see," Bessie said, even though she didn't.

Andrew laughed. "I'm sure you don't," he said. "But that's okay. I just want you to try to explain to Doona how sorry I am. I didn't plan on falling for her, you know? But she's a really amazing person and I'd like to think we might have had a future together if things had gone differently."

"Does that mean you're not planning on coming back?" Bessie asked.

"I can't," Andrew shrugged. "Things have just gone all wrong. I need to disappear."

"I'm sorry to hear that," Bessie said, immediately feeling stupid. She simply couldn't think what to say.

"Thanks," Andrew winked at her. "I was going to try to tough it out, but every day feels more dangerous. I kept hoping, after all of my time and effort that I could make it work, but I know it's just a matter of time. I'm getting out before it's too late."

"You know I have no idea what you're talking about, don't you?" Bessie asked him.

"I figured Anne Caine must have told you something," Andrew replied. "I thought that was why you had me over to talk. I thought you were trying to warn me or something."

Bessie shook her head. "What would Anne Caine have told me?"

Andrew sighed. "So many years of hard work," he said. "Ruined by a woman I never even knew existed."

"That's too bad," Bessie murmured, wondering what he was talking about. They were heading up the mountain road, on their way out of Ramsey, and Bessie shut her eyes tightly every time the man sped up and raced to overtake a slower vehicle in front of them. She shuddered; maybe she didn't want to learn to drive.

"Aunt Bessie, I'm going to tell you a story," Andrew told her after speeding past a white van and narrowly missing an oncoming car. "Hopefully, you can help Doona understand if you know everything."

Bessie nodded uncertainly. "Go ahead," she muttered, hoping he was focussed on the road and had missed the nod.

"My story starts, oh, nearly twenty-five years ago. I was only twenty-one or twenty-two years old and I was making my way around England trying to figure out my place in the world. Me dad took off when I were six or seven and mum didn't have much time for us kids. I've two brothers and three sisters and none of us stayed in school long enough to get any qualifications. Me mum didn't care as long as we moved out." He sighed deeply and paused.

Bessie was surprised at the changes in his accent and speech patterns as he talked about his childhood. Andrew Teare's apparently artificial sophistication had vanished.

The man shook his head. "Anyway," he grinned at Bessie, "that's enough sob story. I was in London, hanging out in this pub by the docks, when I made meself a new best friend."

"Oh?" Bessie said, suspicious of where things were heading.

"I'm sure you've guessed," Andrew laughed. "I met a lad called Andrew Teare, born and raised on the Isle of Man, he'd been. He was a great kid. He was meant to be on his gap year, like, but he'd had a huge falling-out with his dad and he'd been thrown out of the family. His dad gave him a small amount of cash and kicked him across the water, like."

"What did they fight about?" Bessie asked.

"You know, that was the one thing the kid never told me," the man driving told her. "When we first met, I was trying to find a way to get my hands on his money and I wasn't that interested in his background. Later, when I found out that he'd pretty much spent it all and we became friends anyway, it was too late to go back over ancient history."

"So, if you aren't Andrew Teare, what should I call you?"

The man laughed. "I guess you can call me Joe," he said after a pause. "I mean, that was the name me mum gave me. We were Jack, John and Joe and me sisters were Jen, Jan and Jess. Mum had this thing about the letter J, you see. Me dad was called Jim and I think mum figured if she gave us names that started with J, he'd stick around and be our dad, even if he weren't exactly sure that he was our father. You know what I mean?" The man gave Bessie an exaggerated wink.

"So, Joe, you were telling me about you and Andrew Teare," Bessie changed the subject away from the man's obviously difficult childhood.

"Oh, yeah," he broke off as he slammed on the brakes as they reached the electric train tracks. A train was slowly making its way across the tracks and Joe anxiously tapped his fingertips against the steering wheel as he watched its slow progress.

Bessie briefly considered trying to climb out of the car and run away, but in spite of everything she didn't feel like she was in any real danger from the man, and she really wanted to hear his story.

"Where was I?" he demanded as the train lumbered past and they were underway again. "Oh, well, I met young Andrew and we became fast friends. He was only a few years younger than me, but he always seemed like a kid. And his health was so poor that he always needed looking after, anyway. I guess it was the big brother in me, but I sort of took him under my wing."

"What was wrong with his health?" Bessie asked.

"You know, he told me that no one on the island had a clue about him, but I never totally believed it. He had heart trouble, like his sister. But where Moirrey was coddled and spoiled and taken to see specialists and whatever, Andrew was sort of told to just get over it and toughen up. At least that was how he told the story."

Bessie frowned. "I can just about see Ewan Teare being like that, but I can't believe that Jane, Andrew's mother, didn't step in."

"To hear Andrew tell it, his mum was totally under his father's thumb, like. She was terrified of him and never argued. Once Andrew said he thought his mum had some mental problems, like depression or something, but he wouldn't talk about it. From what I've heard, I guess Moirrey was the only thing that she ever paid attention to; she wasn't really interested in Andrew."

Bessie nodded slowly. What the man was saying fit in with her memories of the secretive family. She could well imagine Ewan keeping his depressed wife and sickly son tucked up under lock and key.

"Anyway, we did a lot of travelling, young Andrew and me. We really did see the world. We spent a few years in Oz and a long time in Canada. Everyone thought we were brothers, see, and we used that to our advantage."

"How?"

"Oh, we ran scams. Andrew was always so weak and fragile-looking, well, he was just plain fragile, really. We didn't have no trouble convincing folks that he was dying of something. And folks love to help the terminally ill, like. We never took no money that people couldn't afford to give, you know. But it was pretty easy to get a few donations here and there as we moved around. People would put us up for a night or two as well if, say, 'our wallets got stolen,' or whatever." He winked at Bessie again. "Our wallets got stolen a lot," he laughed.

"Oh, my," Bessie muttered.

"And Andrew taught me a lot, too," Joe continued. "He taught me how to talk all posh like so people would believe that we were well off and just, you know, 'in a spot of bother,' like. For a kid who grew up with all the material blessings, he was a quick study for the con game, I have to say."

"This is all terribly sad," Bessie said unhappily. "I don't really want to know about how you conned people and taught Andrew Teare to be a criminal. Maybe you could just let me out here and I'll find my own way back home."

"Ah, Bessie, but I have to tell you the rest of the story," Joe insisted. "Whatever else happened in the past, I really have come to be very fond of Doona and I want her to understand. I really do."

"Hurmph," Bessie pressed her lips together unhappily. As they were racing down the mountain road at a speed she didn't want to know, it appeared she had little choice but to listen to the man's story, no matter how unpleasant.

"Anyway, it was in Canada that Andrew got his medications mixed up," the man continued. "We'd been drinking, you see. We were pretty much always drinking," he chuckled to himself, presumably remembering his previous lifestyle.

"What medications did he take?" Bessie asked.

"Oh, all sorts, like Moirrey, really. He was almost as bad as she was, although he kept his in a bag next to his bed, wherever we were staying. He didn't carry them around everywhere he went like his sister did with her stash."

Bessie felt a chill as she wondered exactly how the man knew so much about Moirrey. No doubt Doona had filled him in, she told herself. "So what happened?" she asked nervously.

"One night he took the wrong tablets," Joe shrugged. "He just went to sleep and never woke up. It was really sad, but that's when I started thinking. I'd spent close to fifteen years with the man. I knew his story almost as well as my own. I knew the family had a lot of money. I just had to figure out how to get my hands on it."

Bessie shook her head. "Did you not ever think that maybe you should get a proper job and earn your living honestly?" she demanded.

The man laughed. "You know, that thought never crossed my mind," he chuckled.

A sharp reply sprang to Bessie's lips, but she bit her tongue. After a moment, Joe continued his story.

"Anyway, I thought about it, and I made my plans, and then circumstances intervened." He paused again as they rounded a sharp curve and began the descent into Douglas. The view was breathtaking, although Bessie didn't really appreciate it in this instance.

"Sorry," she said. "What circumstances?"

"Let's just say that I spent some time as a guest of her Majesty, shall we?" Joe gave her another wink.

Bessie nodded, understanding the reference to time spent in gaol. "I see," she replied.

"Anyway, I did my time in Canada and then headed back to London. Once I got there, I did my research and found out that Ewan and Jane Teare were both dead, as was Robert Hall. Only Moirrey was left, and from what I could find out, there was some sort of trust set up. That had to mean that Andrew was the heir, and I was all set to convince everyone that I was Andrew."

"Except you could never convince Moirrey that you were her long-lost brother," Bessie inserted. "So you had to wait for her to die."

Joe laughed. "Not quite," he told Bessie. "I figured it would be easier if I skipped pretending to be Andrew and just got her to fall in love with me."

Bessie gasped. "You were the mystery boyfriend?" she asked.

"Mystery boyfriend? How did you know Moirrey had a boyfriend?" Joe demanded. "We never went out in public together and Moirrey promised me she wouldn't tell anyone. Don't tell me she told you about me?"

"No, she never said a word," Bessie assured him. "But her housekeeper saw your car multiple times and some neighbourhood kids actually saw the two of you together."

Joe laughed. "I should have known," he shrugged. "Moirrey

told me that there was no keeping secrets on the island, but I didn't believe her."

"I guess she was right and wrong," Bessie answered. "People spotted you and Moirrey together, but no one knew that Andrew Teare had a heart condition."

"I suppose it was easier twenty-five years ago to hide things, and children were easier to control as well. No one had mobile phones and they couldn't text their friends," he shrugged again. "Everything I heard from Moirrey and Andrew suggested that Ewan went out of his way to keep his family isolated from everyone and everything. Andrew also told me that his father's estate manager was fiercely loyal. I'm sure Robert Hall knew about Andrew's medical condition, but he wouldn't have shared that knowledge with anyone."

"And he must have made sure his daughter kept quiet as well," Bessie mused.

"I don't understand that," Joe told her. "Andrew never even mentioned that Robert Hall had a daughter, and yet as soon as we were introduced I could tell she knew I wasn't who I claimed to be."

"So you cut through her brake lines."

Joe flushed. "I'm really not a bad guy," he insisted. "I didn't mean to kill her. I just wanted to get her on my side."

"I have to say, you chose a very strange method for doing so," Bessie commented.

"I was desperate," he admitted. "I'd spent years planning for this job. This was meant to be my retirement plan, like. I knew Andrew Teare's life story better than my own. And yet, there she was, standing in my way."

"So you tried to get rid of her."

"So I tried to warn her, like. I followed her across the mountain and I went to see her at Noble's before the police got there. I told her if she kept her mouth shut, I'd make it worth her while."

"What did she say?"

"She told me that she'd keep quiet if I signed her cottage over to her."

"And you agreed?"

"Well, sure. I still had the big house and the rest of the property. I thought she'd want more, really."

"And maybe she would have in time," Bessie sighed. "What happened between you and Moirrey?"

Joe sighed. "Oh, I tried," he told Bessie. "I came to visit her and told her how I'd known her brother. He'd never rung or written home after he left, so I, um, didn't mention what all Andrew and I had done over the years. Getting her to fall for me was so easy, it was scary."

"She was a very lonely woman," Bessie told him. "And I don't think she ever dated."

"No, she definitely didn't," Joe replied. "Anyway, I wasn't me, I was Chuck Powers, a handsome American businessman."

Bessie couldn't help but stare at the man as he slipped easily into an American accent while he talked about the identity he had used while dating Moirrey.

"She fell hard and fast for my charms and believed everything I told her about my company in the US and how successful I was. And I did try, I tried to make myself fall in love with her and when that didn't work, I tried to at least like her a little bit. I was hoping I could marry her and get access to her fortune that way, but in the end I just couldn't stand it anymore."

"What do you mean?" Bessie demanded.

Joe frowned as they hit a long queue of traffic heading into Douglas. From what Bessie could see, there were ambulances and police cars up ahead.

"I better not miss my ferry," he muttered. "What I mean is that I had to give up," he told Bessie. "I couldn't take any more of her whining and whinging all the time. She hated everyone and hated everything and in the end I just couldn't stand it."

"So you switched her tablets for something else," Bessie concluded. "I'm guessing you got the idea from Andrew's accidental death."

"Um, yeah," the man glanced at Bessie and then looked back at the road. "And I'm not actually the least bit sorry I did it. I wasn't sure it would kill her, but I didn't care anymore. She was just a horrible woman."

"She didn't deserve to die," Bessie said quietly.

"But while she was alive, I couldn't become Andrew Teare," he told Bessie. "And I'd put so much effort into becoming him."

"And then, once you'd tried it, Anne Caine stood in your way."

Joe sighed. "It wasn't just her," he told Bessie. "I mean, I think I could have kept her quiet, but Matthew Barnes became a problem, too."

"Why?"

"He never believed I was Andrew," the man admitted. "He never actually came out and said that, but he was openly hostile when I arrived and he only warmed to me when I offered to try to find a solution that might work for both of us."

"But if you were really Andrew Teare, you shouldn't have had to do that."

"Exactly, but he had already figured that out. The better question is why he was willing to make a deal with me anyway. I suspect that once the Teare family estate is settled someone is going to discover that Matthew Barnes was stealing from Moirrey in a big way. I already suspected that when Moirrey and I were together, but I couldn't do anything about it at that point."

"I thought you submitted a sample for a DNA test," Bessie questioned. "What was going to happen when the results came back?"

"I'd have been vindicated," Joe chuckled. "The sample I gave came from Andrew Teare, after all."

Bessie stared silently out the window, processing that fact. "You took hair from Andrew Teare when he died?" she asked eventually, shocked that the man had been planning all of this for so long.

"I told you, by the time Andrew died, I had figured out that he was my retirement plan. His health was so bad, it was just a matter of time before he'd pass on and I could take his place."

The queue of traffic moved up a few feet and then stopped again. Bessie decided that once they reached the police she was going to jump out. In the meantime, she settled in to find out as much as she could.

"If you have the DNA on your side, why leave now?" she asked.

"It's just too risky," Joe shrugged. "If anyone had any reason to take my fingerprints, I'd be sunk."

"Oh."

"Besides, you probably won't believe me, but I've really fallen for Doona. She's an amazing woman, she is. But I can't be with her and live a lie. She deserves someone special, not an old con like me."

"She certainly does," Bessie couldn't help but reply.

"Yeah," Joe sighed. "You know I only started taking her out because I thought she might be able to give me an inside line with the police. Then she got suspended and wasn't any use to me, but I didn't want to stop seeing her. And now I'm chucking it all in and running away because I've fallen hard and she deserves better."

An ambulance left the scene in front of them, closely followed by two police cars. Suddenly traffic began to move again, albeit slowly. Within a few minutes, Joe and Bessie were through the previously blocked junction and back on their way to the Sea Terminal. Bessie never had a chance to get out of the car.

"Anyway, I just wanted you to tell Doona all of that," Joe continued as he steered through the streets of Douglas. "I want her to know that I really did care and I really wish things could be different."

"I'll tell her," Bessie promised, wondering exactly how she'd word things when she had the chance to talk to her friend.

"I'm really not a bad guy," Joe continued. "I'm just a con man who never learned to make an honest living. If I'd known Doona was in my future, I guess I would have tried harder."

Bessie stayed silent as they reached the car park for the Sea Terminal. She had no idea what she could possibly say to the man.

"What is that?" Joe asked her, gesturing towards the small structure in Douglas Bay.

"The Tower of Refuge?" Bessie asked, confused by the sudden change of subject.

"I guess," Joe shrugged. "I kept seeing it every time I was down here with Doona and I always wondered what it was, but I figured I probably ought to know since I was meant to have grown up here."

"It's a small structure that was built to be a safe place for shipwrecked sailors to find shelter during storms in the bay," Bessie explained. "It's been there since the 1830s, so you would have known about it if you actually grew up here."

"I guess I'm glad I never asked Doona then," he told Bessie. "Anyway, this is my last stop. It's Andrew Teare's last stop too, I guess," he smiled at Bessie. "It's good news for Matthew Barnes though, I suppose. There's no one left in the family to sue him for mismanagement."

"I'm going to do everything I can to make sure he's caught and punished," Bessie assured him. "There must be a distant relative somewhere who can benefit."

Joe shrugged. "He never would show me Ewan Teare's will. I'm not sure what he's hiding, but if you can get a look at it, I would bet it's interesting."

"I'll get my advocate on it first thing," Bessie said.

"Is your mobile phone in your handbag?" he asked.

"Yes," Bessie nodded. "Do you need to ring someone?"

"Not at all," he said. He reached onto the floor and picked up Bessie's handbag. He glanced inside and then pulled out her mobile. He turned it over in his hands and then shrugged and dropped it back in her bag.

"Come on, then, you can come in and see me off," he told Bessie.

Bessie climbed out of the car, her legs stiff from the long journey. She watched as Joe emerged as well, still holding her handbag.

"Sorry about this," he told Bessie. "But I need to keep you from ringing anyone until I sail."

He opened the boot of the car and pulled out a suitcase. Then he dropped Bessie's handbag, with her mobile phone inside, into the now empty space. He slammed the boot shut and pocketed the car's keys.

"By the time the ship docks I'll be a totally different person," he told Bessie. "I've got a handful of identities to choose from and I've booked a cabin so I'll be able to change my hair and clothes as well."

"You will get caught," Bessie told him.

"Maybe, some day," he shrugged. "Come on," he told Bessie, taking her by the arm. "You can keep me company if I have to wait for a bit."

They walked into the Sea Terminal together. Bessie tried to look around casually, hoping to spot a familiar face, but she recognised no one. With Joe still holding her arm, they made their way to the ticket desk.

"Good afternoon," Joe smiled at the ticket agent. "You're holding a ticket for me. I'm Andrew Teare."

The agent flipped through a pile of tickets on the counter. "Ah, yes, Mr. Teare, here you are. The ferry sails in about twenty minutes. You're welcome to board at any time."

"Ah, that's great, but, well...." he lowered his voice and leaned in towards the other man. "I've got my granny here, you see," he said softly. "I don't want to leave her all alone. My sister is on her way. Is it possible for me to take her with me for now? I promise to get her off the boat before we sail."

The agent sighed. "Let me ring someone." Bessie and Joe stood silently as the agent stepped away to confer with another staff member and then make the call. After a moment he returned.

"If you'd like to wait in the lobby for a moment," he told Joe. "One of our staff will be down to help you find the best solution to your problem."

"Just go and don't be silly," Bessie hissed to Joe as they moved into the lobby. "I promise I won't ring anyone until the ship has sailed, if that's what you're worried about."

"You could promise me anything," Joe shrugged. "But I have no reason to believe you."

Bessie sighed and looked around the terminal. There had to be someone there who knew her. She really didn't want to cause a scene. After a moment another young man in a ferry company uniform approached them.

"How can I help?" he asked Joe.

Joe pulled him to one side and the two had a whispered conversation that Bessie couldn't hear. Joe never took his eyes off Bessie. She thought about just walking away, but she didn't know what the man might do. She knew he was desperate; it was better to let him get on the boat and then ring Inspector Rockwell.

"I've got to go now, Granny," Joe said to Bessie when he returned to her side a moment later. "Sue will be here soon to look after you. You be good, you hear?"

Bessie nodded her head and kept her mouth shut. Joe patted her arm and then turned and began to walk away. An announcement came over the tannoy.

"Today's afternoon sailing for Liverpool is now final boarding. If you are planning on sailing as a foot passenger on this sailing, please make your way through security and on board at this time."

Joe glanced back and waved at Bessie and then disappeared through a door marked "Security."

Bessie blew out a long sigh of relief. She'd never really felt like she was in any danger, but she was still glad to see the back of the man.

"We've got to ring the police," she said to the uniformed man who was still standing beside her.

"Yes, dear, why don't I take care of that once your granddaughter arrives," the man said soothingly.

"I don't have a granddaughter," Bessie told him. "And the man who just left is a wanted criminal. We have to ring Inspector Rockwell in Laxey, and quickly."

"Now, now, don't get yourself all excited," the man said in a soothing voice. "I'm sure your granddaughter can get everything straightened around when she gets here."

Bessie sighed. "Look, I don't know what he told you," she said, carefully enunciating each word. "But I'm not crazy or senile or any such thing. My name is Bessie Cubbon. I've lived in Laxey almost my entire life. I've never been married or had children and I couldn't possibly have grandchildren. The man who just got on the ferry is wanted for murder and attempted murder and you standing there, being an idiot, is preventing him from being caught. If you want to wait here all afternoon for someone who doesn't exist, that's your business, but I'm ringing the police and getting that ferry stopped."

The man blustered a bit more, until Bessie just turned and began to walk away. "Ma'am, I'm going to have to insist that you wait with me for your...."

Bessie held up a hand. "Don't say it, just don't. Ring the police; ask to be connected with Inspector Rockwell at the Laxey Constabulary. I guarantee he'll vouch for me and...."

The sound of the ferry's horn cut her off.

"Well, now you've done it," she sighed. "He's away. I just hope the inspector can find a way to get the boat turned around or catch him at the other end."

It took a few more minutes for Bessie to persuade the man that she really wasn't senile or crazy and in the end, she wasn't sure if he believed her or simply got tired of arguing. Inspector Rockwell didn't seem to have any doubts when she finally reached him, however.

By the time the inspector heard the entire story, stopping the ferry was deemed impractical. Instead, the inspector made sure that the boat would be met by a full contingent from the Liverpool Constabulary.

CHAPTER FIFTEEN

Time seemed to drag on endlessly as Bessie waited. First she had to wait while the police contacted the hire car company. Then she had to wait while they sent someone to the Sea Terminal to open up the boot of the hire car and return Bessie's handbag to her. After that, she was ready to grab a taxi home, but she was asked by the Douglas police to please wait at the terminal for John Rockwell to arrive.

Inspector Rockwell finally turned up with Hugh as Bessie nursed her third cup of tea and began to think seriously about getting some dinner from the small café.

"Bessie," Rockwell smiled and gave her a hug. "I hope you didn't suffer too much in your ordeal?"

Bessie shook her head. "It wasn't an ordeal," she told him. "Aside from the man's driving, I felt perfectly safe. He wasn't really dangerous and besides, he wanted me to talk to Doona for him. He wasn't going to hurt me."

"He's wanted for murder and attempted murder," the inspector said seriously. "If I'd had any reason to believe that he was responsible for Moirrey's death, I never would have had you meet with him yesterday."

"It's fine," Bessie told him. "But did they catch him at the other end?"

"I don't know yet," Rockwell told her. "I'm going to have Hugh take you home and I'm flying across to see if I can help with the questioning. We're assuming they're going to get him."

Bessie nodded. Hugh drove her home, back along the coast road. "I assume the inspector rang Doona and filled her in?" Bessie asked Hugh.

"I'm not sure what all was said," Hugh replied. "But I know he rang Doona and they talked for a very long time."

Bessie nodded. She would ring her friend as soon as she got home. She couldn't begin to imagine how Doona must be feeling.

Unfortunately for Bessie, she didn't get to find out right away. Doona's answering machine picked up Bessie's call and Doona didn't ring her back. It was quite late when Inspector Rockwell finally rang from Liverpool.

"We've got him," he told Bessie, sounding as tired as she felt.

"We had to let the passengers off one at a time and it felt like we spent hours verifying everyone's identity, but we finally found him."

"Was his disguise that good?" Bessie questioned.

"I didn't spot him and I was looking hard," Rockwell admitted. "He cut his hair and dyed it black. He used green contact lenses to change his eye colour and he added a black moustache that was an excellent fake. He used makeup to add a few lines and wrinkles so that he looked significantly older and he changed his clothes from what you said he was wearing when he left."

"Well, you had to guess that he would do that," Bessie replied.

"We did, but your description of his suitcase was a big part of our finding him. I guess he didn't even think about that while he was planning the rest."

"Thank goodness he made that small mistake."

"It made us pay him a bit more attention than some of the others," the inspector told her. "And he pretty much collapsed under questioning. He kept asking me to tell Doona that he was sorry."

"I can't reach Doona," Bessie told him. "Do you think I should be worried about her? She isn't answering her home phone or her mobile and she doesn't ring me back when I leave messages."

"I'll make sure I talk to her. I'm her boss, she has to talk to me," Rockwell assured Bessie. "If I think she needs you, I'll ring you back."

He rang her back anyway, just a few minutes later. "I talked to Doona and she's pretty much okay," he told Bessie. "I think she feels like she was an idiot to fall for the man and she's more embarrassed than broken-hearted, but I could be wrong."

"That sounds like Doona," Bessie remarked.

"Anyway, I'm tied up here until some time tomorrow afternoon or early evening. I've suggested to Doona and Hugh that we have a dinner meeting at your cottage on Tuesday night and talk it all through."

"That sounds great," Bessie consented eagerly, happily agreeing a menu that had her guests bringing the main course and the pudding. "I'll supply a bottle of wine and tea and coffee," she told Rockwell.

The next day, she rang Marjorie Stevens to check on the class that evening. She wasn't sure if Doona would be up to attending and if she needed a taxi she wanted to get one sorted as early as possible.

"Marjorie, it's Bessie," she said. "I just wanted to check whether there's class tonight or not. I wondered if you'd heard anything from Doona?"

"I was just going to ring you," Marjorie laughed. "Doona rang a few minutes ago to say she wasn't feeling well. She said she was going to ring you later and let you know. Anyway, Liz has two kids with chicken pox and Henry was asked to work at a special evening event at the castle, so he can't make it either. I was going to ask you if you mind if we reschedule tonight's class. We can simply add it on to the end of the session, if that works for you."

"That's absolutely fine," Bessie assured her, feeling like a small child with an unexpected snow day like they'd had during her childhood in America. Learning Manx was often more like hard work than fun.

Bessie felt slightly better later that day when Doona finally rang. It was a short chat, just enough to confirm the cancelled lesson and their plans for the next day.

"I'm fine, Bessie," Doona insisted when Bessie asked. "I really am."

Bessie didn't press her on the telephone. She would see for herself the next day how her best friend really was.

Tuesday seemed to drag on endlessly as Bessie paced around her cottage, trying to fill in time. She usually loved her own company, but today she found herself bored and restless on her own. Just before lunchtime she finally walked up the hill to the little shop to buy herself a magazine or two. She was surprised to find Anne Caine behind the counter.

"Anne? You got your old job back?" she asked.

"I'm just helping out for a bit," Anne replied. "Georgie, the new girl, has some sort of flu or something and my old boss rang and asked if I could fill in for a few days."

"And you said yes?" Bessie asked incredulously. "After the way he treated you?"

Anne laughed. "After being cooped up in hospital for so long, I wanted to get out and see people," she told Bessie. "It's only for today and tomorrow and then I won't ever do it again."

The door buzzed as another customer walked in. Anne smiled and said "hello" to the man who grabbed a television listings magazine and a few bars of chocolate and was quickly out the door again.

"Bessie, I need to talk to you," Anne told Bessie as the door shut behind him. "We can't talk here, there are too many people in and out. Can I stop by later, after I shut the store for the night?"

"Inspector Rockwell, Hugh and Doona are coming around tonight," Bessie told her. "I don't know what time we'll finish. Tomorrow night might be better if that's okay with you."

Anne gave Bessie a thoughtful look. "Maybe I'll stop tonight anyway," she replied. "What I want to talk to you about will be all over the island by the weekend anyway. And it concerns Doona and the police as well." She sighed. "I might as well get it over with in one telling."

"Suit yourself," Bessie shrugged. "You're more than welcome. If you hurry, you might even be in time for some pudding. I can't promise, though, as Hugh has been known to finish off an entire cake on his own."

Anne laughed. "My Andy is much the same," she told Bessie. "Which reminds me, he said if I saw you to tell you that he'll be around one day very soon to make shortbread and talk."

Bessie smiled. "He's one of my favourite people," she told Anne. "He's more than welcome any time."

The door buzzed again and Bessie was surprised to see her advocate, Doncan Quayle, walk in. "Doncan? What brings you here?" she asked.

"We ran out of milk at the office," he said to Bessie. "And I wanted a word with Ms. Caine, so I offered to come and get some. I can kill two birds with one stone this way."

Bessie smiled. "I'd better get out of the way," she laughed. "I'd hate to be in the way of flying stones." She gathered up her shopping bag, now full of the sort of gossipy "celebrity" magazines that she only ever read in dentists' waiting rooms. They were perfect for her unsettled mind today, however. She could look through them and not worry about actually retaining anything that she read.

During the walk home she puzzled over what Doncan Quayle wanted to talk with Anne about. It had to be something to do with Anne's cottage and the Teare estate, Bessie decided. But what?

She ate a light lunch and caught up with which second-rate soap opera actor was currently married to which page three model and where the minor royals were planning to spend their summer. A lavish multi-page spread covering the wedding of two people who had both appeared in television shows Bessie had never heard of amused her for several minutes. The guest list included a few names that Bessie recognised as having had their fifteen minutes of fame a good many years earlier. She had to assume that the rest were still wallowing in their artificial importance.

By the time six o'clock rolled around, Bessie had had enough of modern celebrity weddings and had turned her attention back to Henry VIII and his brides. They were much more interesting and of more lasting import, after all.

Her guests were prompt, and Bessie was relieved to see that Doona looked perfectly fine as she emerged from Inspector

Rockwell's car. They made their way into the cottage as a group.

Doona gave Bessie a big hug. "I'm so sorry that I put you in danger again," she told Bessie with a sigh.

"I wasn't in any danger," Bessie insisted. "The man wanted me to tell you how much he cared about you. He wasn't going to hurt me."

"I'm not so sure about that," Doona replied.

"I'm more worried about you than I ever was about me," Bessie told her, studying her intently.

"Bessie, I'm fine," Doona laughed. "You can stop staring at me, really."

Bessie blushed. "I'm sorry, but I'm really worried about you."

Doona sighed. "I won't say I'm not upset," she told her friend. "But it was all starting to feel a little bit, um, strange, I guess. I was starting to think that there was something not quite right, but I didn't know what it was."

"Bet you didn't guess that he was a conman and a murderer," Hugh interjected.

"Hugh," Bessie scolded.

"It's okay." Doona gave what looked like a forced smile. "I know the whole island will be talking about how I fell for a man who turned out to be a conman. I'm ready to be laughed at."

"No one better laugh at you while I'm around," Bessie said stoutly. "The man was charming and he had his story down pat. He fooled everyone."

"Not you and not Inspector Rockwell," Doona argued.

"But I'm naturally suspicious," the inspector said. "And I'm starving."

Everyone laughed, and Bessie passed out plates while the inspector and Doona opened up container after container of the mouthwatering Indian food that they had brought with them.

Bessie was relieved to see Doona eat her fair share of the feast as everyone focussed on food and let the conversation drop. Once Hugh had sliced generous helpings of the treacle sponge pudding he'd brought and passed them around to everyone, the conversation resumed.

"This is delicious," Bessie sighed as she spooned up a

mouthful with hot custard.

"Me mum made it," Hugh told her. "I asked her to make me something nice to bring."

"You need to learn to make it yourself," Bessie told him. "Men should be able to look after themselves."

"Oh, aye," Hugh agreed. "And I would have had a go myself, only I thought it might not come out right and I didn't want to disappoint everyone."

Bessie smiled at him. "Next time, make it yourself," she told him. "I'm sure it will be fine."

Hugh blushed and ducked his head. "Yes, ma'am," he muttered.

"So if the inspector is naturally suspicious," Doona said, "what made you distrustful of the man who claimed he was Andrew Teare?" she asked Bessie.

Bessie shrugged. "I'm not sure," she admitted. "There was just something about him that seemed not quite right. And Anne Caine had a strange reaction to him as well."

"Anne Caine could have put us all out of our misery a lot earlier if she'd just told us what she knew," Rockwell told the others. "To make matters worse, she still isn't talking."

"Well, she's meant to be coming over here after she shuts down the shop up the road," Bessie told him. "She said she had a lot to tell me and that it concerned Doona and the police as well. Maybe you'll finally get your answers."

"That would be nice," Rockwell replied.

"Did Joe confess to everything once you caught him?" Bessie asked.

"Well, he admitted to being Moirrey's boyfriend, although he denied deliberately switching her tablets. To hear him tell it, they were, um, spending nights together. He's claiming that somehow she must have picked up some of his medication and mixed it up with hers," Rockwell replied.

"That doesn't sound like Moirrey," Bessie remarked. "I can't see her sleeping with him without being married. Besides, he told me he did it. He said that she was driving him crazy and he couldn't take it anymore."

"That certainly sounds like Moirrey," Doona said dryly.

"He admitted to cutting Anne's brake lines when we talked as well," Bessie reminded the inspector.

"He's not admitting that either, now," Rockwell replied.

"I suppose that figures," Bessie sighed.

"We have more than enough to hold him for now while we investigate," the inspector said. "And if we run out of things to charge him with, the authorities in both Canada and Australia would like to talk with him as well."

Doona sighed deeply. "I finally meet a guy who ticks all the boxes and he turns out to be wanted in three different countries."

Bessie laughed, but Inspector Rockwell looked serious. "The Canadian authorities are taking another look at Andrew Teare's death," he told them soberly. "It's entirely possible that his medications were switched deliberately as well."

"But they were best friends," Bessie protested.

"Maybe," Rockwell shrugged. "I find it interesting that Joe had the foresight to cut off some of Andrew's hair, just in case he ever needed it for DNA testing."

"That's just creepy," Hugh said.

"He claims he kept it as a keepsake," Rockwell told them. "I think that's pretty creepy as well."

Doona shuddered. "It's all creepy and I can't believe I was dating the guy. I'm so glad we were taking things slowly, but I wish now that I hadn't ever laid eyes on him."

"He was very good at hiding his true character," Bessie told her. "I didn't like him, but I didn't think he was a murderer."

"The more information I've been able to gather, the more it looks like that is exactly what he is. It seems that he was very skilled at causing 'accidents.' The Australians want to talk to him about the sudden death of an older woman that he and Andrew Teare were staying with at one point, as well. Apparently he was very good at disappearing whenever it looked like anyone was getting suspicious."

Doona sighed again. "Just like he did this time."

"Exactly," the inspector agreed, giving Doona's hand a squeeze.

"I didn't like him and I didn't trust him, but I do believe that one of the reasons he left was because he was genuinely falling for you," Bessie told Doona. "I don't think he would have given up so easily otherwise. He'd planned this impersonation for a very long time."

Doona shrugged. "I don't know if I want to believe that or not," she replied. "I'm not sure if I'd rather think he was just conning me or that a man who could kill people actually fell for me. They're both pretty awful notions, really."

Bessie smiled at her friend. "Tell yourself that you managed to bring out the little bit of good in a man who has had a difficult life," she suggested. "I believe that's true and...."

A knock on the door interrupted their conversation. Bessie let Anne in and got Hugh to bring a chair from the sitting room into the kitchen for Anne.

"Before I forget," Anne said as she crossed the room. "Here's the cheque you gave me for Moirrey." She handed Bessie back the cheque that Bessie had written weeks earlier.

"Should I write another one to someone else?" Bessie asked. "I don't want you to lose your home."

"It's all fine," Anne assured her as she sank into her seat. "Thank you, though, I really appreciate your willingness to help. Ah," she sighed. "I'd forgotten how tiring it is standing all day in the shop. I'm glad tomorrow is my last day."

Bessie offered Anne some treacle sponge and she accepted eagerly. "I brought some sandwiches from home for my dinner, but that was hours ago. I very nearly treated myself to a huge bar of chocolate at the shop, but we were just busy enough that I never really had the time."

Everyone sat and waited politely while Bessie cut a piece of the sponge for Anne and added a spoonful of custard. Anne took a bite and sighed.

"This is delicious," she told everyone as she looked up from her plate. She burst out laughing then, as four pairs of eyes were staring at her with ill-disguised impatience. "I'm sorry, I suppose you're all waiting to hear why I didn't tell anyone that I knew the man was a fraud." She sighed again and then blinked hard several times.

Bessie got up and found a box of tissues, which she set down next to Anne on the table.

"Have you ever worked so hard at keeping a secret that, even when it really didn't matter anymore, you still felt like you couldn't tell?" Anne asked, looking at each of them in turn.

Bessie nodded. "The older a secret gets, the harder it is give it up," she said.

Anne sighed and pushed her plate away. "I don't even know where to begin," she said. "Doona, I am so very sorry that I didn't warn you. I never intended for you to get hurt. I knew he wasn't Andrew Teare, but I wanted to see what he was up to before I said anything. I didn't realise that you two were dating, I just...." she trailed off and buried her face in a tissue.

After an awkward moment, Inspector Rockwell cleared his throat. "Why don't you start at the beginning?" he suggested. "Start with the first time you met the imposter and go from there."

Anne nodded from behind her tissue and then wiped her eyes and sat up straight in her chair. "I can do this," she said loudly.

"Of course you can," Bessie answered emphatically.

Anne gave her a small smile. "Okay, well, I first met the imposter at *La Terrazza*, the night that Bessie was there having dinner with Doona and...." she sighed. "What's his real name?" she asked.

"His real name is Joe Watson," Inspector Rockwell told her.

"Thanks, that might help move the story along," Anne said. "I met Joe at the restaurant that night and almost blurted out that he wasn't Andrew Teare. He interrupted me and offered to sign my cottage over to me, so I held my tongue. Mostly, I was curious as to what he was up to; I never suspected that he'd killed Moirrey."

"No one thought he'd killed Moirrey," Hugh told her.

"Anyway, he met me after work that evening and we had a long talk. He told me that he'd been Andrew's best friend. I'm not sure where the conversation might have gone if my Andy hadn't turned up just then, but he did. My son was hoping I could lend him some cash so he could go out for a drink or two with his mates. Joe took one look at him and knew he had me right where he wanted me." She sighed again and began to pick at her pudding with the spoon.

"He threatened to hurt Andy?" Bessie asked angrily.

"Quite the opposite," Anne told her. "He promised that if I kept my mouth shut he would make sure that Andy was taken care of. He told me that Andrew Teare had made him promise that he'd look after me and my family."

"He told me that Andrew never even mentioned your name," Bessie replied.

Anne flushed and bit her lip. After a long minute, she wiped tears from her eyes and spoke again. "That's probably more likely to be the truth," she said with a catch in her voice. "Anyway, I promised I would keep my mouth shut and Joe promised he would make everything right and I wouldn't be sorry." she shrugged. "It wasn't long after that that he tried to kill me."

"You had to know who'd cut through you brake lines," Inspector Rockwell said in a carefully measured tone. "I can't understand why you didn't tell us at that point."

"Joe was following my car across the mountain," she told him. "He followed the ambulance to Noble's and the staff let him in to see me even before the police arrived. He told me that if I said anything to anyone that he'd kill Andy. There was absolutely no doubt in my mind that he meant it, as well."

Doona shuddered and Inspector Rockwell patted her hand gently. Bessie gave Anne's hand another squeeze as Anne continued her story.

"I was glad I was able to get police protection, but all I really wanted was some protection for Andy. I made him stay with me as much as I possibly could and I worried constantly when he was out of my sight. I didn't finally relax until they told me that Joe had been arrested."

"You could have sent him to stay with Jack across, couldn't you?" Bessie asked.

Anne laughed sharply. "Even if I knew where Jack was, I wouldn't have done that," she said.

"You don't know where he is?" Bessie queried.

Anne sighed. "All sorts of secrets are going to come out

tonight. No, I don't know where he is. He left me in February and moved to Birmingham to be with some slut he met at *The Cat and Longtail*. He kept in touch long enough to send divorce papers through, but now everything is being handled by our advocates, and I don't have any idea if he's still with her in Birmingham or if he's moved on. I don't really care, either."

"Surely Andy wants to stay in touch with his father?" Doona asked.

Anne shrugged. "He never got along with Jack," she replied.

"I'm not sure I understand all of this," Bessie said after a long silence. "There's a piece of the puzzle missing somewhere."

Anne smiled at her. "Absolutely, and it's one I have to fill in, even though it isn't easy. You need to know before Andy comes to see you later this week, because he knows and he'll probably want to talk with you about it. He always loved talking to you about the problems in his life. He said you were the only one who ever really listened."

Bessie smiled. "Parents are so busy doing the job of raising their children that they don't usually have time to listen to them as well. When kids come here to visit, I have nothing else to do but listen. I don't have a telly and I don't let them use their phones while they're here. They have to talk and then they have to hear what I really think of what they've said," she laughed. "Some of them only visit the once, because of it."

"Well, you certainly did your fair share of raising my Andy," Anne told her. "And I never did thank you for it, so let me do that now. Thank you for everything that you did for my son."

"He's a great kid," Bessie told Anne. "And I'm glad I got to be a part of his life."

"Okay, enough prevaricating," Anne shook her head. "I've been keeping this secret for so long that I don't even know if I can tell it."

Bessie took her hand. "Maybe I should guess?" she suggested. Anne looked at her curiously. "You named your son after his father, didn't you?" Bessie said softly.

Anne burst into tears and buried her face in her hands.

"I thought his father was called Jack?" Hugh said in a

confused voice.

Doona rolled her eyes at him. "Andy Caine's father was Andrew Teare," she explained to the confused constable.

"He was?" Hugh asked.

"Yes, he was," Anne answered, as she ran a tissue over her tear-stained face.

"Do you want to tell us the whole story?" Bessie asked. "Or have you had enough for tonight?"

"I think I'd like to tell you, if you don't mind listening?"

The other four exchanged glances and Bessie could tell that they were all dying to hear the story. Bessie took Anne's hand again and patted it gently. "We're happy to hear it," she assured the woman.

"I was sixteen," Anne told her. "Andrew was eighteen, and practically a stranger. He came home from boarding school for a few months before his gap year and, well, we...." she sighed. "I suppose it's melodramatic to say that we fell in love, but we really did. He was kind and sweet and sensitive. His health wasn't great, so he wasn't rushing around drinking a lot and driving too fast like all the guys I knew from school. Andrew liked to sit and talk about books and just hold hands and watch the sunset. I was head-over-heels, madly, passionately in love with him. I suppose I still am."

The others sat quietly and waited while Anne composed herself after another short round of tears.

"We were both so young," she said eventually. "We were both so stupid. When I found out I was pregnant, I told my dad, and he went and talked to Ewan Teare. Before Andrew and I knew what was happening, Andrew was being sent away without even being allowed to say goodbye."

Anne paused, her face reflecting pain that was still felt even after so many years. "We managed to write back and forth for a little while," she told the others. "But when Andrew found out that I was marrying Jack Caine he wrote me a horrible letter telling me that he never wanted to hear from me again." Anne took a long drink of water from a glass that Bessie handed her.

"I understand that he was hurt," she said softly. "But I didn't have any choice. I was sixteen. I couldn't possibly have brought up a baby on my own. My father said he'd throw me out if I didn't marry Jack and I simply didn't have anywhere to go."

"And I'm sure Andrew understood that eventually," Bessie murmured reassuringly.

"I don't know," Anne shook her head. "I'd like to believe that, but I just don't know."

"You have to believe that," Bessie told her. "Because you have to convince your son of that. It's important for Andy to think that his father cared and would have been a part of his life if he could have found a way to do so."

Anne nodded. "I know you're right," she said.

"I can't believe you kept all of this a secret for so long," Doona said.

"Neither can I," Anne replied. "Andy looks so much like his father that I always thought someone would guess. I suppose no one ever really saw Andrew Teare that much, but that was one reason why I was happy for Andy to move across as soon as he was old enough. As soon as Joe saw him, he knew, though."

"I assume Jack knew he wasn't the baby's father?" Bessie asked.

"Oh, he knew," Anne answered dryly. "And he never let me forget it, either."

"So why did he marry you in the first place?" Doona asked.

Anne blushed. "My father promised him a free home," she admitted. "Dad and Ewan Teare made some sort of verbal agreement that we could all stay in the cottage and he would mark the loan as paid each month, without any money changing hands. I guess Ewan was supposed to leave the property to me when he died, but he didn't."

"So you suddenly had to start paying Moirrey every month," Bessie said.

"Yep. Anyway, I guess that brings us to the last big Teare family secret."

"There's more?" Doona asked. "I'm not sure I can handle anything else."

Anne smiled at her. "As it happens, Matthew Barnes was the

one keeping this secret and he was happy to use Joe to hide behind rather than reveal it."

"Go on then, what was that horrible man hiding?" Bessie demanded.

"It seems that Ewan Teare left his fortune in trust for Moirrey, but on her death it all goes to his only grandchild, my son."

"He disinherited his son?" Rockwell asked.

"Apparently it's more complicated than that, but it seems that Ewan didn't expect Andrew to ever come back. Maybe he assumed that his heart condition would kill him or something. Anyway, my Andy is the Teare family heir."

"Finally, some good news," Bessie cheered.

Anne smiled. "What we don't know yet is how good," she sighed. "Doncan is doing his best to figure it all out, but it seems that Mr. Barnes might have misappropriated funds here and there over the years."

"I knew it," Bessie said. "I knew that man couldn't be trusted."

Anne smiled. "From what I understand, the family fortune wasn't as much as everyone seemed to think to begin with," she told the others. "It seems my father wasn't the best estate manager around, either," she flushed. "And once he started drinking he let a lot slide as well. Ewan insisted on living in the big house and that cost a fortune to run," she shrugged. "And I gather that Moirrey wasn't a fan of living within her means."

"Now why doesn't that surprise me?" Bessie asked.

"Anyway, it appears that Mr. Barnes found some, shall we say 'creative' ways to keep both Moirrey and himself happy by selling land that shouldn't have been sold under the terms of the trust and by borrowing heavily against the property. Doncan is going to figure it all out and then we'll see where we are. Andy is feeling totally overwhelmed, of course."

"Of course," Bessie patted Anne's hand. "I hope I can help him get his head around it all."

"I'm sure you can," Anne told her. "Doncan's son, Doncan, Junior, wants to buy the big house. Andy and I don't have any use for it, so I think we're going to let him have it at fair market value. Doncan reckons once we've sold that and squared away all the debts that Moirrey left behind, Andy should have just about enough to put himself through culinary school. If he's lucky, he might even end up with a small down payment for his own little restaurant or bakery once he's finished."

Bessie smiled happily. "I love a happy ending," she told everyone.

"This one seems to have been a long time coming," Anne sighed.

"At least we all got there in the end," Doona told her. "Joe wanted things to end up very differently."

"That's why us good guys are around," Hugh said with a grin. "To step in and save the day."

"How about stepping in and washing up?" Bessie suggested, pointing to the sink full of dishes.

Hugh laughed, but he quickly began to get the job done. Anne slid back in her chair and finally dug into her pudding. Bessie looked over at Doona, who smiled and mouthed, "I'm fine," at her friend. This time Bessie decided to believe her.

She sat back in her chair and watched her friends as they relaxed and began to chat amongst themselves. Hugh washed and rinsed the dishes, and after a moment, Inspector Rockwell grabbed a towel and began to dry and put away the clean items. Doona and Anne began to talk about Andy's suddenly brighter future. Bessie smiled. A happy ending indeed.

Glossary of Terms

Manx Language to English

by vie lhiam ushtey	I would like some water.
fastyr mie	good afternoon
gura mie ayd	thanks
kys t'ou	How are you?
moghry mie	good morning
oie vie	good night
quoi uss	Who are you?
slane lhiat	goodbye
ta mee braew	I'm fine.

House Names – Manx to English

Thie yn Traie	Beach House
Treoghe Bwaaue	Widow's Cottage (Bessie's home)

English/Manx to American Terms

advocate	Manx title for a lawyer
aye	yes
biscuits	cookies
bacon butty	bacon sandwich
bank holiday	public holiday
booked	made a reservation
boot	trunk (of a car)
car park	parking lot
chemist	pharmacist
chippy	a fish and chips take-out restaurant
chips	french fries

comeover	a person who moved to the island from elsewhere
container lorry	large truck for hauling goods
crisps	potato chips
cuddly toy	stuffed animal
cuppa	cup of tea (informal)
estate car	station wagon
fairy cakes	cupcakes
fizzy drink	soda (pop)
flat	apartment
gaol	jail
hire car	rental car
holiday	vacation
indicators	turn signals
jab	injection (immunization)
journal	diary
lift	elevator
longtail	rat
loo	restroom
Oz	A British slang term for Australia
pavement	sidewalk
pensioners	retired people
prang	crash
pudding	dessert
queue	line
saloon car	sedan
skeet	gossip
solicitor	lawyer
stroppy	easily annoyed, difficult to deal with
tannoy	public address system
telly	television
trainers	sneakers
whinging	whining
windscreen wipers	windshield wipers

Other notes:

The British (and Manx) number their building floors starting with ground level, which is essentially level "zero," therefore the floor above ground level is the "first floor" and they continue up from there. (In the US, the ground floor is generally referred to as the first floor, the floor above would be the "second floor," etc.)

Reception is the first year of formal schooling in state-run schools in the United Kingdom, roughly equivalent to a US kindergarten. Children begin in reception at the age of four, turning five during the year. (Unlike most American kindergartens where children don't begin until after their fifth birthday.)

A character refers to meeting her husband at "uni," which is short for "university." In the UK you would go to university after you've completed your GCSE (formerly O-level) and A-level exams. Universities award bachelor's degrees as well as providing graduate level education, like US colleges and universities do.

A "gap year" is time taken out after finishing A-level exams and before beginning university study. Traditionally the time is spent travelling to allow a student to learn more about the world before returning to academic learning. Today students who choose to take a gap year do everything from travelling to volunteer work to taking on a full-time job to help finance their future university studies.

CID is the Criminal Investigation Department of the Isle of Man Constabulary (Police Force).

"Noble's" is Noble's Hospital, the main hospital on the Isle of Man. It is located in Douglas, the island's capital city.

When talking about time, the English say, for example, "half seven" to mean "seven-thirty."

A charity shop is a store run by a charitable (non-profit) organisation that sells donated second-hand merchandise in order to raise funds for their particular cause. They are great places to find books, games and puzzles as well as clothing, knick-knacks and furniture.

Someone says to Bessie, "I thought you'd have popped your clogs ages ago," which means died.

A "pensioner" is someone old enough to be collecting his or her pension. In the US the term "retiree" or "senior citizen" might be used instead.

When island residents talk about someone being from "across," or moving "across," they mean somewhere in the United Kingdom (across the water).

The emergency number in the UK is 999, rather than 911, as used in the US.

Hospitals in the UK have "Accident and Emergency" departments (A&E) rather than Emergency Rooms.

Cars in the UK that are over three years old are required to undergo an annual MOT (Ministry of Transport) test to ensure that they are roadworthy and safe. This does not apply on the Isle of Man, although motorists are expected to maintain the roadworthiness of their vehicles.

A "page three model" appears topless on the third page of certain British daily newspapers.

Aunt Bessie's story continues in:

Aunt Bessie Considers
An Isle of Man Cozy Mystery
by Diana Xarissa

Aunt Bessie considers it an honour to be giving a presentation about her research at a conference at the Manx Museum.

Miss Elizabeth Cubbon is known as "Aunt Bessie" to nearly everyone in her hometown of Laxey. While she never earned a college degree, she's become something of an expert in the history of the island that she's called home for all of her adult life. Once she turned sixty, she stopped counting how many years that includes.

Aunt Bessie considers it unfair when the entire conference schedule is thrown into disarray by Mack Dickson's sudden arrival.

Mack promises that what he has to say is important enough to warrant the upheaval. Even more turmoil follows when Bessie discovers Mack's body only a short time after he's finished giving his speech.

Aunt Bessie considers Police Inspector Peter Corkill a poor substitute for her friend, John Rockwell.

But the Manx Museum is out of Rockwell's jurisdiction and that means Corkill is in charge of the investigation, no matter what Bessie thinks. With Corkill insisting that Mack's death was probably an unfortunate accident, Mack's slides that shocked the conference disappear. Bessie finds herself drawn into another investigation, and she's determined to drag her friends, Rockwell, Doona and Hugh, in with her.

Aunt Bessie Decides
An Isle of Man Cozy Mystery
by Diana Xarissa

Aunt Bessie decides that she and her closest friends should have an enjoyable night out.

Elizabeth Cubbon (known to almost everyone as Aunt Bessie) has made many friends over the lifetime that she's lived in the village of Laxey, but few have been as close as the ones she's made recently. Bessie relied on Doona Moore, Hugh Watterson and John Rockwell to help her through several recent murder investigations she's found herself caught up in. Now she wants to treat them all to an open-air performance of a Shakespearean play on the grounds of historic Peel Castle.

Aunt Bessie decides that it doesn't much matter what show the troupe is performing as long as she and her friends can relax and have fun.

Two members have recently left the theatre company. Now the troupe has thrown aside its usual repertoire in favour of a play written by one of their own. When those two former members appear in the audience, though, someone decides to get rid of one of them for good.

Aunt Bessie decides to give the show another chance, but a second performance almost ends in a second tragedy.
With all of the suspects blaming one another, and several of them turning up on the doorstep of Bessie's cottage, it's time for Bessie to decide to solve this murder herself.

The Isle of Man Cozy Mystery Series

Aunt Bessie Assumes
Aunt Bessie Believes
Aunt Bessie Considers
Aunt Bessie Decides
Aunt Bessie Enjoys
Aunt Bessie Finds
Aunt Bessie Goes (Release date: October 16, 2015)

By the same author
The Markham Sisters Cozy Mystery Novellas

The Appleton Case
The Bennett Case
The Chalmers Case (Release date: December 16, 2015)

The Isle of Man Romance Series

Island Escape
Island Inheritance
Island Heritage
Island Christmas (Release date: December 1, 2015)

ABOUT THE AUTHOR

Diana lived on the glorious Isle of Man for more than ten years before returning to the United States with her family. Now living near Buffalo, New York, she enjoys having the opportunity to write about the island that she loves so much. It truly is an amazing and magical place.

Diana also writes mystery/thrillers set in the not-too-distant future under the pen name "Diana X. Dunn" and fantasy/adventure books for middle grade readers under the pen name "D.X. Dunn."

She would be delighted to know what you think of her work and can be contacted through Facebook, Goodreads or on her website at www.dianaxarissa.com.

Printed in Great Britain
by Amazon